PATCHWORK OF ME

Patchwork of Me

A NOVEL BY

Gregory G. Allen

ASD PUBLISHING

PATCHWORK OF ME
Copyright © 2012 by Gregory G. Allen. All rights reserved.
www.ggallen.net

All persons and places described in this novel are fictitious. Any similarity to persons alive or dead is purely coincidental.

No part of this publication may be reproduced or transmitted in any form or by any means electronic or mechanical, including photocopying, recording, or by any information storage and retrieval system without the written permission of the publisher except in the case of brief quotations embodied in articles and reviews.

Published by ASD Publishing
ISBN: 9780983604945
Library of Congress Control Number: 2012900346

Cover Design by Janie Bynum www.bynumcreative.com
Author photo by Tom Schopper
Manufactured in the United States of America

Praise for

PATCHWORK OF ME

"*Allen weaves an intricate tapestry of characters, successfully transporting the reader into his world...a compelling read.*"
~ Joanne Huspek
Blogcritics

"*It's a kaleidoscope of unexpected twists and turns, emotional and psychological. It's soul-searching; self-discovering, humorous and romantic...it's a Patchwork of Me!*"
~ Arthur Wooten
Author of *Leftovers*

"This book is for anyone who treasures friendship, asks big questions, looks for the truth, or simply enjoys a great story."
~ Pamela Milam, MA, LPC
Author & Columnist

For the women who have inspired me with their personal journeys

CHAPTER ONE

I stood at the edge of the soothing water, the atmosphere a marked contrast to the violent and ferocious scene of that day. How could this same place be the setting for such different scenes? I felt Gracie run past me in the child life-vest we insisted she wear, and I, as always, tried to wipe away the blood that smeared across the back.

But Gracie wasn't really there with me that morning. She was gone – taken by a freak shark attack off this very coast. Carol had begged for us to move away from this place, but I had been raised here and couldn't leave my small town Maine roots.

I lifted the coffee mug to my lips, smelling the aroma of my favorite Colombian-blend, and a soothing heat engulfed me as it made its way down my throat. The seagulls squawked overhead, and the sun slowly came up over the water. At home, Carol was still in a deep sleep – but I could barely nod off all night. Each morning, I retired to this spot to greet the sun, thinking perhaps that Gracie would appear and would return home with me, as if it all had been a sick practical joke.

I enjoyed being the only person standing on that beach, but knew any pleasure in my solitude was but an illusion. The birds seemed to taunt me as they spoke back and forth to each other –

laughing at the human who could not connect to anyone, even his own wife.

"And then I wake up," I said as I stared at the tiles on the ceiling, cognizant of the star-shape at the center of where the four points joined.

Six months into my therapy sessions with Dr. Pingleton, and I was just noticing how pronounced that guiding star was.

"Do you think it's a story you are trying to tell?" he asked.

Naturally, you ass, or why would I be telling you?

"I'm not a writer, I don't know anything about telling stories," I said.

I thought I must have really been going crazy to have dreams like that. I don't mean like the yummy chocolate-scarred singer Seal saying 'we'll never survive unless we get a little crazy' – I mean certifiable.

"I think it's the child we need to concentrate on," he said.

"Really," I asked. "You don't think the fact that I'm dreaming I'm a man married to some woman named Carol has any pertinence?"

"Sara, I don't think you're a lesbian if that's what you mean," he said.

Do you have a strange desire to wear flannel and combat boots, Sara?

I knew I wasn't a lesbian. I had a few boyfriends through my twenties that could more than attest to that. But I was still waiting to find Mister Right.

That's a joke, Sara, and you know it.

I wasn't going to find him here. Not in Phoenix. Maybe if I ran off to another state, he'd be there – but my dip in the Arizona relationship pool had always been a fight to stay afloat. Oddly enough, I had never even been to Maine ... except in those nightly dreams that freaked me out and kept my therapist's pockets full of money.

Money wasn't growing on the cactus outside my one bedroom condo on Barber Street, but I wasn't starving. I had a decent job as an office girl working at a metal industries shop. How lame – not even a cool Arizona job like running a gallery or making Southwestern jewelry.

We hate that turquoise shit.

And I wasn't even a "girl," still perky like I was younger, using Clairol to keep my long straight hair as red as could be, and spending mornings at the gym to keep my weight under 125 pounds, so as not to become some fat old maid eating Oreos and drinking whole milk. But the truth was that I had become a 33-year-old woman in search of some deeper meaning, teetering on the edge.

Pretty stupid, Sara.

Oh yeah, and I had a habit of talking to myself. I wished I could turn that voice off in my head, but she spoke out whenever she wanted to. I imagined that at least it was better than blurting out crap from my mouth.

I surrounded myself with three close friends, two gay men and a woman I had befriended at the gym, who, in fact, acted like a gay man. Our gay mafia. I guess being a fag-hag at my age didn't help my dating life much either, but there were no straight men taking me out to the Olive Garden on a regular basis. And I felt safe inside the fortress I had created with this bunch. As dysfunctional as we were, we served as support systems to each other – even if it felt at times like it was strictly superficial.

I didn't want to think about the girl in the dream or her childhood. I didn't want to think about my own transient past. I counted more square tiles on the ceiling. Anything to keep my mind from the questions Pingleton peppered me with. My family. My past. My future. What I was eating for breakfast.

What did any of this have to do with my ailment? Sharing of dreams. Sharing my thoughts. No one believed me anyway. I had never met anyone else who had this problem – other issues, yes, but not this strange issue that I fought with.

"You haven't said anything in five minutes," the doctor said, interrupting my rambling inner monologue.

And what have you been doing for those five minutes as the clock ticked away my money?

"I was thinking about your last question," I said.

What was his last question? I couldn't even remember.

"Did you ever watch the swearing in of Sotomayor on YouTube?" I asked him, changing the subject, which he never seemed to mind, analyzing the digressions as if they were dreams themselves.

"I think I saw it back when it happened."

He thought I was a freak for digging up events that were years old. I had to make it seem relevant.

"I had a strong sense of pride in that historic moment witnessed by her mother standing there at her side, mixed with bouts of giggles. You know, when a Hispanic person who speaks perfectly good English says their own name and the thickest accent comes out just on that name?"

Crap. Pingleton. Hope there is no Hispanic in his background anywhere.

"Would you like to have your mother around to witness your triumphs?" he asked.

Jesus – just enjoy my joke for a moment with me. Lighten the mood.

"I don't think about my mother being around … so, no, to answer your question," I said.

A child of the foster care system doesn't usually think about parents. At least I didn't. I had more "parents" than anyone I knew. A different set each time I ended up in a new home. But none of them were real. None of them were mine. And not a one of them, I sensed, would remain in my life.

Why had I agreed to see a shrink?

I began to scratch the place on my arm where it always started around my elbow. It soon worked its way down toward my wrist. It was like a tingle that cried out to be scratched. And if I didn't give in, it would pulsate more and more intensely until I paid attention to it. Alone in my bed, in the stillness of the night, sometimes it was the only thing I could sense in the room – the need, desire, impulse to attend to the area. I hadn't been able to pinpoint what brought it on; I wasn't even sure there were triggers for it. At times, it just beckoned me to tend to it– like some twisted Siamese growth attached to me. Other times, I clawed at it until it bled, but I was not about to give Dr. Pingleton the pleasure of witnessing any of this. So I stopped scratching; I endured the growing itch.

"Something in your past must be eliciting these outbursts," he said.

They are not outbursts. My life is not a musical! I'm not busting out into song.

"This didn't happen to me as a child," I said, shifting positions on the sofa.

Thank God I had thought of something to say, but the itch on my arm was calling to me to scratch it. Now! But must not give in to its taunting.

I resisted.

I remembered when Dr. Smythe had suggested I see a shrink. He had given me a thorough examination, expecting to find hives of some sort. But get this crap: he was unable to come to any type of diagnosis. No plague on my skin. No signs of anything. Just as I couldn't see anything, neither could the man who had spent a huge fortune to go off to medical school. He figured it was something in my mind. He wrote out Pingleton's name and number on a prescription pad, shoved it in my hand, and sent me out the door.

"Tell me what you remember as a child," he said.

Here we go again. As I had done on previous visits with Pingleton, I settled for the easiest lie. With my freakin' shrink! The man had no idea I had bounced from foster home to foster home since I had left that small detail about my past out of our conversations. He thought I had the picture perfect past with parents that had died in a plane crash when I was in my early twenties. Morbid, I know. But I had to make up some shit not to have a mother or father. Isn't that who gets half the blame for things?

The lies had become a game.

"I remember my bedroom, my favorite stuffed animal, my parents painting my ceiling bright pink," I said, almost proud of the fictional details.

"All things that make you happy," he said. "Now what about painful memories?"

Here we go with the pain. It always has to go to that.

"I remember getting braces at ten years old," I said.

I actually had perfect teeth and never wore the things.

"I don't think that would be causing this. Many children get braces."

Now, any sane person would have told me I was not participating in my own recovery; and I understood it, even then, on some deep, emotional level – but people would have to recognize where I was coming from. Annoyance: pissed off that nothing was emerging from these sessions after all the money I had thrown into them. And, truthfully, I didn't really believe dredging up crap from when I was a kid was gonna help my itch to go away. That was the number one reason I was here. Not to deal with being a product of the foster care system. Not to learn some big lesson about being *a little girl lost*. I just wanted to get rid of this fucking itch!

I obviously would have to live with my problem, and that was that. Some people cut themselves in private; I would go on scratching something that wasn't there. A closet scratcher. That's what I'd be. Let's at least give it a name, I decided, "the invisible pandemic of Sara Butler."

"I'd like to try hypnotizing you again," Dr. Pingleton said. "To get to the root of these dreams."

If a doctor can't get what they want out of someone's mouth, they always think they can get it from their subconscious. Great.

"We tried before and it didn't work," I responded, knowing that it was me who didn't allow it to work.

Too much truth would have come out, and Pingleton would have sent me off to the loony bin for all the lies I had fed him.

"I think we need to go back further. Next time you come, we'll do it then," he said.

Sure. Whatever.

"OK, next time," I said, studying the strange patches of his beard. He needed to get a grey colored pin and fill in those spots.

"Try and think about that child you lost in the dream," he said.

The moment Pingleton said it, my mind went back to ten years earlier when I had literally lost a baby. I wasn't pregnant long and in the end, it was best that I not bring a child into the world. What did I know of being a mother?

He looked at the small clock conspicuously placed over my shoulder, and before he could say it, I stood to leave his office.

"See you in two weeks, Ms. Butler," he dismissed me in his formal way.

We did our awkward goodbyes- something I never quit e got the hang of (I wasn't saying adios to a friend) – and I was out his lobby and into the dry air of my "lovely" city. Each time I finished a session, the guilt came over me something fierce. Why did I lie to this man who was just trying to help me with my issues? And why did I keep paying to go back and see him every other week? None of it made much sense to me, but then again, neither did the freaky dreams or the elbow that was screaming for me to attend to it with my fingernails. And so I did, as I walked back to my car.

CHAPTER TWO

I told Erick I would meet him at our favorite spot in Paradise Village at the vintage clothing shop. Although these days, I mostly went to Target. PV was a collection of boutique-type shopping places, a Chinese restaurant, and oh yes ... a pawn shop. We were known for those places all over town. Spend money on something you can't afford, and go hawk it at the pawn when you need to pay your water bill – all part of the American dream.

Erick (with the silent "k" he had added on his name at twelve years old – a sign of how pretentious he would become) was so much more like a girlfriend than I had ever had. He was 36 years old, striking good looks, tall, and blonde-haired – well let's just say "God." If Brad Pitt and that McSteamy guy from TV had a child, it would have looked like Erick. His monumental good looks aided in his job as a massage therapist where both women and men would request his services at the spa. He enjoyed clothes shopping as he was always dressed in the most up-to-date style, just as if he had walked out of a magazine – no matter where we were going. He also loved to act as my personal shopper to find fabulous outfits for me to wear – and with

Halloween coming up in a month, who knew what kind of costumes we could come up with at the old clothing shop.

"This is so 1983," he said as he held up a white glove.

"And people still dress up like the man all this time after his death," I said.

"I don't know what I want to be," he said. "I was thinking maybe Wendy Williams."

"You are so much prettier than that drag queen," I said. Wendy Williams was a radio slash television slash dancing with the stars personality who (while female) looked like a man in drag to my sanctimonious eyes.

"Don't you talk about Wendy like that," he said. "That girl will cut you — or if she doesn't, I will."

We laughed and kept sifting through the old clothes.

"Punk chick from the eighties?" I asked.

"Your girls would pop right out of that top."

Erick was right. When men talked to me, I never saw their eyes. They were always stuck on the 36 double Ds that seemed to greet them long before they had a chance or cared to see my face. (I always had to take them in account when weighing myself, since each girl weighed at least two pounds and had a mind of its own.)

"How about a biker witch?" I said when I found a bomber jacket and then a witch's hat nearby.

"Now you're just making up shit."

You're not even trying, Sara.

Obviously my mind wasn't on clothes shopping.

"Do you and Ron want to come over for dinner Friday night?"

"I can come, but I never know what Ron is doing these days."

Ron Gilmore was the epitome of a 80s club kid. He was somewhere in his fifties, and Erick had been with him for ten years. He had the look of a Ken doll that had cooked a little too long in the easy-bake oven. A plastic-like skin, constantly tanned. His dark hair never out of place. And I know he was making his way over to Monroe Street to see Doctor Sickler Botox for the Stars. The lines on his forehead had been disappearing little by little during the past three years. But we weren't supposed to notice it.

"He's your husband. How can you not know what he's doing?" I asked.

"Do you see a ring on this finger?" he asked, giving me his middle finger instead. "And it ain't legal in Arizona, so I don't think we need to worry about that just now."

"Come on," I said, tugging on his tight black t-shirt that made his arms pop out. "You know you love him."

"Is that what the kids are calling it nowadays? Love?"

"Then what the hell was that big to-do about flying off to Palm Springs last month for your anniversary?"

"Honey, that was just a weekend getaway for my half-a-century old lover to recapture his glory days."

Erick had told me the entire story about that trip. The clothing optional resort where they had stayed sounded like something right out of a Roman orgy scene. How Ron would go for "a walk" and come back to the room hours later with friends that enjoyed poppers, cocaine, and everything that his golden decade had brought him.

"If I hear Ah-ha, Bronski Beat, or Erasure one more time, I think I'm gonna scream," he said. "That man doesn't know the name of any new group after 1989."

The two of us laughed, and I knew it was time to change the subject. Erick had a good heart, and deep down, I knew he was hurting over the changes in his relationship with Ron. But certainly, standing in the middle of Decades of Haberdasher Clothing wasn't the place to discuss his love life. It brought up too much shit.

Wonder what inner monologue he has going right now about Ron.

"I'll call Matty and ask him to join us," I said.

"You know I love hanging out with you guys, but if the man hits on me..."

"He's not gonna hit on you," I said.

"Because if he gets enough alcohol in me, I just might take him up on any relief he needs," Erick said as he kissed my cheek and went to the next aisle.

And people wonder why you stay alone.

There were no decent role models for relationships as I was growing up, and the friends around me offered nothing worthy of taking note of either. I found it best to stay clear of any romantic relationships; just stick to sex.

Note to self. Send booty text to Steve tonight. Needing it badly.

Back to Erick. He was the one requiring my attention. Stuck in a relationship with Dr. Plastic-stein. Maybe I should have sent him to see Pingleton. Given him one of my sessions so I wouldn't have had to go. And Lord help the day if I ever told Erick about my wild dreams of being a man. He'd crown me as a tranny and have me as Grand Marshall of the Phoenix Gay Pride Parade. No, that was something that was best to leave for me and my shrink. That was sort of bothering me more than the itching arm.

"We need to do some more training this weekend on the bikes," Erick said.

You are so stupid, Sara, for getting into this.

"I hope I'm able to do it," I told him.

"You'll be great. Don't you love pushing yourself?"

Pushing yourself off a cliff.

"It'll definitely be a challenge."

Erick and I had bonded early on with our love of bike riding, but I had been kicking myself ever since I had let him talk me into joining him on a cancer bike ride from Phoenix to Sedona. We worked hard to get sponsors for the 113-mile bike ride. and I had been working even harder on building my stamina for the event. I was a pretty healthy chick (if we don't count mental health), but I had never done anything like that before.

"Well, we don't have much more time and it'll be here," he said.

"I'll be glad once it's over."

"Then, we'll start training for a triathlon," he teased.

"Yeah, can you imagine these gals in the water?" I asked, grabbing my chest.

"You could use 'em as a flotation device," he said.

"I'm not finding the right costume," I said, frustrated with my lack of involvement in the day of shopping. "Let's head over to Veggie Delight for a tofu burger."

Erick was the one person who had the same eating habits as me, and it was nice to see someone who totally understood the disaster that was the fast food market in America.

"Sounds heavenly," Erick said, wrapping his arm in mine and escorting me to his black Mustang convertible. "I'll pretend I'm Matty and feed my inside instead of my hunger for shopping."

"I can take my car," I said.

"No, let's drive together ... so much more fun when I have a hot babe in my car."

"Confuse the people in town who recognize your bat-mobile," I joked.

There was something about riding in that Mustang with the top down that made all a person's problems drift away. Most gals would scream about their hair being all windswept and mucked up, but I couldn't care less. The music was blaring, the sun was beating down on us, and we could enjoy the time without even trying to talk over the wind and the music. It was heaven. It blocked out the conversations in my head. I was a normal girl, riding with her gay friend on the way to eat a nice tofu burger.

Normal, Sara.

CHAPTER THREE

It was the day before my session with Dr. Pingleton, and I swore I was making myself sick. The thought of being hypnotized by him again was enough to send me over the edge. Not a good place for a crazy gal like myself. Living on the edge, maybe – but not over it. I had played out several different scenarios of how I could get out of the session, or disrupt it like the last time. Death in the family. No good. He knew I was all alone. Chicken pox. But he has never even seen me scratching. Maybe a work emergency – a metal industry emergency? It's all so transparent.

My legs were getting tired from the miles and miles bike ride I had done around the park, so I stopped at a bench to stretch. The iPod in my ears was pounding out an old Black Eyed Peas song; it was time for a cool-down. I noticed the men who looked at me and smiled, but I always looked away. Finding someone to date was not at the top of my To Do List. I think an opener like, "Hi, I dream I'm a dude married to a woman," might send them running the opposite direction. Now, if I said, "I'm a chick wanting to get with a chick," they'd be all over that to watch. But there was something deeper in that dream.

I had my leg up on the back of the bench stretching out my hamstring, switching off one leg with the other. The sun was just starting to set, and it was in the high sixties. I had worked up a good sweat – but not in the way I preferred with my booty text guy. A tall blonde ran past and turned his entire body my way as he watched me bend low for my final stretch.

Tell him to go for it. Do it!

"Hey buddy," I asked. "Wanna go at it right here on the bench?"

The man turned, momentarily befuddled, then ran away as fast as he possibly could.

I sat down on the grass laughing, switched my music to something much softer, and did some deep breathing. Anything to calm me down over the impending session the next day. I had tried the yoga classes, and while I didn't stick with them, I remembered many of the poses.

Breathe deep. You'll be fine tomorrow.

I was still concerned about the dream. If only it would just stop and I could dream about something else – but it felt too real when I was in it. It was almost as if I could smell the sea air, but the only time I had ever experienced anything close to a marine breeze was in the Gulf of Mexico, when I had taken a cruise after a bad breakup.

Bad breakup? Isn't that an understatement?

I was a clingy mess with that man. Questioning his whereabouts all the time. Thinking I wasn't good enough for him. The two of us had been originally booked in that cruise. I was just as nuts then. Begging him to stay, thinking that would help things.

Don't you get that was exactly what drove him away, you ass?

Obviously, I don't know how to be in a relationship; I just couldn't admit to it at the time. The trip was paid for, so I said screw him, flew to Galveston, Texas, and went on it alone. But that was back when I actually had the nerve to date anyone, and I wasn't allowing myself to travel that path again.

The breathing wasn't working, nor was the music in my ears. And as always, the arm started to itch. Perhaps it was just from the sweat … or perhaps something really was wrong with me that Pingleton was about to uncover.

~~~

"Sara, tell me what you're feeling," Dr. Pingleton's voice sounded as if it were coming from inside a well.

My body tingled, but I was as relaxed as I had ever been in my life. My breathing was comfortable and deep. It felt as if he were peering through a tunnel but watching the scene at the other end.

"Darrin needs to stop lifting my dress up in school," I said. "It makes me mad."

I hated that the teachers never made him stop. And I didn't dare tell Mrs. Rivers. They might have just sent me to another home if I became a problem.

"Have you told Darrin to stop?" came the voice.

"He doesn't listen to me. He just does what he wants," I said.

Darrin was the biggest bully in all of Harden Elementary School. I knew he picked on other kids, too, but it seemed like I was his favorite target.

"What does your mother think about Darrin?"

I couldn't answer the voice. I had no mother. The kids at school all made fun of me. They had mothers and teased anyone who was different from them. I knew it.

"Did you tell your mom what Darrin does?"

I think the voice knew the truth. It must have seen me in the River's home with those other kids who belong to them. I sleep on the upper bunk in the bright yellow room with the little girl who is younger than me. I had been with another family before, but they didn't keep me long. I can't remember anything about where I was before that other family. But I had to have come from somewhere. I didn't just appear at their doorstep. I wished Darrin would get away from my dress and leave me alone.

"Sara, why are you crying?"

Crying? I reached up and felt the tears on my face. Was it about Darrin or was it about my parents? What happened to them? I wished I could wake from this nightmare; I was afraid what else the voice was going to expose.

"Can you tell me what bothers you the most in your life right now?" he asked.

He was determined for me to tell him about how much I hated going to different homes and not having real parents. That's what the voice wanted. I wished more than anything I knew where I came from – to be connected to someone in life. With these families, they didn't belong to me, and I didn't belong to them. Then, I realized I was crying harder.

The voice counted and told me to wake, remembering everything that had happened. I opened my eyes, and they were wet. But there was Dr. Pingleton's ceiling squares that joined at the points. I was back on his comfy green sofa, back to myself, and I could recall everything that had just happened. It was just luck that I hadn't blurted out any of the truth from my past to this man. He was getting too good at this hypnosis thing.

"How do you feel?" he asked.

"Fine."

"You didn't want to talk about your mother ... do you know why?"

Of course, I know why. I'm a big liar.

I could smell fresh paint, and my eyes began to dart around the room to see where it was coming from anything to keep my mind off of the task at hand. How do you tell a shrink that you had lied the past six months? Or do you even admit it, even if you are caught? The whole point of therapy is to come clean, spill your guts, and get to the root of the problem. (I also didn't need him to know that I was capable of lying the way I had.)

See, I had another huge issue in my life that was probably at the root of every decision I made. I had a gigantic and pathetic need to be liked. There. Said it. It's a classic foster kid syndrome because you meet so many new people and just want someone to like you. But if Pingleton discovered my deception, any kindness he might have felt about me would be history. I'd end up on some sort of shit list. Sick, I know. Totally stupid and works against the entire reason for going to therapy. But it was my issue, so it was real.

At least that's what Oprah would have said.

"Is our time up?" I asked, sitting up and still looking for the culprit of the paint smell.

"We still have five minutes," he said in that tone that said I had yet to make even a minor breakthrough in this visit.

I had nothing more to say. Being a foster kid was not the reason for the dreams I was having or for the phantom rash that no one could see. America was full of foster kids, and I was sure they didn't all go around pawing at their arm.

And so another game would begin. Dr. Pingleton and I could either sit and stare at each other and say nothing or I could give him what he wanted about some kind of "discovery."

"Did you experience something that you want to share with me? Something I may have missed?" This self-deprecatory technique was one of his favorites.

"I found out that I can cry over something that happened many years ago," I said.

"Hypnosis makes you believe you are right there again."

"Wonder where that bratty kid is today," I said. "Hopefully, he's sitting on a shrink's couch discussing what he did to me."

"Perhaps," he said, dismissing my attempt to veer the conversation away from the issue.

The irony was that in hindsight, Darrin was a shrimp of a kid who picked on others because of his Napoleon complex. Probably grew up to be a closet case serving in the Republican party.

Then, that dreaded pause.

Found it. All the trim in the room had been painted a light, soothing blue.

"Do you spend much time thinking about your parents? What life would have been like now had you not lost them in that plane crash?" he asked.

Maybe it was time to let Pingleton in on all my secret lies. Tell him there were no parents. There hadn't been since I was three years old. That I had made up the entire plane crash story after watching DVDs of the television show *Lost* – just so he would stop quizzing me on the parental units.

Or maybe I just needed to go buy some more cream for my arm.

"I try not to think about it," I said as I got up. "Goodbye, Dr. Pingleton. Thank you for your help."

"Good session, today." He gestured for me to stop. "You know, I think you need to come in every week. So why don't you come this time next week?"

Change in schedule definitely means he thinks I'm nuts – big time.

I gave a half smile with no answer and walked out the office door with its newly painted trim and into his waiting room. As soon as I crossed the threshold, I scratched the hell out of my arm. The desire to get to the spot was so great, it momentarily overwhelmed me. Yet still, there was nothing there. No rash, no bite, nothing. I felt like an idiot, an idiot who could really go for a set of sharp knives right about then to help me gouge the spot where the root of the itch plunged into my arm. But nothing was helping. And it was obvious that Dr. Pingleton wasn't helping the problem either.

I realized I did have a breakthrough in that session – the decision that I would not come back. I had experienced almost sharing something I didn't want to, and I had no idea how much deeper into my past he could go during this hypnosis. I pulled the sunglasses out of my oversized purse and left his office for the final time as I shaded my swollen red eyes from the hot Arizona sun.

CHAPTER FOUR

"The next round's on me," Erick said as he left the table for the bar to get four more shots of tequila. As he walked away, he allowed the pounding club music to take over his body, and he danced his way across the room.

"Watch it wiggle, see it jiggle…" Matty sang as he watched Erick's ass.

"Hey, the guy is married," I said, smacking Matty on the hand.

"Doesn't make him invisible," he replied.

"Matty, you look at everything," Hahn said as she lifted her tiny Asian head off the table.

"Too many shots there, Hahn?" I asked her.

"I can't keep up with you fuckers," she said. "Tequila is not my drink. In San Fran, we…"

"God, I'd love to go there for a visit," Matty interrupted. "I want to walk down the street of Castro and feel the history of that city."

"Psssshhaaaa," Hahn blurted out, surging with new energy. "History, fistory. They'll gang bang you in that town coming in and going out."

"Sounds like fun," Matty quipped.

Hahn and I had made a pretty good connection through our gym workouts the past few years. From what the guys and I could gather, she seemed to be around my age and had gone through things in her life none of us could fathom. Forced to work in a sweatshop as a child, she never set foot in a real school until she was in her mid teens, high school age. By that point, she had left her parents' home to live with an aunt. She ended up getting a GED and then put herself through Berkley. A lot of survival skill packed into 5 feet and 2 inches. And what a kick! Literally! Watching her in a kick-boxing class was like seeing Jackie Chan rehearse for one of his movies.

"I don't ever need to see that Pacific coastline again," she said. "Perfectly fine right here in good ole Arizona."

"Oh yes, that Arizona desert is so much more appealing than the rolling hills of San Fran," Matty guffawed.

"And here's the drink of Arizona," Erick bellowed, returning with our shots and more limes.

"I love how you three are the picture of health," Matty said and paused for effect. "Except on Friday nights at Passions."

Yes, that was actually the un-ironic name of this establishment: a local hang out where gay men and the women who love them could come and let their hair down, a dark place tackily decorated with too many hand-made signs of glitter and neon markers announcing the drink of the night or an upcoming event, several mirrored balls hanging above the dance floor, and the smell of stale cigarettes that lingered in the air and had penetrated the upholstery from the days people could actually smoke in a club. To us, it was home.

"We're getting our fruit," Erick said as he sucked on his lime.

"I got some fruit for ya." Matty leaned in a little too longingly just before I stopped him.

"There'll be none of that on my watch."

I shoved him back into his seat.

"Don't play all prim and proper with me, missy," Erick said grabbing my cell phone. "Let's just see how many texts I can find on here from Steve."

"Give me that," I said, yanking the phone back.

"Who is Steve?" Hahn asked, a glazed tequila look in her eyes.

"No one!" I glared at Erick.

"Booty text," both men said in unison.

"Girl, you should not give it up to someone who doesn't put a ring on your finger," Hahn interjected.

"Now that should be a fortune cookie," Erick said.

These guys yammered about sex all the time, but I was still embarrassed for them to be delving into my sex life. Especially when what I did was so secretive it was like having a drug dealer come to my house and giving me just enough to dull the pain – but always leaving me longing for more.

"More gym time. That's what I do. When I feel the urge, I just get to the gym," Hahn said.

"Yeah, that's what I tell myself, too," Matty said, patting his paunch as he reached for the nuts on the table.

"Like I've said a hundred times, you can get rid of that if you'd just follow mine and Sara's lead," Erick said.

"You ain't getting me to drink no grass of the meadow or eat a soy chicken wing, or all that other nonsense you guys do."

"You should have seen what I had to grow up eating," Hahn said.

Matty sucked in his gut a little as Erick patted it. Matty wasn't obese or ugly by any means. He was just a regular guy who would always look average next to Erick, who had the sun streaked hair while Matty was a dirty blonde. Erick had the piercing blue eyes, where Matty's were a muddled hazel. And whereas Erick looked as if he had walked out of the pages of Vogue, Matty owned a few old faded jeans and a handful of t-shirts that needed the attention of an iron and were marked with the ghosts of an assortment of foods.

Matty was my age but still lived at home with his mother. We could usually find him with his iTouch not too far from his possessions. He was addicted to online poker. A stranger would have surmised he was just a nerdy techie middle school science teacher and out of touch with other gay men in the city. But then, something completely queer would come out of his mouth, and we'd be reminded that he was a card-carrying-member. Erick rode him hard about his eating habits, but I really didn't care that he was slightly overweight. I loved the guy like a brother, and he would do anything for me and vice-versa. Well, except setting him up with Erick behind Ron's back. That wasn't kosher.

"What's with all the marks on your arm, girl?" Hahn asked, looking at the scratches.

"Oh, I had some sort of rash last night and got a little crazy scratching it," I said.

Note to self: Clip my fingernails.

"Hahn, have you ever known anyone to get hit in those tsunamis overseas?" Matty asked.

The science brain was never far from an assignment for his students.

"Why would you ask that?" she replied, stating the obvious.

"I just thought…"

"You white people," she said. "You think all Asians are related?"

"No! No!" Matty fumbled. "I was covering that in class today, and I've never known where you are from."

"And I ain't telling. Part of my charm. Maybe you'll get it on my reality show. Wherever I get in. Oh, by the way, I got a rejection from another one."

"How many more videos are you going to send out?" Erick asked.

"I've told you, until one of them accepts me," she said. "I don't care which one it is."

"Do you sing?" Matty asked. "There are a million different singing contests on TV."

"Have you heard her at karaoke?" I asked in an incredulous tone.

"Where else can you try then?" Matty continued.

"There is one out there for me," she said. "They should just follow me around with a camera. What does Margaret Cho have that I don't?"

"Her own shows," Erick said.

"A comedy routine," Matty said.

"A gay throng as a fan base," I said.

"I got these two," Hahn said, putting her arms around Erick and Matty.

"Step back bi-otch and get your own," I told her.

I was glad Hahn enjoyed spending time with my boys, just as long as she stayed in check on who was the number-one gal in their life. I looked out on the dance floor at all the men grinding their bodies together, some making out, whispering into each other's ears, but mostly enjoying the music. Sprinkled throughout the room, you could spot the women who were there with their guys. Most, if not all, of the girls were fated to be dumped by the end of the night when their men would hook up and head home with each other.

This is the type of relationship you deserve, Sara. No strings – and men who can only love you to a certain point.

Guess I was lucky to have a guy who had a man waiting at home, and then Matty, who was so busy pining for Erick that he wouldn't even look at any of the other guys in the room. I knew I wouldn't be left alone come closing.

"I'm thinking I'm gonna start wearing a ribbon on my arm," Erick piped up.

"Like Lance Armstrong?" Matty asked.

"For Kabbalah?" Hahn threw in.

"Nah. A shiny lavender one in support of Michael Kors," Erick said. "Have you seen his new collection?"

Hahn smacked Erick's arm as Matty let us know his feeding clock was ticking.

"Are we planning on eating tonight, or are we just drinking the night away?"

"We can go to my place for food," Hahn said, raising her head from the table again and pushing her long straight hair from her eyes.

"Forget it. God only knows what you'd feed us," Matty said.

"You seem to be the only one who's hard to please," I said.

"So why don't you three just run out to graze on the small patch of grass next to the building and drop me off at the Bell of Taco," Matty said.

Erick laughed and grabbed Matty in a head lock.

"I am gonna sway you yet, my friend," he said.

"The only tofu I'm gonna eat is if it's served on your ballsack," Matty said.

-31-

"Ahhhhh ... I don't need to hear that," Hahn said, covering her ears. "You tea bagging freaks."

While everyone was laughing at Hahn, my cell vibrated on the table.

All three of them lunged, but I beat them to it.

I read the text from Steve and smiled.

"Guess we know what Sara will be eating tonight," Erick said.

The song changed into a remix of that Bryan Adams eighties classic, *Heaven*. The guys started singing along with the singer, belting it out simultaneously.

"I love this song!" Erick said. "Takes me back in time."

Erick looked around at us.

"Oh, you kids were just starting elementary school then," he said.

We all looked at Hahn since no one was really sure of her age.

"What?" she said. "A woman? Age? How rude!"

We laughed, and the boys kept singing. I hadn't thought about elementary school in so long. It was a part of my life I tried not to revisit. Then, it felt strange, as if someone had poisoned the air. None of us were in our twenties anymore, and the entire scene, our Friday night happy hour, had a pathetic hint of trying to recapture some other, better time in our lives. Much as Ron did with the eighties. Or perhaps it was just friends having a good time, and I was letting the tequila and the therapy sessions make me too morosely analytical.

In any event, I was somewhat happy with my makeshift family of friends. Even if they didn't know the demons that were attacking me from the inside out, perhaps it was best if they didn't find that out about me. I took a swig from the Corona sitting in front of my "brother" Matty and watched as he slid his arm right up next to Erick's and let it rest on the table, almost grazing as long as he could.

CHAPTER FIVE

There was hardly ever any talking where Steve was involved, which was good since my mouth had been known to get me into trouble. I never even knew where he was coming from when he arrived. It could have been playing cards with the guys or on a date with another girl for all I knew. He would show up, say his, "Hey, Red," remove his clothes to show his perfectly 6'2" chiseled body, and feed the part of me that my friends could not supply. Even though the shame of the clandestine scene gnawed at my mind, his muscular back felt good under my freshly clipped fingernails as I ran them up and down the length of his spine. The hair on his chest would make my nipples hard, and he knew exactly how much I liked for him to bite on them.

This is the safest way for you to have any kind of relationship, and you know it.

Both me and the voice in my head knew I wasn't good enough for a real relationship, so I could tell myself that Steve and I were using each other.

His thrusts were not that of a young man, but of a seasoned professional who knew how to please a woman. I arched my back, meeting him midway as he filled me with something that was larger than most other men I had dated. Maybe that was one of my reasons for always responding to his texts. As much as women protest that size doesn't matter, it did to this woman.

Show him how much you like it, Sara.

I never wanted to confuse what we did with making love. I wasn't that much of a fool. We were satisfying needs. That's it. There was no tender caressing, no kisses on the nape of the neck, just pure unadulterated sex. Sessions that could go for a long time. And it felt good for a long time.

You've got an itch to worry about.

But this particular night, my mind wandered. He was out of me and had moved down to do some of that virtuoso tongue-work that I always enjoyed. But I was thinking about the girl in my dream. The man standing on the rocks on the beach. For a moment, the man looked like Steve.

Stop it! Enjoy the face between your legs.

His tongue and fingers were invading my body, and the pleasure quotient was intense.

You should never have left that therapist.

He had ripped off the condom and thrown it on the floor, so I knew that meant he wasn't heading back to that area for a while with his mammoth stick. He could stay where he was for days as far as I was concerned.

And Gracie ran past me in the blood-stained life preserver. The overwhelming feeling of her being mine made me want to reach out to her, but she disappeared.

What the hell was going on? The images had never appeared outside of my dreams before.

You're crazy, girl. Why do you think you wouldn't be seeing Gracie all the time?

I took his head in my hands, tugging his dark, wavy hair as I pushed my pelvis deep onto his tongue. I wanted him to encircle and pierce me with it to wipe my mind clean, remove all images that were playing there by using my vagina as the entrance to my soul and my brain.

Sara, we need to think about this...

Was the invisible rash simply a sign that I was going crazy? Dreams that occurred when I was not asleep. Children who didn't exist. A part of me that thought I was a man. What the fuck?

Sara!

And just like that, something happened that I had never experienced before. The myth of the female ejaculation made itself known that night in my very own bedroom. And it was quite obvious that Steve was just as shocked as I was.

CHAPTER SIX

While certain parts of the country were enjoying the start of fall weather on this October day, in Phoenix we were still reveling in the warm 80 degrees. I could have gone down to the condo pool and jumped in if I felt inclined, but I didn't. This type of climate was some of the draw for people to live in this part of the country. I got sick of the "but it's a dry heat" justification – like that was supposed to make things better. But an 80-degree day was much better than 100. Luckily, it was morning, and we hadn't gotten to that warmth yet.

Hahn and I had just finished one of our early morning kickboxing classes, and the sweat was running down my back heading for that infamous region of the ass crack. The sweat meant the job was working. I had tried to ignore the latest voicemail on my phone from Dr. Pingleton's office. I hadn't talked to him in over three weeks.

You have to tell him what happened with Steve. You're a dude inside.

He sounded genuinely concerned. And why not? A crazy patient of his had simply stopped coming in for her biweekly sessions. He probably had visions of me mauled to death by self-infliction with shaved head and/or having joined a lesbian cult.

Or he hasn't even thought much about you, and his assistant is the one clogging your voicemail.

Hahn and I were doing a cool-down stretch on the mats and talking about heading off to each of our jobs.

"If I could just get on a TV show, I could walk away from E&Y," Hahn said.

She had a strange way of breathing during those stretches, and I almost laughed at her tiny body lifting up and down on the floor like some sort of blow-up doll.

"If it's meant to happen, it will," I said, not really sure if I believed that old saying or not.

"Like Obama said – *just dream it and go for it,*" she said. "And this little Asian is following right in his footsteps."

"I don't think he was talking about trying to get your Asian ass on TV," I said. "There's a big difference between running our country and grabbing those dreaded 15 minutes of fame."

"Bitch, I'm going for way more than 15."

Hahn laughed and fell back on her mat.

"But I thought you didn't want to head back to California," I said. "You know if you get anything, you're L.A. bound."

"That's a risk I'm willing to take, as long as it's southern California. I can endure it for my art."

"Your art," I laughed. "Hell, which art is that?"

Hahn shot me one of her stoic dirty looks and changed the subject.

"Oh, I meant to tell you that I have a friend coming from San Fran for Halloween," she said.

"Great. Will they be stopping at the mansion?" I asked.

"Samara will love the party at the mansion," she said. "She'll fit right in."

"Is she a Halloween nut, lesbo, or a hag?"

"None of the above. She is an eccentric mystic who performs palm and chart readings and even hypnosis. The boys will be all over that."

The mere mention of the word hypnosis, and I was back on Pingleton's couch, feeling the guilt over having abandoned my therapy. How could I confide in him that his sex-crazed client wasn't sure if she was straight, gay, or Chaz Bono. I allowed my body to stretch all the way and exhaled out the air that had filled my lungs during my class.

"Do you believe in all that?" I asked.

"Of course. You've never had your cards read? You think it's all a sham, right?"

"I believe in working on my physical well-being; hence you see me at the gym. That metaphysical stuff, not for me."

"Samara will have to read cards for you when she is here."

I nodded, a dubious expression on my face.

"It'll be great!" Hahn continued. "People will love her at the party."

"Why don't we charge a fee for her services and make a buck or two," I said with a laugh.

But the laugh was merely to cover up an uncomfortable feeling. Someone reading my cards, telling me things about my future or my past. This was not the kind of situation that got me all warm and fuzzy. I preferred to leave the future and the past exactly where they were – out of my immediate purview. It made me think of New Orleans voodoo or some witch from one of those stories in the Salem trials.

You're just a chicken, Sara.

I preferred to live in the here and now and deal with concrete things in my life – my job, friends, the gym, sex with Steve.

Trying to ignore me.

"God, I wish I could win the lottery so I wouldn't have to go to work," Hahn said, heading for the bathroom.

"You and me both, sister," I said.

We walked through the swinging door into the gray and purple-striped room with the old vanities and mirrors. The place was in dire need of a makeover from one of those television shows that could bring the woman's changing room up to the current decade.

"This locker room stinks," Hahn said. "Whoever said that women smell better than men? Lies!"

I knew all about lies, that was for sure. But no need to fill my friend in on that. I caught Hahn looking at me as we both were doing our "after workout comparison" in the mirror.

"What?" I asked.

"God, I wish I had your tits," she said.

"I'll gladly give them to you."

"I'm cursed with these freakin' kumquats over here," she said trying to pull her boobs up in her spandex top.

"Men drool over your petite little body," I said. "And that jet black straight hair."

Hahn started to undress to ready herself for the shower.

"They just want me to tickle their balls with this hair and then giggle like a stupid geisha movie. Ain't happening. Single is fine by me."

She made her proclamation and went into a shower stall. I went into the adjacent one, trying not to laugh at her as she attempted to sing some Lady Gaga song. As the water poured over my body, my mind kept thinking about what was locked inside, venting to get out. From the moment I had encountered the freaky sex release with Steve, I questioned if there was a man in there about to break through in some science fiction movie scenario.

Sure you don't need to get back to therapy?

~~~

I had agreed to meet Matty for lunch at Applebee's near my office. I could find a salad on the menu while he could eat whatever fat-laden food he wanted. The televisions over the bar were playing CNN; someone had decided it was time to recap top stories of the past ten years. Images of the small boy and the homemade flying saucer hoax popped up.

"I had forgotten all about that silly family," I said, looking over Matty's shoulder at the TV.

"While my science brain applauds the parents for building something like that, I think they need to be a little better at what they teach their kids about their search for fame via television appearances," he said.

We both looked at each other and instantly shared the same thought.

"Hahn," we said and laughed.

"I'm glad I don't have kids," I said.

"Thank God for this fall break. Spending two months with those heathens, and I'm freaking ready," Matty said as he bit into his spinach dip.

"Do you enjoy your job?" I asked.

"I love teaching. They are the future of tomorrow," he said.

"OK, Laura Bush, take a pill."

"No, seriously. There is something exciting about imparting knowledge to those who really want to learn. But the half who have no desire to be sitting in the room? That often makes it difficult to get through the day."

The waitress refilled my iced tea as Matty slurped down a root beer and piled his chip with the gooey concoction.

"What?" he asked, noticing me staring. "It's the dip of spinach. Have some."

"With a shitload of cheese added to it," I said. "And you impart knowledge?"

"I'm working on a super Halloween costume for this year," he said.

"You are such a kid sometimes," I said with a laugh.

"My students keep me young."

"My gym keeps me younger."

"Jim is a boy's name," he joked.

"Don't forget. You have something major to do before Halloween night gets here – drive to Sedona to pick up me and Erick."

"You think I'd forget something like that?" he asked. "Besides, I won't pass up the chance to see your aching body at the end of the ride and … maybe give Erick a back massage or something, you know, if he needs it. He's always doing that at his job, I think he needs to let someone work him over."

"You're too much," I said.

The phone in my purse vibrated.

"Don't look at it," he said. "You need to cut it off with him."

"What are you talking about?" I said. "It's the best sex I've ever had."

"Don't rub it in."

"But it's just sex, nothing else."

"Exactly," he said. "And what good can come of that?"

I looked at my friend who had always been so full of sexual innuendos in every situation we found ourselves in.

"I'm waiting for your zinger to that," I said.

"I know I talk the smack; comes from hanging around kids all the time. But between you, me, and this plate of gooey cheese dip – something more meaningful would be nice."

Matty was right. How was I ever going to be able to find a normal relationship when my dark nights were full of cheap, tawdry sex? But I wasn't a normal gal and didn't deserve normalcy.

I caught his eyes following a group of business men who had walked in for lunch. We were both checking them out.

"Your team," he said.

"Why don't you try meeting someone?" I asked. "We go out every Friday, and you look at no one. You're a computer nerd type. You could probably even find someone online."

"Gee, thanks," he said. "I'll remember that the next time you call me for the support of tech."

"I just worry about you, Matty. We want to see you happy."

"I am happy."

"You just said you want more…"

"If it happens. But do you think meeting some guy would really help anything? I don't see you hitting the dating scene."

He has you there.

Matty had never known me back when I actually dated. I had not been on a real date in … well, I couldn't even recall how long. Prior to Bill and the ill-fated singles cruise, there had been Robert Michelson the third. Yet one more notch in my crazed list of attempts at love. Fifteen years older than me, good looking with his onset of salt and pepper hair, great job as a financial analyst – and did I mention married with three kids? Yes, I had been the proverbial other woman in my early twenties thinking I could actually find true love with a man who was at the top of the "unavailable meter." But Robbie made me believe I was special – and I fell for every line he gave me. From our chance meeting waiting for our oil changes at the car dealership to the numerous nights I spent in a hotel room catering to him to the ugly ending where I threatened to call his wife – it was one big mess of a relationship. He would have been the father of the child I never had, which would have made it all so much worse. So in a "self-fulfilling prophecy" type of move once in my thirties, I stopped trying to find that one man who would be different. Instead, I spent more time with gay men and one really hot straight one late at night. But I guess none of what I had could compete with an honest to goodness relationship. Though I still had plenty of reasons for staying to myself (not to mention a terrible track record).

Crazy chicks don't make for good girlfriends.

"This is about you, not me," I said. "Stop waiting around to massage Erick."

My salad and his burger arrived to the table, and the server grabbed the empty bowl of dip. Matty tried to catch the last bit of falling cheese from the bowl as she took it away.

"I'm not waiting for anyone," he said.

"I know you have it bad for him; you always have."

I had basically introduced the two of them when I caught Matty sitting alone at Passions one night and invited him to join us. I never intended for his passion to grow for Erick, but from that moment on, he became something much more than a bar mate.

"Maybe it makes it easier for me to want something I can't have," he said. "Flirting with Erick is safe."

Boy, didn't I know about that. The fact that Steve and I would never have to go out on a date or leave the bedroom made it much easier to stay with him.

The itch on my arm started to flare up. I wondered if people would notice if I took a fork on the table and started to gnash away at my arm.

That would be a little dramatic, even for you.

"Okay," I said. "No more men talk."

"Good idea, or you'll just get me jealous over your late night shenanigans."

"Oh, my God, you sound so old, using that word."

"Comes from living at home with my mother," he said. "Ever watch a group of old chicks play gin with safety pins as money? Enthralling!"

I cracked up over my friend and his life at home with his mom. He continued to eat and fill me in on the quirky Mrs. Reiner. There are those moments in life when you realize that perhaps you are not the only crazy one in the world. It's just that some of us keep it in our heads while others have no problem letting it all hang out there.

    Matty was one of the latter.

CHAPTER SEVEN

"When are you coming to pick me up?" I asked Erick as I continued getting dressed in my bedroom.

Erick and I loved catching an early movie on a Saturday night before the young crowd arrived, who annoyed everybody with their phone calls, conversations, and constant texting through the movie. Yes – we were officially part of the "older" crowd.

"I should be leaving shortly. Just waiting for Ron."

And then it started – the conversation I felt I should not be hearing. You know how people say "I wish I were a fly on the wall" so they can overhear something? Well, I got the chance to do just that, and it wasn't pretty.

"Where the hell have you been?" I heard Erick say to Ron through the phone, completely forgetting he was talking to me.

"Out with my friends," I heard Ron say in the distance.

"Are you falling in love with that guy? First it starts as a drug connection, and next you're fucking his girlfriend."

What the hell was Erick talking about? Ron is gay.

There were slamming of doors and screaming through them.

"Use that damn face exfoliation thing all you want! You're still gonna die someday!" Erick yelled.

"Like you would fucking care," came Ron's muffled voice.

"I don't care anymore; you're right! I'm just waiting for the call that you have overdosed somewhere!"

I hung up the phone. I didn't want to be involved to that extent. I knew Erick was having problems, but he wasn't discussing them with me. And I had no idea it had grown to this. I guess it was the same way I kept so much from him. What kind of friends were we that we weren't there for each other? So many people just deal with surface issues and never try and delve emotionally. I wished I could tell the guys about my dreams, my rash, my crazy thoughts.

You have me to talk to, Sara.

My inner voice talked to me, but I tried not to talk back.

Sometimes, I wondered what it would be like if I completely disappeared. Who would care? Notice, even? My friends had their own lives. And it was obvious we were not as tight as I thought, or we'd be sharing our deep dark secrets with each other. I wasn't sure I'd be missed at all if I were gone. I was certain that when I walked away from the foster homes, they never thought twice about me again.

The story of your life, Sara.

When you get right down to it, who is there in life that you can truly count on outside of yourself? People let you down eventually. I knew that all too well. As much as I enjoyed my friends, there was no blood between us to connect us. We could pretend all we wanted to be a tight-knit family, but if things got really complicated, I was sure they would bolt. They each had so much going on that my silly life wouldn't matter if I was gone. Maybe the gang would start to wonder after a week and come into my condo to find me clawed to death by any sharp object, whatever I had found most convenient. Or maybe one gadget would be all it would take to end the entire thing.

What the hell are you talking about? You could never kill yourself.

I shrugged off the pity party and went about my business. It had become second nature by then to walk through my condo scratching my arm. I didn't even notice I was doing it until I went into the bathroom, turned on the light and noticed streaks all over my arm. I decided to change shirts before I saw Erick and put on a long sleeved blouse to hide the marks.

Now, you're a real freak, hiding your secret obsession.

I opened up the windows in the condo to let some of the Arizona fall breezes in to clear the stagnant air in my place. Maybe there was some force that was tickling my arm, and it just needed to be released from the living room.

Double freak.

Forty-five minutes passed before Erick arrived. I opened the door and could tell he had been crying.

"Sorry we missed the movie," he said.

"I don't care about the stupid movie. Get in here."

I made my friend a dirty martini and went into the back of the pantry where I kept the "emergency junk food." In this case, a bag of popcorn and some corn chips with salsa seemed to be calling out to us.

"If you tell Matty I keep this in my condo, I'll kill you," I said, bringing the stash to my friend who had curled up on my sofa.

"Your secret is safe with me."

"So is yours. Now, do you want to share what's been going on?" I asked, reaching out for it.

Seeing Erick in need brought out a side of me I was unaware I possessed. But it was time that he and I went below the surface of our relationship and took it to a new level.

"Ron has been going through some major changes lately," he said, taking a big gulp of his drink.

At 50, Ron had decided to give women a try. Like my gender was dying to make it with the plastic-man. But it was all wrapped up in the new set of friends he had made, which also meant a new set of drugs. I was sort of shocked by the fact that a gay man could so easily sleep with a woman. Maybe my lesbian dreams really were trying to tell me something about myself that I was trying to hide.

"Why does he say he wants to do this?" I asked.

"He said he thinks he is pathetic for making it to 50 and never having screwed a girl. I told him he was more pathetic for doing it in his fifties."

"Do you think you could do that?" I asked.

"Are you coming on to me, honey?"

"No," I said with a laugh. "I just always thought people were born gay ... and stayed that way."

"We are, dear. He's using this as a way to get to someone."

Whew. You're straight, Sara.

"What?"

I should have known there was a man involved. No matter what Ron had done or what my dreams were saying – people are who they are. Erick told me that the "friend" Ron had been smoking pot with and doing God-knows-what other drugs with was a gorgeous straight guy Ron was trying to get to. By starting with the guy's girlfriend, Ron was hoping he could eventually talk the guy into a threesome.

"Is this the kind of open relationship you two have?" I asked.

"Not that I was aware of."

"Your life with Ron seemed so different when we first met."

"It was. We were happy. We were the perfect couple, and he was a great guy. I guess years can really change you."

"Then, why are you staying?" I asked.

"I've been with him for ten years. I ain't getting younger."

"Stop right there. Hundreds of men would want you. You don't have to deal with this."

I looked at the gorgeous guy both men and women adored wherever we went and could not believe he had any doubts about finding someone else. If this guy had problems, there was no hope for the average people in the world.

"I can't imagine starting all over, finding my own place, all the rest of it."

"That's not a reason to stay with Ron, and you know it," I said.

"The man has money." He smiled in the manner of someone caught in shame.

"Oh ... so are you a kept man?" I said as I hugged him in my arms.

"He does keep me in a certain lifestyle that I've become accustomed to."

"I'll drink to that," I said taking a drink from my martini glass. "Now, find me a sugar daddy?"

"You need to meet someone, hon."

"Nope. We're not turning this on me," I said.

"But what else is there to say about me; you now know what I've been going through. And amazingly enough, I feel relieved that you know. And that you're not judging me."

"Of course, I would never judge you."

How could you? You have the most screwed up life of all.

"Are you worried about him?" I asked.

"I'm worried he'll piss this guy off at some point, Ron will end up dead, and I'll never even know. Who would know to reach out to me? Whatever chick he's banging?"

Erick started laughing at the absurdity of the situation, which made me laugh as well.

"I have to admit, you yelling at him about his skin exfoliation was priceless," I said.

Erick continued to laugh.

"The bitch is gonna die no matter how tight he makes his skin," he said.

"Do you still love him?" I asked.

Erick looked at me.

"I'm not in love with him anymore, but I still love him. We have a long history together. So much time ... the life we've built. But I can't stand all the lies. It's taken a toll on me, and I feel like I'm reaching my limit."

Lies can really push someone to the edge. How much had I been lying to my friends? I certainly didn't want to be the one causing more stress in someone's life.

More drinks were poured, and then, it finally came out.

"I've been seeing a shrink for six months," I said.

Erick spit his drink out.

"Bi-otch, watch my sofa!" I said.

"How have you kept this from me? For what? You are the sanest person I know."

Oh, Sara, you have them so fooled.

I let it all out. The trips to the doctor for the "rash," which eventually led me to Dr. Pingleton. The jaunt down memory lane on his sofa, full of lies. The fact that I then stopped going and never even called.

"It's like you skipped out on a bad date," he said.

"Oh, God, can you imagine if I were dating my shrink?" I asked.

That is so something you would do, Sara.

"There could be worse things," he said.

"I do feel guilty."

"Don't. When you're ready for it, you'll try it again. The process is for you, not for him."

Erick was good for my self-confidence; he made me feel better about myself.

"But why did you lie about being in foster homes?" he asked. "You told me that several years ago, and I didn't flinch."

"I don't know," I said. "Really. I just didn't want to go there with a stranger, I guess."

The truth was that I was scared of my past, of what came before the foster families. I was afraid Pingleton was going to get too close to that life, and I'd learn something I didn't want to know. I wasn't ready to talk to Erick about that either.

Erick jumped up to shake up another batch of cocktails while I flipped channels on the television.

"While we're sharing so much and the alcohol is pumping through me, I have to admit something," he said.

"What?"

Erick stopped his bartender act and stood still.

"I think I'm slightly attracted to Matty."

"I can't hear this," I said, covering my ears. "You two are good friends. Why would you screw that up?"

He had no answer, nor did he seem to get the gist of my question and went back to the pouring of cocktails.

"He's so attentive to me. And such a great guy."

"Friend."

A new drink was put in my hand, but the corn chips and popcorn were not soaking up enough of the last one as it was.

"Be careful with that," I said. "Someone will get hurt."

"I'm not looking to hurt anyone."

"I have one more to share with you also," I said.

"Lord, girl, what more can there be? Are you a dyke?" he said with a laugh.

"Well, in my dreams, I'm close."

"What?"

I explained the whole dream set in Maine where I was a married man with a dead child. Even saying it out loud made me feel like an idiot.

"Damn ... but you are one hot mess, aren't you?" he asked in that loving way that only Erick could.

"I've never been to Maine."

"Maybe you have."

"What?"

"You told me you don't know where you came from before you were in foster care. Maybe you were born there."

He said it so dismissively, as if it were meant as a joke, but something made sense through my drunken haze.

I loved the fact that we had opened up in a way we never had before. But we had shared enough secrets for one night, so we spent the rest of the evening laughing and watching episodes of the cancelled *United States of Tara*. The character of the schizophrenic woman made me wonder if schizophrenia was what I was afflicted with. After all, the dreams had started to happen while I was awake. I had heard it was hereditary. Maybe my real parents had it and passed it to me before they dumped me off at some orphanage. Or perhaps I had a sister somewhere named Gracie.

Stop analyzing so much.

It was after midnight when Erick said he had to go.

"Are you sure you want to go home?" I asked.

"I'm fine. Sobered up and ready to face him … if he's even there."

I grabbed him at the doorway.

"If I went missing, would you come looking for me?" I asked.

"Of course." He paused. "Who else can I eat tofu with and share dirty secrets?"

He had said the right words. Why was I so scared of believing someone could care?

"You know how much I love you?" I said.

"Backatcha."

He kissed my forehead, and out he went. I picked up the mess that was left in the living room and took it all into the kitchen. I thought about all we had talked about – the men we chose to be with, the past that was knocking at my memory's door, the dream of me switching teams. Then, I went to the bathroom to start my nightly routine. Taking the white pill was a daily reminder that I had high blood pressure. I flossed and brushed and started to remove the make-up from the day.

The doorbell rang; I figured Erick had forgotten something.

"Did you change…"

"Hey, Red."

It was Steve.

"I sent you a text. Didn't you get it?" he asked.

I had been nowhere near my phone all night. And it felt good to not be on constant standby for his little missives.

Send him away. Tell him we're not in the mood.

I stood there with half a washed face. But here was this hot guy standing in my door, and I felt another itch in dire need of a scratching. I moved aside in the doorway and watched him strut to my bedroom, removing his clothes as he went.

CHAPTER EIGHT

My boss stood over my small cubicle regaling me with weekend stories, but I only feigned a slight interest. I couldn't care less that some cigar-smoking fat-ass bought a new riding lawn mower when most of Phoenix was full of rock beds!

Thank God the phone rang.

"Widdleton Industries," I said.

The fat fuck stood over me watching how I spoke to a client. The smell of stale cigar and old cologne floated down to my desk.

Really?

"Yes sir. I'll put you through to Rick right away."

"Rick is one of my best salesmen," lard-butt said, still hovering.

"Yup. He's good all right."

If you really care about how much metal someone can talk someone into buying.

Maybe this is why my brain liked to escape to weird dreams at night: My day was full of idiotic moments like this. The door opened, and there was the delivery guy. I tried not to let my face light up in front of Mr. Widdleton when I saw that it was Steve coming in with that gorgeous chiseled face that had been buried deep between my thighs several times the weekend before.

"Good morning," I said, reaching for the pad I knew I'd be signing.

"Hey," was all that Steve said.

Get out of here, Widdleton!

"I better leave you to your job," Mr. W said as he made his way back to his office.

He heard me!

The voice in my head was doing a victory dance for being heard. Sick.

Steve was leaning over me in two seconds, allowing his hand to make its way inside my blouse, even as I signed the form and tore off my copy. I stared at his huge forearm sticking out of my top with the thrill of knowing anyone could walk in at any moment. It was the brazen act in which he claimed me which also shook me. Here was a man who would not even take me out to lunch during the day but felt he could touch any part of my body (and had) whenever he felt like it. I was property that was good enough to get his rocks off, but nothing more. It became too much for me, and I pulled his hand away.

"Thanks for your business," I quipped with a smile.

"Saturday night was amazing, Red," he whispered in my ear and vanished out the door.

I was completely hot and bothered by his breath on my neck and his scent in the air.

Way to get my engine going, Steve.

I picked up the phone and dialed.

"Guess who tried to get a little something-something right in the middle of the day?" I said.

"Did you get a delivery at work?" Erick asked.

"Almost turned into more than a delivery the way he was touching me," I whispered.

"Ewwwww. Are you wet?"

"Sara!" came the voice from the other room.

"Gotta run," I said. "And yes ... I am!"

I hung up the phone and went into Mr. Widdleton's office. Here was a man who loved to act like administrative assistants still took dictation. I think he just wanted me to be near his dick. The man, like all men, couldn't keep his eyes off my breasts.

"I have a huge favor to ask," he started, stumbling over words while he looked at my cleavage. "And I know it's not part of your job description, so I'm embarrassed to even bring it up..."

"What do you want to buy her?"

I wanted to get away from the office, and shopping for his wife would fill up half the day. At that moment, I didn't care if I was setting the women's movement back by several decades.

"You know me too well," he said with a laugh, putting a hefty, sweaty hand on my shoulder.

Lower it any, and you lose a limb, mister.

"Whatever you think she'd like. All up to you."

I gave him a small jiggle of the girls, took his credit card, grabbed my purse at my desk, and went out to my car. It felt like getting a furlough for the day. I grabbed my cell phone from my purse and called Erick.

"Wanna meet for lunch? It's on the company credit card."

The two of us laughed and joked on the phone as I made my way down Pierce Street. I must admit, I wasn't paying much attention to the road between the radio blaring and my conversation with Erick. All of a sudden, the car in front of me sped up through a yellow light turning red, and the oncoming car smashed right into its side, sending it flying.

"Oh shit!" I yelled, slamming on my brakes.

I dropped the cell phone and froze, witnessing the careening sounds of metal on metal, broken glass spraying, and everyone heading toward the intersection in panic mode to stop their own cars. I hyperventilated and heard Erick's faint voice screaming for me. I picked up the phone quickly.

"I'm okay. I'm okay," I said. "But there has been a terrible accident on Pierce and 15th."

"I'll be right there," he said.

"No. Don't come. Too many people. Call you later."

I hung up and got out of my car, joining the others, who were all surveying the scene. The driver who had the right of way was out of his car, but the person in the car in front of me wasn't moving. It was a man, probably around my age. Stuff from his car was strewn across the intersection. Obviously, he had plans to go to the lake since there was fishing equipment on the street and falling out of the back of the car. A child's car seat was strapped in the backseat, but thankfully, there was no child.

This could have been you, Sara. You could have gone through the light.

Suddenly, the thoughts I had about vanishing popped into my head, as well as the three amigos I called family. I knew at that moment that I would have missed them dearly.

Others had called the police, and I heard sirens in the distance as good Samaritans began to offer help. I turned toward the wreck of the car with its shattered glass and crushed metal once more and lifted something that was at my feet. A child's life vest.

My mind flashed to Gracie.

CHAPTER NINE

It was an amazing Saturday morning, all the bike riders coming together to fulfill a common goal: not only raising money for cancer research, but pushing themselves to finish the strenuous ride. The previous Saturday night drinking with Erick hadn't been a good idea, knowing our bodies had to be in top form for the task, but he and I were only part-time health nuts. The professionals had trained much harder than we had, so I told myself to make sure and do some of my riding directly behind them to grab their wind speed and save some of my energy. Team Sarick (Matty and Hahn) were doing their part – driving to meet us later at night and bring us back to Phoenix with our bikes. Erick and I made the most of it by staying in the pack with the others, taking breaks when needed and laughing and chatting along the ride.

I had been to Sedona before, but I always forgot what a breathtaking trek it was to go on that highway. Visions of deserts and red rocks in the distance, passing some of the famous swimming holes from the area, counting the different animals roaming Verde Valley – anything to take my mind off my legs pumping the pedals on the hillier part of the trip.

"We are lucky that the intensity of the warm weather has died down," Erick said.

"My ass wouldn't be on this seat if it that weren't the case," I joked.

"You'll have to get booty text to massage that ass later on," he said.

"After this ride, I'm not gonna want to have sex for weeks."

Speaking of sex and my speed-booty text, I saw a jack rabbit on the side of the road that seemed to be racing us. I just missed hitting a lizard that darted out in front of me. Hawks circled above, making me laugh to think they were waiting for one of us to just pass out.

It will probably be you.

I seemed to be the weakest link on this animal/human food chain that had all gathered on this highway.

The ride was supposed to be ten hours, and I tried not to count as each morning hour passed. Everyone seemed so into what they were doing that at times, Erick and I were too embarrassed to talk. This would leave me alone in my muddled head having conversations with myself.

Not a good place for you to be.

Sometime around one o'clock, I was feeling an intense burn in my legs, knowing a scheduled stop was coming up. Power bars and water were supposed to be enough to sustain us until we got to the end, and oddly enough, it had been doing the trick. It was the ache and burn that needed some attention. I kept telling myself there were only four more hours and it would all be over. I'd be able to check this off that invisible "I've done that list" that we all keep. The group stopped near rock terrain that overlooked a valley below. Everyone got off their bikes to walk around and work out the cramps in their legs.

"I'm scared I won't want to get back on the bike," I told Erick.

"You can do it, girl. Don't even think about it."

He's lying, Sara. Your ass is gonna end up in a hospital.

I tried not to listen to that voice in my head and walked up on the rock overlooking the desert land below. Instead of dirt, my mind drifted to water as if I were standing on rocks overlooking the ocean – much like in my dream. How different from my real life. My eyes viewed red rocks and patches of dead grass while my mind saw waves and sea foam. Perhaps my craziness was becoming stronger and I simply was not aware of it.

"Sara, time to go," Erick called from behind me.

"Holy crap," I said.

We were back in the groove, legs all going in motion as we worked our way to the final stretch. There were drenched areas of my body that I never knew could sweat. Thank God they made the Lycra outfits large enough for a woman of my chest size to soak in what my body was pumping out. At times, I just coasted down the highway, allowing my legs to rest from the constant pumping of the pedals.

I would be a fool to not admit the beauty of the setting sun as we made our way into Sedona. The sky was magnificent; stretching as far as the eye could see, a canvas of purples, my favorite color of orange, yellows. It was slightly after 5:00 p.m. when I saw the finish line in sight. I thought I could possibly cry over the fact that we had done it, finished, and several people did break down in tears. There were friends and loved ones lined up along the road in Old Town as we came in. I saw Matty and Hahn wearing Team Sarick shirts they had made – waving to us to cross the line. Signs reading *Cure Cancer* and *You Can Do It* filled the sides of the road. The jubilation of the ending was quite intense.

"We did it," Erick said as he smiled at me.

"Yeah, we did," I said.

The feeling of accomplishment was overwhelming to me. Sometimes, that voice in my head didn't let me believe I could finish something I'd started. But I had – and it was exhilarating.

The bikers all got off their bikes, pushing them out of the way. People were handing us water, and doctors were checking on some to make sure they were okay. Others were popping open champagne bottles, and men and women were hugging and congratulating each other. It was a magical moment in my life that made me feel even closer to Erick. I had been able to achieve something that I had never thought I could and was almost able to let go of crazy Sara in the process.

But she had reared her head a little.

"I can't believe you fucking did it," Hahn said as they made their way to us.

"Congratulations," Matty said, hugging me and grabbing my bike.

"Nice shirts," I joked.

"Mr. Science talked me into it," Hahn replied.

"I'm exhausted," I said.

"She was a trooper," Erick said.

"Do you need me to peel you out of that tight suit?" Matty asked Erick.

"You ass," Hahn said to him.

"It was the hardest thing I've ever done in my life," I said. "But we did it!"

"I can't even imagine," Matty said.

"We know," Hahn said, smacking his gut.

"How did you know I was ready for dinner?" he asked.

We all laughed, and Erick and I made our way to the check-in table to finish up everything we had to do before taking off. So many hours – my entire day – all ending with a medal and certificate stating that I had completed the journey in such-and-such time. We snapped some photos, and I noticed Erick drifting toward the cute men and camera crews who were on hand to capture the event.

"There goes our whore," Hahn said.

"He needs the attention," I said, knowing how little he was getting at home.

We watched Erick work the TV people, and then Matty helped him load the bikes on the back of Hahn's car. I sat down on a bench outside of one of those tourist shops, beginning to feel the exhaustion of the trek.

"I'm just going to run in and get our friend something for the car," Hahn said.

"You're a good person," I told her.

"You know he'll think he's starving if he doesn't eat right away."

I was shocked that I wasn't hungry, but I wasn't, just tired beyond belief.

"Congratulations," a woman said to me.

"Thank you."

"That's a pretty amazing feat."

She was one of the locals, you could tell – an older crunchy granola lesbian who had probably visited Sedona at some point and then just made it home. You saw those types of earthy women all the time in these parts.

"You are in a great place right now," she said. "Your mind and body are at its most open."

"Okay..." I said, giving her a strange look.

"Oh, sorry, I read palms so I always think of that type of thing."

I laughed.

"Sorry. I had no idea what you were talking about," I said.

"I'm a survivor of breast cancer, and I can't say thanks enough."

I sort of liked putting a face to the horrible disease I had just helped raise money to combat.

"It was completely worth it," I said.

"Let me read your palm," she said, grabbing my hand.

"Oh, no."

"No charge. I just want to give back something."

Even though I despised this kind of crap, I was too tired to fight her, and she seemed to really want to do it. The woman took my hand, read the lines, and discussed my life with regard to what she saw. I believed none of it until she said something that confused me.

"You have a strong tie to water. Mother Earth claims you as her child in this area of rock and land. But you must have sailed the seas in a previous life since the ocean is the stronger current of your life."

I stared at the woman who looked me deep in my eyes until I felt one of us had to move.

"Got it," Hahn said, coming out of the store. "The child can now be fed."

I got up quickly, gave a feeble attempt to thank the woman, and walked away with my friend.

"What the hell was that?" Hahn asked. "Thought you abhorred that sort of thing."

"The lesbo grabbed my hand; what was I to do?"

"Am I gonna have to marry you off to some older lesbian? What will all the available men in Phoenix think?"

"I couldn't care less what any of them think right now. I'm too exhausted to even contemplate men … or sex."

"I'm proud of you, kiddo," Hahn said as she wrapped her hand around my neck. "You did a good thing today."

I was shocked by my friend's public display of affection, but my mind was still on what the woman had said about my palm. I had no idea who that woman was or what she meant, but something told me she could see inside my dreams. She saw the same coastline.

CHAPTER TEN

The thought of trying to get out of bed that Monday morning and get to the gym was the equivalent of motivating oneself to go to the dentist for a root canal. My body had decided to fall apart two days after the triumph of our bike ride. I decided I needed a day to just stay at home and pamper myself. I made the obligatory call to work and then shuffled my body toward the kitchen, pausing to turn on *Good Day, Phoenix* for the local news. I was sure they would be covering the cancer ride, and I was still hoping to hear something about the man from the car wreck.

Coffee was calling from the next room. Thank God, I had set the timer to have the pot waiting for me in the morning. I poured a large cup, added some non-fat soy milk, and limped back to the sofa. The newscaster was talking about how much money had been raised over the weekend at the ride, and then, like a beaming Hollywood star, our little Erick was front and center.

My phone rang.

"Do you see him?" Matty panted.

"I've got it on," I said. "We should have known he would be the one to get his face on air."

"The camera loves him."

So do you, Matty.

"They look for the pretty boys," I said.

I was worried as soon as I made the comment that Matty would take it as a personal dig.

"Even after biking all those miles, he still looked good," Matty said in a longing and muffled voice.

"What are you doing?" I asked.

"Eating a bowl of Pebbles of Fruity … it's the real breakfast of champions," he said.

"You sick puppy, have a good day at school," I said and hung up without telling him that I was playing hooky. No need for Mister Reiner to come down on me. I was glad there was nothing in his voice that said I had offended him with my "pretty boy" remark. I kept the TV on until the program ended, but there was no mention of the victim who continued to plague my mind. I was tormented by thoughts of switched positions, him being behind me and pushing me out into that intersection. What would I have done? How quickly something can happen and change everything in your life.

You always jump to a morbid place.

I needed to rest my mind and rest my ragged body. I decided it was a good day for a massage and made a call to Erick's place, asking for the woman I liked. I always thought there was something strange about having my friend massage me. They had an opening in the early afternoon.

My morning was saturated with television. I was glued to my spot. Maury Povich, court show after court show, game shows, *The View*, anything to keep my mind from death, dying, and small children with blood-stained clothing.

The phone rang again.

"What happened to you this morning?" Hahn asked.

"Sorry. My body has been beaten up from that ride on Saturday. There was no gym in the cards for me."

"You little sleaze."

"Yup."

"There better be no house calls from that text guy of yours," she warned.

"Goodbye, Hahn. I'll talk to you later," I put the phone down. Back to mindless daytime television. Before I even realized it, I was half asleep on the sofa – drifting in and out.

I drove down a coastal road in my Mustang convertible. The warm sun kept the temperature just right, coming off the water to my left. All my fishing equipment was in the car, and it was going to be a great day. I looked in the rearview mirror, and Gracie waved and smiled to me, her blond locks blowing in the wind. I smiled back as we pulled into the parking lot. I lifted her out of the car and safely to the ground before I unloaded our gear.

We walked along the jagged rocks out on the jetty so we could fish from the edge, showing her how to hook a worm, cast the line, the patience it took for the right fish to come along. I drank a beer from the cooler while she had an orange soda, which turned her lips a vibrant color. Quickly, she grew bored playing hopscotch along the rocks. I reminded her to be careful, and she decreed how she was a big girl and was fine. The seagulls wavered overhead, hoping for us to toss them a breadcrumb or something from the sandwiches Carol had packed for us.

It felt as if something had bitten me and reached down to scratch my big hairy forearm. Just then, my line tugged, and I had a bite. I stood and worked the reel slowly to keep the fish interested in the bait – waiting for just the right moment to pounce, to bring him on in. I called out for Gracie to watch Daddy. But as I looked around, she was gone.

Nowhere to be found.

This couldn't happen again. I had gotten her back. Right? She was here after being gone for so long. I called out her name, and as I did…

I was awake and back on my sofa in my living room.

What the hell is wrong with you? Who is she?

I suppose on some level I could have thought she was my unborn child from a decade ago, but that would have been too simple an answer. Besides, I could have understood if it had just happened – but I never had these dreams back then. This was all new to me, and I certainly didn't enjoy the crazy implications these dreams were making on my life.

CHAPTER ELEVEN

It was raining like a bitch on that Halloween night (a remnant of one of our Arizona monsoons), which cast an entire different mood on the evening, causing everyone's costumes to cling to their bodies like wet suits. The poor kids who were combing the neighborhood in search of candy had it the worst. At least we were all indoors. My body had healed from the torture of the previous weekend, and I had almost completely recovered from that mammoth victory.

Windsor Mansion was decorated to the hilt, every corner covered in a cobweb or ghostly image. The place had been a part of the town for years and had been donated to the Historical Society once all the Windsors had died off. It had the look of one of those incredible mansions out of an old movie – one you knew had secret passages behind some wood-paneled wall. It was beautiful in décor and kept refurbished to look as if you were stepping back in time through its huge leaded door. By the time of our visit, it was used for seasonal events, and the annual Halloween party was always a hit.

The best part was that it was a party where straights and gays could go together and have a good time without anyone feeling out of place. The room was full of every recent pop icon or headline-stealing current event you could think of. Erick was painted head to toe as the hottest skeleton you'd ever seen. Every muscle of his lean body popped, causing many heads in the room to turn. Matty, who was always years behind, was dressed as the Joker. Hahn had shown up as a scary midget Sumo wrestler and was bouncing off of everyone in her fat suit (blaming them for bumping her). I had donned a black wig and tight orange satin dress that really showed off the gals and became Khloe Kardashian, who, along with her sisters, had created quite an empire. Oh yes, and Ron was there dressed as … well, himself.

"What the hell is Ron supposed to be?" I whispered to Matty.

"I think he is Bruce Jenner with that tight face," he said.

"I don't even know why he bothered to come," I said.

"Exactly. I could be Erick's date with no problem," Matty said, kissing my neck.

Those boys were gonna be the death of me. I just knew it. How long could I keep them away from each other?

Not your problem, Sara.

Erick walked up to us and started inspecting Matty's plate.

"How many carbs are on that plate, Mr. Reiner?" he asked.

"It's a holiday," Matty said.

Matty forced some hot pastry filled with something into Erick's mouth.

"I swear to Buddha that I'll hurt you if you don't do that again," Erick said with a smile.

Erick grew up in a family that never took the Lord's name in vain, so he adopted someone else's leader to swear to.

"Ah-ha, I knew it," Matty said. "You secretly crave the carbs."

"I crave a lot of other stuff, too," Erick said.

I noticed Ron walking over to Erick, whispering in his ear, and Erick's skeleton lines wrinkled into a scowl as he told Ron to go ahead. Ron was out the front door into the downpour, headed for the next party, I supposed. Erick turned and took another bite off Matty's plate and caught my eye.

"I need to reapply," I said.

"I'll take you to the bathroom upstairs," Erick said. "Hold my spot, Matty."

Matty was thrilled to oblige as I put my arm through Erick's to head up the huge staircase at the end of the parlor.

"You okay?" I asked.

"Ron can do what he wants," he said.

I got to the restroom, and Erick followed me inside. A woman came out and smiled at the two of us, thinking we were going to get it on or something.

"If she only knew," I said.

"I ain't Ron. Don't even think I'm gonna make out with you in here," he said.

"You know it's fine for you to have a good time ... even if he's not here," I reminded him.

"Abso-fucking-lutely," he said. "And I intend to."

I added some lipstick to my oversized Kardashian lips and turned to look at him.

"I'd kiss you, but I don't want all that skeleton makeup all over me," I said.

"Girl, there are plenty of demons and gargoyles downstairs for me to devour," he said.

"He died, you know," I said.

"Who?"

"The guy from the car accident. It was in the paper."

"Yeah, I was hoping you wouldn't see that," he said.

"What a waste," I said. "Just to try and save a few minutes at a red light."

"Let it go. Nothing you can do. Let's just have a good time."

I realized the man was a stranger, but I was affected by his passing in a very odd way that I couldn't explain to Erick. We made our way back down the long staircase where Matty patiently waited for Erick at the bottom like a doting puppy.

"I'm gonna go to the bar," I said, walking away from my boys.

I tried not to allow the death of the unknown man to get to me, but I couldn't help but feel connected to him. Not only had I witnessed him leaving this life, but the child's life-vest felt strangely tied to my own dreams of Gracie. Was there a message there? Was there a morsel of profound knowledge that I was supposed to take from this event?

Or are you just whacked in our head?

There were so many people at the party; the rooms were packed and hopping. Witches and demons and vampires- oh my! People were laughing, dancing, and living it up. As I passed through the hordes of people, my mind drifted to the man who left a wife and daughter when he died at that intersection. Surely, so many people were upset that he was gone. I tried to think about who would flash before my eyes if I were dying. I had no family other than my friends.

The poor pitiful Sara song.

Then, someone dressed as a *True Blood* character moved out of my way, and I saw a small girl in a life vest. I pulled the black wig from in front of my eyes to get a better look, but the crowd engulfed her, and she was gone as suddenly as she had appeared. My brain told me she wasn't real, but Gracie was definitely out of my dreams and suddenly haunting me during the day. Who the hell was she? I managed to get through the people and made my way to the coffin-bar and ordered myself a vodka tonic with a splash of blood-orange juice for the festive occasion. I figured alcohol was just the thing to wipe my mind clear so that I could enjoy myself.

Hahn was there with her friend, Samara.

"So who has more fun? Red-heads or your impression of brunette tonight?" she asked me.

"Depends on the fun you're talking about, dumpy," I said. "I think I noticed some hottie looking me up and down."

"Sara Butler, my friend Samara Mansour," Hahn said introducing the two of us.

I couldn't tell if the woman was dressed this way because it was Halloween or if this was just her usual attire. She had straight jet-black hair, the palest skin, and layers and layers of loose fitting clothes from the 1960s. Almost as if she was single-handedly trying to resurrect Woodstock here in Phoenix. There were more bangles, jewels, and beads around her neck and arms than on any of those young Hollywood leading ladies that you see in the magazines. I sure as hell hoped she was dressed like a gypsy and didn't feed into the stereotype of the psychic that Hahn said she was.

"Nice to meet you. How do you like Phoenix?"

"Hahn has been showing me around. The Art Museum, Pueblo Grande, Heritage Square."

Her voice had a soothing quality, and I couldn't quite make out the accent. Perhaps she was hypnotizing me, and I didn't even know it.

"I hope she wore a better outfit," I teased.

"Shut up, slut," Hahn said. "I was a great tour guide."

"It's no San Francisco, but we try," I said.

"It's a beautiful place, full of a completely different history than you get from other parts of the country," Samara said.

"Samara has traveled everywhere," Hahn added.

"Glad you could be with us on Halloween," I said, searching for anything polite to say.

"Too bad I didn't get a chance to pick up an appropriate outfit for the party," she said.

Guess this *was* her regular dress. Note to self: Never fall into the trap of looking like what people expect. I wouldn't want to be the old hag with the cat on my lap. Ever.

"I was telling Sara all about what you do: palm reading, crystals, hypnosis, all this cool shit," Hahn said.

"Are you a believer?" she asked me.

The poor pitiful Sara song.

"I've never given it much thought," I quickly stated.

"Many people are scared of it. Think it's the devil's thing or the occult, but it's not really. It's just getting in touch with your subconscious and letting it come to the forefront of your consciousness. There is so much locked away that we never pay attention to," Samara said.

Don't share what's in your mind, Sara.

"There are some scary bats in my belfry," I said. "Not sure I'd want to disturb their sleep."

"Come on," Hahn said. "She's done me before. It's really great to find things you forgot."

"The past is intricately connected to the present and the future," she said. Her soothing tone had become a subtext. "That's why I enjoy hypnosis as well as palm and card reading. It's all channeling different energy."

Erick and Matty walked up.

Thank you, guys.

"You guys hoarding the bar area?" Erick asked.

"Sara just met my friend," Hahn said.

"Isn't she the coolest chick ever?" Matty asked. "I think I talked her ear off when I met her before."

"I'm sure she doesn't want to be bored with your online poker talk," Erick said, putting his arm around Matty.

"I am a wealth of knowledge. Just ask any of my students."

"We better not see any of those rugrats around here," Hahn said.

"I think Sara is a little frightened by the thought of what I do," Samara said.

How the hell did she know that?

"Not at all," I demurred. "It's a party. Who wants to talk about work and jobs?"

"I have a question," Erick said. "Can you read Hahn's palm for us and tell us how old she is?"

The guys burst out laughing and pushed the little wrestler back and forth in her costume like some sort of human piñata.

"Bitches, you will know that information when it is time for you to know," Hahn said.

Erick ordered a drink, and the conversation shifted. I could feel Samara's deep, dark eyes on me, as if her gaze were penetrating me. Perhaps she really knew what she was talking about. Maybe she could help me unleash whatever it was inside that I was so afraid to learn. My eyes caught her eyes as the others spoke around us. The noise of the room melted into a dull drone as the bond between our eyes strengthened. I could feel she was trying to communicate, as if telling me I had nothing to be afraid of. Finding out my past was not going to kill me. And maybe the invisible rash would go away as well. My connection to her eyes was broken when someone bumped into me, and I turned.

"Oh, sorry about … Sara?" the man said.

It was Steve, dressed as the sexiest pirate with an open shirt for all to see his body. That hairy chest that had touched my skin so many times glistened in the glow of the eerie lights.

"Steve."

At the mention of his name, all three of my friends turned to get a look at the person they had never seen. Then, everything seemed to happen at once. I knew my friends would want to speak, but I was trying to talk over them anytime they had a chance. And Steve was busy doing his own backtracking as well. He pushed the woman on his arm forward to meet me.

"Mandy, this is Sara. Sara works at one of the companies where I make deliveries," he said.

He was speaking so quickly, I was trying to process it all. She had to be his girlfriend. It was true. There was someone else in his life. It was Robert Michelson the third all over again. Ten years later, and I was still playing the role of the other woman. I tried to get a good look at her through the Cleopatra-like costume she was wearing. She was tall as a model next to my 5'6" stature. She had wavy blonde hair that was so much more striking and full than mine. Her legs seemed to go on for days underneath the gorgeous dress, and her lips were naturally full, where I always had to fake mine with lipstick. What the hell was wrong with this guy leaving her to come to me? Or what was she not offering him?

I feel like the whore of Babylon.

"It's nice to meet you," she said as she shook my hand.

"You, too," I said.

He placed his hand on the small of her back, as only a boyfriend would do, to lead her through the crowd. But as he passed me, he whispered in my ear.

"Hang on to that black wig, Red, for the next time I come over."

I fell from Babylon status to just a cheap call girl in one instant. I had always enjoyed my times with him, but suddenly – there was her.

"Fucking hot," was the first thing I heard Erick say. "He needs to be on a calendar for all twelve months."

"Brawny called and they want their model back," Matty said.

"Who's the bitch?" Hahn asked.

Too many questions – questions I didn't want to answer. I put on my best poker face and turned to them all.

"Let's leave mister text in the phone where he belongs– and no more questions," I said.

We made our way to the bar, and I felt Erick's hand on my back. It comforted me, sensing that he understood I was just as surprised to see this Mandy person as they were to see Steve. Music blared from the speakers above the bar. And again, I felt Samara's eyes piercing me. That was something I tried to avoid the rest of the evening: the one person who could get to my secrets probably even better than I could. But I'd be damned if I was going to allow her.

CHAPTER TWELVE

Carol sat across from me at the table, eating each bite as slowly as she possibly could. Not speaking. Not looking up. Studying her food and chewing, as if she were afraid of choking to death. I reached across the table to try and comfort her, but she did not want her husband to touch her that night. Between us was the empty chair with a small plate and cup at the table. Why did she insist on setting a place for Gracie each night? Our child was dead. Didn't she understand that?

Not that I could ever forget my own child.

What parent could? But how in the world were we supposed to be able to move on as a couple? How could we get past this horrible black splotch across the canvas of our lives? I could go on doing my job, coming home to this tomb, and listening to my wife sob herself to sleep. Or perhaps it would be best if I left. Maybe that was what she wanted. If I left her, both Gracie's memory and my own could be wiped from Carol's brain.

I sat up in my bed and looked at the clock. 2:00 a.m. I was trembling. Dreams are supposed to be about actions. But mine were about thoughts, thoughts in someone else's head – a man's head at that. I felt like I was going crazy. Where was this stuff coming from? Was I reincarnated and thinking about a past life?

Or was this my life from when I was a child, before the foster homes?

But lack of sleep was not going to help anything during the day. If I kept this up, I'd be crashing and burning by 3:00 p.m. every day. No, I needed to do something. And as much as I had protested on Halloween, I knew it was to talk to Hahn before Samara left town. I wanted to see what she could do for me, but I didn't want Hahn to be in the room. I couldn't imagine someone I knew witnessing whatever I might uncover.

Just make it until morning, and you can give Hahn a call.

There was no going back to sleep. My mind was racing between Steve and his woman I had met, the dead man I saw in the car, the people from my dreams, and the stupid invisible rash. I went into the living room, turned on the TV to one of the all night infomercials, and went to the kitchen to find a Red Bull. I was determined that the next morning was the day I got some answers.

~~~

I took a personal day off at my job and hoped Mr. W wouldn't miss his daily glances at my breasts too much. Hahn had gone to work, leaving me in her luxurious house with Samara. It occurred to me I had never been inside of Hahn's home before – and wondered why that was. Looking around her beautifully decorated environment gave me a glimpse into my friend. Everything seemed to match and have its proper place to dwell. I was almost afraid to mess up the pillows that lined the back of the very expensive sofa where I sat. The initial fear, embarrassment, and weirdness of the "meeting" were slowly leaving my body. Candles were burning in the living room, and a sweet, familiar smell filled the air. Samara sat in a chair with crystals she had strategically placed around me.

Hahn's house is so much better than our small condo.

Even my inner voice couldn't get away from our lush environment, but I had to focus. I had to get my head in the game to get to the bottom of all of this. I suppose the crystals that were surrounding me were supposed to do something magical.

"You don't need to be nervous, Sara."

"Sorry. I can't help it. I've been dealing with some bad…"

"No, please. You can actually stay quiet for a while."

Samara sat in silence, breathing heavily and "taking in my aura" … or so she said. I wasn't really sure what was happening. I just knew that I needed help, and if this stranger could do it, I'd be very grateful. She flipped through a deck of cards she had me shuffle and touch. Finally, she spoke.

"The man is not good for you."

Great. Men are bad. You're supposed to be a lesbian.

"All men or one in particular?"

"You know. We all saw him Saturday night," she said.

Well, I didn't need any cards to tell me that.

"Your future can only be as good as your past allows it to be," she said.

What the hell did that mean? Was something or someone holding me back? Damn that Darrin in grade school!

"I've had a pretty screwed up past," I said.

"It was hard without parents, wasn't it?" she said.

Wow. Who told her that?

"Yes. But I had some nice people raising me through the foster care system. But this never made up for my real parents."

"And you don't even know who they are or what happened to them."

"No."

"You need to know," she said in that soothing voice, both a question and a command.

I had never admitted to the loss I felt from not having parents. I was quite good at meandering my way through life and leaving that all on the inside.

"At 33 years old, it is holding me back – so I guess I do."

"I want you to lie back on that sofa, Sara. Concentrate on your breathing."

This was it. The reason I had come. She was going to let me know why I was having these dreams. At least I hoped she could.

Samara lowered the lights in the room, and that sweet smell somehow seemed to lull me into an intoxicated state.

Are you going to fight it, Sara? Why?

I needed my inside voice to stay quiet so that this could work. I recall Samara counting backwards, giving me certain directions along the way – things I'd seen work on television shows but never believed. Dr. Pingleton had gotten very close as well. And here I was in my friend's apartment with a stranger digging into my mind. I was no longer afraid.

Before I even realized it, I was back in time, in my youth. We discussed some of the foster families I had been with – what it was like in each of those homes. I was truly lost in a world that I had tried for so long to forget. I conveyed events in my life, reliving them with Samara. Living with strangers and trying to find my place within their family. Playing the game "I'll show you mine, if you show me yours" with one of the boys I had lived with. Starting school over and over again. Having people make fun of me as the new girl. The pillowcase I carried from home to home with the few belongings I actually owned. The constant thoughts of running away. Wondering when I'd be asked to leave.

Then, she took me further back to when I was three years old. Memories that I didn't even know I had. Only they were real. It felt as if I were right there, suddenly in a place I don't ever recall living in. I didn't know what to share with the woman asking me the questions.

"Can you tell me where you are?" she asked.

"I don't know," I said.

"Describe it to me," the woman said.

"I'm sitting on the floor, and I hear noises in the other room."

"What kind of noises?"

"The lady is screaming."

"Are you scared?"

"Yes."

I wished I had a puppy to hold in my arms. Or my Teddy Bear from home.

"Mama!"

"Where is she?"

"In the room with Daddy and that lady."

"Do you notice anything around the room that you recognize?" she asked.

"We've never been here before. What? I wanna go home."

"What happened?"

"Mama came into the room and yelled at me to stop making so much noise."

"Where are the lady and your daddy?"

"In the other room. She keeps screaming, but it sounds far away. There is something big and shiny in Mama's hands when she goes back in the other room."

"Is there anything in your hands?"

"No, only see those marks," I said.

"What marks?"

"The ones left after they smash those smoky things on me."

"Do you want to stay in this house, or do you want to come back to where I am?"

"I want someone to take me away. I don't like these visits. Last time we did it, the man had red stuff come all out of him and it got on Mama's dress."

"I'm going to count to three, and when I do, you're going to wake up and not feel frightened. But you are going to remember everything that happened," Samara calmly said. "Now, just relax. One. Two. Three."

I was back in Hahn's living room. The fragrant smell made me feel safe and sound. But I could recall everything. Suddenly, I was overcome with embarrassment lying in front of Samara.

"I'm sorry about that," I said.

"You have nothing to apologize for," she said.

Could that really have been your past? Your family?

"Are you OK?" Samara asked.

"I don't think I want to know who my real parents were anymore," I said as I sat up on the sofa.

"Why? You need to embrace your past. It's part of your destiny."

I looked into the eyes of the stranger, but she no longer felt foreign. She had just witnessed something truly horrendous. Those people were not good people. I hoped to God they were not my parents.

"Was that what you expected?" I asked.

"I had no expectations," she said. "More importantly, was it what you expected?"

"I have not been able to recall anything in my life prior to being in foster care," I said.

"Then, this was a breakthrough," she said in that same smooth voice.

"I don't know what it was," I said out loud.

My stomach began to do flip-flops, and I knew I needed to get out of Hahn's house.

"Thank you, Samara for your ... help today," I said standing up. "You certainly did what you said you could do, and I shouldn't ever question that line of work again."

I couldn't get out of the room quickly enough.

"Sara, you don't need to rush…"

"I need to get back to work ... I shouldn't have taken off. Thank you."

I was out the door, leaving her standing in the foyer of Hahn's house while I slammed the door shut. I still wasn't certain if I believed Samara had gone into my past or if she had pulled some type of trick on me.

I secretly hoped it was all just another dream.

CHAPTER THIRTEEN

Whoever thought it was a great idea to bus in pumpkins from other parts of the country to create a faux pumpkin patch in Arizona must have been smoking crack. But there we were. A park had been converted into Autumn Central, with every possible cliché thrown up on the entire landscape– fake fall foliage, scarecrows, straw hay, pumpkins and other gourds. My two boys and I traipsed through it as if we were on some country meadow in Pennsylvania, passing by the cornstalks and mums that didn't quite fit with the short sleeves we were still wearing. If lucky, we might have seen 50 degrees at night, but to me, it wasn't what autumn was supposed to be, with that sense of a dirt-clay smell in the air. No one who was raised in Arizona noticed it, but I always did. No fresh rain. Or a flower garden with honey dew. No, it smelled like dirt.

But at least Thanksgiving is right around the corner.

Shut up!

I hated the fact that I was responding to the crazy voice in my head.

"Tell me again why you have to create the centerpiece?" I asked Erick.

"Hello! The gay gene! My family wants it to look fabulous, and who better to do it?"

"I don't even want to imagine what Thanksgiving is like at your house," Matty said. "No stuffing. No cornbread. A carb-free zone in the Warren house."

"Nah, my family is all carb-eating peeps. There'll be plenty," Erick said.

"I hope you have something for me to eat as well," I said.

"I'll have a stash just for you and me."

"Jealous that you two are gonna be together, and I'll be with my mother and her old friends," Matty said.

"You'll be fine," Erick said, throwing on Matty's head some of the hay that had been used in a display.

I knew that Matty wanted an invitation, but I also knew he would never abandon his mother on a holiday. He pulled out a Butterfinger from his pocket, and his sulking was transformed into voracious eating. The smell of peanut butter and chocolate filled my own nose, and I was transported to my past when I would turn to candy to make myself feel better as well.

By this point, I was turning to late night sex. I thought about how I should really work out those issues with a new therapist.

Matty looked like a cute little boy who wasn't getting his way in his crumpled ASU red devil t-shirt and tattered jeans. In contrast, mister model had obviously ironed the FCUK designer shirt he was sporting. I found myself laughing at my gay Bert and Ernie.

"Hey, Mr. Reiner," a student said, running by.

"Hi, Alicia. Enjoying the pumpkin patch?" he said in a completely different voice.

"It's cool!" she said. "See ya Monday," and she was off and running.

"What a teacher-voice you have," I said.

"Think of me as Clark Kent. Mild-mannered teacher by day, and by night – he's Super Gay," he said.

"To be super gay, you gotta be having super gay sex," Erick said as he lifted a puny looking pumpkin.

"Are you offering to tutor me?" Matty asked.

The never ending banter between the two began. I wanted to scream at them to just do it already. But like many of my favorite TV shows, it was always best before the two leads actually got together.

"Why didn't Hahn come?" Erick asked.

I hadn't invited Hahn. I hadn't talked to her since Samara had left two weeks before. I felt too weird about the whole thing. The last two weeks had played quite a mind game on me. I was well aware of my past in foster care and could recall those memories at a moment's notice. But the reflections I touched on from my early years sent shivers down my spine. From those horrendous things I had learned at Hahn's house to trying to make some sense of my idiotic relationship with Steve, to doing it all alone without Dr. Pingleton, the entire process that was my life … completely sucked. My body was beginning to show it as well, since I hadn't made it to the gym in the morning for a while.

"She's got some project at work she had to get done this weekend," I lied.

Don't start lying to your friends now, Sara.

I felt guilty that I was not returning Hahn's calls or reaching out to her. It wasn't her fault she introduced Samara to me or that I had recalled those flashes of the past ... but I was sure Samara had shared everything with Hahn, and I wasn't prepared for her smartass remarks.

We made our way through wooden display tables, fall wreaths, and assorted scarecrow-type knicknacks. I found myself laughing at the people who were actually wearing sweatshirts; trying to force themselves to believe it was cool outside. I lifted my hand back from the table when a gentleman next to me was reaching for something with a cigarette in his hand, and it grazed my wrist.

"Owww," I protested a little too loudly.

"I'm sorry," he said, trying to brush off my arm.

"It's OK, it's OK," I said.

"No it's not," Erick said. "Keep your cancer stick to yourself."

"Erick, please," I scolded.

The three of us walked away from the man before he decided to kick some gay ass right there on the bales of hay.

"Insensitive people piss me off," Erick said.

"Well, damn, lookie at the manly man in action," Matty said. "Me likey."

"I'm fine," I said, checking my arm for a burn. "Nothing there."

But something burnt in my brain. It came back to me like a faint photograph that had been tarnished with age, so that I could just make out the picture through the blurred paper.

I had been burnt as a child.

The sensitivity on my arm. Someone used to put cigarettes out on me. No. Never truly touching. They would hold them over my arm as a threat, and the ashes would sometimes fall on me. But who would do that to a child? I could feel the heat from the tip and my fear of it stinging my skin. I remembered crying hysterically, and someone yelling at me that little girls deserve it. Where were these memories coming from?

The invisible rash. Could that really be something from my past? Had I been trying to scratch away the invisible scars from something that was 30 years old? I wished Samara was there so that I could get her to hypnotize me again. Or did I dare call Dr. Pingleton? What would he say since I had allowed so many weeks to go by? I needed to talk to someone, and I wasn't sure the guys would understand this sort of thing.

I wasn't sure that I even understood it.

CHAPTER FOURTEEN

I knew it wasn't therapy. I knew it wasn't good for me. But the moment I got the text, I told him to get to my condo ASAP. He felt wonderful in my arms. It was something I could physically hold onto, and I needed something real next to me. I knew Steve wasn't my boyfriend. And no matter how I tried to close my mind to his girlfriend, to what my friends would say – the words that Samara said about him kept popping up in my brain.

"Where's that wig from Halloween, Red?"

"Threw it out," I said, as I pushed his head down on my breasts. How he loved to nuzzle himself between them, caressing, licking, kissing.

He pulled me up in a mock-rough way by my neck and over to the side of the bed where he pushed me on all fours on the soft mattress. I heard the rip of the condom wrapper, and soon after, he was entering me doggy style, yanking on my long red hair. Sweat dripped from his body and landed on my ass as he continued to pound me from behind.

I could be anyone to him at that moment. He couldn't see me, and I couldn't see him. I wanted to look in his eyes. I needed to connect to him. I pushed him back and flipped over, lifting my legs around him and pulling him inside. I was staring deep into his eyes, wondering what he was thinking about. Did he want to call me Mandy? What kind of feelings did Steve really have for me – if any?

I put my arms around his neck, holding on for dear life, lifted my body up onto his, and before I knew it, I was kissing him as hard as I could. I thought he would have fought me, but he was a man and was too far past the point of no return. His tongue thrust into my mouth as forcefully as he filled me below. I couldn't seem to kiss him enough. My entire body wanted to stay linked to his for as long as possible. And like it was timed out perfectly, we both came, and he fell over me on the bed, panting.

"Damn, Red. That was fucking hot."

"I had a lot of pent up aggression I needed to get out."

"You can take it out on me anytime," he said, as he smacked my ass and went to the bathroom to flush the condom.

I pulled the sheet up over me and again had the worst empty feeling.

Steve came back into my bedroom, slipped on his underwear, and was pulling up his jeans.

Ask him, Sara.

"Do you want to stay?" I asked.

The clingy, needy girl was back. This was not good.

He stopped. I had crossed the line, and I knew it.

"Ah ... I got work tomorrow, Red," he said, as the shirt went over his head.

"Where is Mandy?" I asked.

Why are you pushing this? You knew what it was.

The stupid voice had told me to do it, and she was taking none of the blame.

"Mandy? Oh, Mandy. She's at her place. Don't worry about her. She was just…"

"Don't, Steve. It's fine. I've no claim."

"You're the best piece of ass I've had in a while," he said.

Great. That's what every gal wants to hear before the money goes on the nightstand.

"Yeah ... so are you," I said weakly.

I sat up in bed with the sheet just below my breasts. I had nothing to hide, nothing to cover. The man had seen and visited every part of my body time and time again. Steve came over to the side of the bed, sat down next to me, and took my face in his hands.

"I really love what we got going here," he said.

You thought he was gonna say he loved you, crazy Sara. Really?

"Me, too," I said.

"Then, let's keep it as it is. Don't ruin it by trying to bring anything else in."

With that, he did something he had never done before and kissed me goodbye. It was sweet, soft, and nothing hard like our sexcapades.

"Text you later, Red," he said and left the bedroom.

I heard the front door close, and I wondered with all the firsts that we had tonight, was this really gonna be the last with me and Steve?

CHAPTER FIFTEEN

I needed to make sure that the fact that I had felt no itching on my arm in the last week wasn't a fluke, so I went to Rite Aid to find some cream. I just wanted something to put on as a precautionary measure. Maybe it was really gone. Maybe the breakthrough of realizing that I was possibly traumatized with cigarettes as a child was all I had needed. Or maybe it was but a respite and would soon grow worse.

I was hunched down on the ground reading the ingredients on the side of one of the boxes of medicine when I heard her.

"So the bitch is still alive after all."

"Hahn," I said, standing up.

"No, stay down there. Don't get up on my account. Wondered where you were each morning at the gym. Thinking you must be really sick, and it looks like you just got some genital disease or something that you need some fucking cream for."

"It's not like that."

"God only knows what that prick Steve might be giving you."

"Hahn."

"I don't deal well with people just blowing me off," she said.

"I'm sorry. It's not about you. It's about Samara."

"Samara? What the hell?"

Hahn stopped speaking, trying to stare at my insides, and then she spoke.

"She freaked you out, didn't she? You couldn't handle whatever went on between you two."

"Oh, I handled it; it was just way more than I ever expected."

"You said you wanted to have a session with her," she said. "I gave you what you freakin' wanted."

You are a terrible friend.

"I know! I know. But the session brought up stuff ... strange stuff ... and then, I was embarrassed to see you. Afraid she had shared it with you, and I didn't know how to face you."

"Sara, how can you possibly be embarrassed with me? After I told you about my childhood in a sweatshop?!"

She was so right. How stupid could I have been pushing her away like I did. I felt horrible.

"I'm sorry."

"I don't care what you learned about yourself, what freaking shit you're into – I just missed hanging out with you."

"I really am sorry, Hahn."

I went to hug her, but Hahn wasn't one for physical attention.

"Don't go getting all gushy with me."

I picked up the cream and walked to the counter to pay for it.

"So, you're looking a little flabby," Hahn said, as she followed me. "Am I gonna see you in the gym tomorrow morning?"

"Absolutely. Bright and early," I said.

"And you just leave whatever kinky stuff you learned about yourself between you and Samara," she said with a smile.

I laughed and realized how much I had missed Hahn.

"You cut off your hair," I said, finally noticing.

"See what happens when I don't have a best gal around to seek advice?"

"But all that long, beautiful hair … gone."

"It'll grow back. I needed a new look," she said with a wink.

"It really was pretty heavy with Samara," I said, paying the cashier and walking out the front door with Hahn.

"I told you she was good."

"A little too good. I found out some stuff from when I was a child that pretty much rocked my world."

"We all got our ghosts from the past to deal with," she said getting into her car.

I stood at Hahn's car window thinking about what it was like for her to have worked in a factory at such a young age.

"I suppose we do," I said. "I'm just not sure I want to see those ghosts again."

"Obviously, something has been bothering you to make you reach out to them," she said as she started her car. "Maybe you need to do a poltergeist hunt."

I wasn't sure what to say to Hahn as she started to pull out of the parking space.

"Not to mention a hundred sit-ups, butterball!" she yelled. "See you tomorrow!"

I watched her drive off, and I was happy she forced me to face her. Why was I so stupid about these sorts of things. Hahn was right. I needed to get over that feeling of embarrassment. I just wondered how Dr. Pingleton was going to take hearing from me again.

~~~

"Did you really think I was not going to allow you to come back to my office?" he asked.

"I wouldn't have," I said.

"Why?" Dr. Pingleton asked in that same tone he had always used.

"Because of the lies I told you."

"Don't you think it's important for you to understand why you told those stories? And being able to face the person you told them to is a huge part of that understanding."

"I want people to like me," I said, sitting up and looking him in the eyes. "I'm afraid that if people know the truth about me, they will judge me in some way."

"But I'm not here to judge you. I'm here to help you through issues you may be dealing with."

"I know. And I'm grateful to have that, to have you. But my whole life, people have made fun of me for not having a family."

"So keeping the fact that you were in foster care from me was a way of protecting yourself from more ridicule."

I nodded.

This guy really does get you.

"I need you to realize that I'm not here to ridicule you. The rash you have. The past you've had. Or whatever you are dealing with. I want to help you, Sara, so that you can eventually walk away from here and feel you have the tools to assist you in coping with all the challenges that life will bring you."

Coping with the challenges.

That's exactly what I needed to do. So I spilled my guts to Dr. Pingleton. I filled him in on all the holes I had stepped around during the six months I hadn't seen him. I discussed the crazy day with Samara and what happened when she hypnotized me. I even told him I thought I had discovered what the invisible rash was, but that I wasn't sure because I couldn't recall anything prior to my being with the foster families and I couldn't see burn marks.

"How many different families were you with?" he asked.

"I think I moved every two to three years. So about six or seven different families."

"It's very difficult to form any kind of bonds when you're always afraid of leaving – moving to another place. Uprooting."

"It was. Some I really liked, and I wanted them to adopt me. But then, I'd be on to another family."

"Do you have any good memories?" he asked.

"There are some. Most families were very kind to me. I think they got how hard it was to be the kid coming into their lives. There would be struggles if they had other kids. We didn't always get along. But I remember when I was 15, I had my own room at the Peterson house."

"That must have made you feel special."

"Absolutely. They made a big deal of my 16th birthday. School was just about out, and they threw me a huge party. They were a great family."

Mrs. Peterson popped into my head with her flaming red hair, oversized thick glasses, and that dimpled smile that made me feel warm.

"Did you get to stay with them and finish school?"

"Nope. The system had a cut-off, and I had to go to another family for the last year of high school … not even at the same school."

There was something odd, yet refreshing, discussing this part of my life. It felt like a lifetime ago, but it was also right there on the cusp of my mind, just wanting to be released to someone.

"Have you ever contacted any of the families since you've been an adult?"

"No."

I wondered why I hadn't. To let them know what I was doing. What kind of person I had turned into. I'm sure some of them wondered.

"Were you always in Phoenix?"

"No. New Mexico. I moved to Arizona once I was old enough to get away."

"Why not stay there?"

"New Mexico reminded me of being a transient, and while there were a few good times, there was pain. Frustration. Fear of some of the families."

"So you wanted a fresh start."

"Once I was 18, I was out and on my own. Moved here, took a job to work my way through community college."

"Impressive."

"Didn't feel that way at the time. It was just something I knew I needed."

"Not all 18-year-olds would see the importance of an education, to be able to go out and stand on their own."

"I had no one else," I said.

"This is really powerful stuff you are dealing with, Sara."

"Tell me about it."

The need to talk to myself in my head seemed to vanish after talking to him for 45 minutes. Words I usually would have said only to myself were just coming out of my mouth.

"Why did you mention fear in New Mexico?" he asked.

"Not every family was as nice as the Petersons. There were a few where I just wanted to crawl into a closet and hide."

"You've had quite a life. Very different from the picture you painted before."

"You mean the lies."

"We don't need to call them lies. I think in some way it was the life you wished you had."

"I don't want a pity party. I think I've done great by myself the past 15 years."

"You won't get pity here," he said with a smile.

"Maybe it was the stupid rash that brought me to you, but I'm starting to see there was such a bigger purpose in me being here."

"I think that's true."

"I sort of wish I had scars, just for proof."

"Sounds as if they were smart enough to make sure to leave no marks – on purpose. By taunting you and keeping you hostage by fear, they kept the upper hand."

"I feel that has to be the root of that problem," I said.

"I really appreciate the fact that you are trusting me with your past. I feel that's part of what has kept you at bay with other people, not being able to trust."

"You're right. I have one female friend I feel somewhat close to. My other closest friends are two gay men, so that keeps a comfortable wall up. I'm not dating anyone, but…"

"But what? Go on."

"I might as well put it all out there ... since you're not judging. But I do have a man I regularly see for sex."

"Sex is important."

Why had I been so afraid to tell Dr. Pingleton these things before? I thought for sure he would think me some kind of cheap whore with that little tidbit, but he hadn't even flinched.

"Yeah, but I know that seeing Steve, that's the guy's name, is just another way for me to not confront someone for real. He's just one guy in a list of losers. I have problems connecting to anyone."

"I think it has a lot to do with connecting to yourself, finding the truth of who you were before you went into foster care. And that's what I want us to continue working on."

"Do you think you might want to try hypnotizing me again sometime soon? Just so I can see more of that past?"

"If you want to. But I want you to feel safe and secure with what you share with me in this office."

"You know what? I do. I do now, finally. Thank you, Dr. Pingleton."

"Thank you."

"And I see our time is up," I said.

"You always like to beat me to the punch on that," he said, as he stood and put out his hand to shake mine.

I took his hand firmly in mine, and he patted my shoulder with the other. It felt comforting. Something felt right about this older gentleman caring for me in this way. And I was so glad I had found my way back to his office with the star-pointed tiles on the ceiling.

I felt invigorated from my session. Something had opened up for me in that room, and I was starting to see the importance of having other people in my life, allowing them into the darkest reaches so that I was not alone. I wasn't certain what I was going to find going down this road, but I was ready to head there. No matter what the outcome was going to bring.

CHAPTER SIXTEEN

I couldn't believe after all these years what I was actually going to do. Maybe once during high school, the thought crossed my mind, but never since then. I looked up the number to child protective services, wrote it down, and went to my car on my lunch break to make the call. No need for anyone at work to listen to my conversation. The person on the other end wasn't in a helpful mood when I gave her the year.

"Name's Sara Butler. I'm sure I'm in your records. I was brought there to New Mexico."

"Ms. Butler, we're not allowed to discuss that information over the phone. If you would like to come in and fill out some forms…"

"I don't want to fill out anything," I said. "I just want the truth about my past!"

"I understand your need, I really do."

"Oh, were you in the foster care system too?"

You don't need to get testy, Sara.

"No, ma'am, but I've worked with people for years."

"Then, you understand when someone wants to know where they came from before they were put into your system. That's all I want to know. Where the baby, Sara Butler, came from."

"If you can give me your address or email, I can send you some forms that we need for verification."

I hung up. I was feeling so good about working with Dr. Pingleton, but this person was not giving me any help at all. And I felt my self esteem crashing again. Maybe I should find that guy on TV who can locate people from your past, I thought. He could get through to them, I was sure.

Or maybe your past isn't worth looking into.

I needed to let go of the anger that was building up and concentrate on the good things in my life. I was planning a dinner with my friends, and I still had shopping to do. After work, I planned to go to the store and keep my mind on the present – the things I was thankful for.

~~~

"This has got to be the stupidest thing I've ever allowed someone to talk me into," Matty said.

We all sat around the dining table in my small condo with the diminutive Thanksgiving foliage centerpiece I had made. The golden autumn tablecloth was out, and we used cloth napkins like true adults. With this crew, someone would be yanking my chain before the meal was through.

"I don't even think anyone will touch the dessert I brought," Hahn said.

"That's because it's dyke-food, you short-haired freak," Erick teased.

"Leave her alone," Matty said. "I think it's cute in a *Dora the Explorer* kind of way."

"Come on, I wanted us to be able to share a moment of Thanksgiving before we all go off our separate ways next week," I said.

"But I'm gonna be with you," Erick said.

"Are you all gonna give me a hard time?" I said.

"At least when they did this on Charlie Brown, there was popcorn and toast, two of my favorite carbs," Matty said.

Matty was staring at the healthy food that Erick and I enjoyed eating. There was an organic turkey breast. Fresh vegetables. A cabbage soup for starters, which was steaming in the bowls in front of them. And none of the processed food that Matty so enjoyed. He looked liked someone had killed his puppy.

"This stuff smells," Matty continued.

Erick broke out laughing and smacked him.

"Be nice, and maybe I'll take you out for a pretzel later," he said.

That was all Matty had to hear, and he was slurping down the soup as quickly as possible.

"You're easy," Hahn said to him.

"I'll screw for real food, what can I say?" he said.

"You'll get your real food next Thursday," I said. "Today is really just a day that I wanted to say how thankful I am to have all of you in my life."

The room grew quiet. I hadn't meant to bring everyone down, but this honesty thing seemed to be a buzz-kill to our regular rounds of jabs and quips. Going back to Dr. Pingleton this week had really helped me understand that I wasn't alone. I had him, and I had these great friends to surround me and hold me up.

"Sweetie, you know I feel the same way," Erick said as he leaned over to kiss my hand.

"Hey, hey," Hahn said. "No hand kissing. Swine flu is always a hand-shake away."

Everyone laughed at Hahn, but they got the message. These guys were my family. I didn't need anyone to replace what I had right here. The mood went back to laughing and joking as we made our way through the meal that I had worked so hard at preparing. Finally, Matty pulled out his iTouch.

"No, put that away," I said.

"I'm just logging into the poker game to get my daily money," he said.

"They give you free money?" Hahn asked.

"It's not real," Erick said.

"What the hell are you doing playing with fake money?" she said.

"Do you think I'd spend a teacher's salary playing poker?" Matty said.

"It's really strange. Come on, admit it," I said. "Playing this game with people all across the country who are sitting on their sofas or toilets or whatever – waiting for that perfect straight to come up."

"I'm waiting for a perfect straight to come up," Hahn said, "Is he out there?"

Everyone except Matty said "No" at the same time.

"And those poker people can chat with each other, too," Erick said.

"Well, those freaks need to be able to communicate somehow," I said, patting Matty's hand.

"Let he who is among us who isn't looking for some sort of community cast the first Ace," Matty said.

"I think I dated an Ace once," Erick joked.

"Once, this guy kept going 'all in' each round, and sharing what his cards were," Matty said. "Everyone thought he was nuts, and he said he wanted to lose all his money because the addiction had ruined his life."

"Hello! Delete the game from your little device thingy then!" Hahn said. "How can fake money ruin your life? You people don't know what a tough life is."

"Oh, here we go again with the Asian female stories," Erick teased.

"Hey, I can always fall back on my sewing skills from my youth and make winter coats for all of you," she said.

"That will come in really handy in Arizona," Matty said.

I loved how our gay mafia enjoyed teasing each other, but that was all it was. Nothing was ever malicious. It was just the way we communicated. But in an odd way, Matty was right when he said we were each just looking for where we belonged. Took me a long time to find this group, and I wasn't giving them up that easily. We finished up our meal, and I stood to clear away the dishes.

"Erick, wanna give me a hand with dessert?" I said.

"Sure ... I can serve these people," he said to them.

We went into the kitchen to pull out the carrot milk pudding that Hahn had made.

"This was really great of you to have us over," Erick said.

"I'm back in therapy."

"Really?"

"Yup. I need this doctor's help."

"Good for you, girl. I'm proud of you," Erick said as he gave me a tight squeeze.

"Do you know how important you are to me?" I asked him.

"I feel the same way," he said as he placed the bowls onto a tray.

"I'm sorry Ron didn't want to join us," I said.

"Don't be. You know it's always been you and me," he said.

"Oh wait, one more thing," I said, pulling a small cherry chocolate cake from the fridge. I had made it for Matty.

"You are such an enabler," Erick said with a laugh.

"Hey, he likes this stuff. What's the harm," I said.

I added a dish to Erick's tray so that Matty could cut himself a nice big piece and eat as much as he wanted.

"OK, OK," I said entering the dining room. "Dessert has to go quickly. We have places to go."

"What is that?" Matty asked, looking at the cake being placed in front of him.

"See, I do think of you," I said, kissing his head. "And you're taking the whole thing home later."

"You won't hurt my feelings if no one likes the pudding," Hahn said.

"Are you kidding?" Erick asked, taking a huge bite. "It's great!"

"You people make me ill," Matty said. "But this is delicious. Wanna try a bite, Erick? You can just lick my lips, and it won't be as bad for you."

"I think I'm going to vomit," Hahn said.

"Finish your dessert, people," I said. "We're running out of time."

"For what?" Erick asked.

"Tip it!" I yelled, mimicking one of our favorite comedians.

"Oh, my God, you've got to be kidding me," Erick said.

"She's in town tonight at the Dodge Theatre. We have four seats on the front row," I said.

"I need to run home and get my book for her to sign," Erick yelled like a little girl.

"Kathy Griffin is waiting for us," I said. "Now, let's throw these dishes in the kitchen and get out of here."

"You are a great friend, Sara," Hahn said.

"Think of it as an early Christmas present," I said.

I had never seen the four of us work so quickly as we made an assembly line toward my kitchen, put things away, and were out the door to be entertained by one of the funniest women around.

CHAPTER SEVENTEEN

You couldn't escape the Christmas music in the malls or all the people shopping like crazy. I'd go from the gym to work to home, and it seemed like it always took forever during that time of the year as people used every cut-through street to get to their next shopping destination. I had seen Dr. Pingleton a few more times and had even come to terms with the invisible rash – which was officially gone. I felt cured!

But at the same time, it was a little creepy because I was walking around with new memories in my head from that hypnosis session. And the thought of them added more fear to my already screwed up existence. Memories of me as a small child witnessing an adult whose face I did not know, using their cigarettes as a discipline tool like it was some sort of game.

I could never imagine doing something like that to my child. But I never planned on having children. The world didn't need more unwanted kids. I saw my share as a child myself, and I didn't want to add to that type of population. No, Gracie from my dreams was the closest thing to a child I would ever have.

You know you need a man to have a child, Sara.

I knew that all too well. But Dr. Pingleton was on his way to helping with that, too, working on those "sex-as-escape" issues.

Some day, I would be a normal woman who could handle having a regular relationship and not the fake ones I had been drawn to in my adult life.

Keep telling yourself that.

I didn't hear from Steve for weeks, but he must have needed something because there on my phone was a text from him that I had not returned. I was sitting in my car waiting for my session with Dr. Pingleton to begin and trying not to respond to him, although I wanted to see him. Maybe it was the Christmas season making me feel lonely. Or maybe I just needed a really good screw, and that man was the finest. But he was just as messed up as I was if he had a girlfriend with me on the side. I saw her face in my head. Probably out shopping for his Christmas present, and he was sending me messages about how he wanted to get in my pants.

Don't do it.

Should my needs win out over hers? And how long could I allow Steve to go on using me in that manner and lying to Mandy?

There is that word again. Lying.

My fingers, as if separate from my brain, were trying to type back to him when I decided to go on in and wait for Dr. Pingleton in the lobby outside his office. I stopped typing, left the phone in my car, and went inside.

More Christmas music was playing on the small radio in the corner of his waiting room. Was that really necessary for all the people who were coming into his office? Don't they say the holidays are the worst time for people with emotional problems? He shouldn't be adding to it by playing *White Christmas* on the damn radio. I wondered what a white Christmas would even look like.

Dr. Pingleton opened his door and had me come in. Instead of sitting up to look at him, I plopped right back on the sofa. I knew this would be another hypnosis session, and I was ready. I needed to know more information.

"Are you ready, Sara?" he asked me.

"As I'll ever be."

And then, we began ... the slow climb backwards into my mind. I had gotten rather good at it. As frightened as I was, I wanted to visit this place. I needed to see what was there. He took me back, past the Peterson's house and the River's house. Before I had lived in New Mexico. Back to a place I knew nothing about.

I was inside a home I didn't know. The place was freezing, as if heat had not been turned on for the winter nights. There was a gray linoleum floor and one of those chrome and Formica tables that you would find in a grandparents' house. The vinyl seats around the kitchen table where I was told to wait were sticky. I figured someone must have dropped some jam on them while eating their breakfast. I looked around the room trying to find something that I would recognize, but nothing was familiar. Huge wooden beams ran the length of the ceiling. The place was dark with only a small light streaming in from an adjacent hallway. And then, as if something came over me, I became a small child again – just as I had been when Samara took me back, just as I appeared when the stranger taunted me with cigarettes.

"Are your mama and daddy there?" Dr. Pingleton asked.

"They are sneaking in the other room," I said.

"Sneaking?"

"They told me to be very quiet and play the game with them."

There was silence while I waited at the table, staring at the thick wood boards across the ceiling. I bet Daddy could hang a swing from that big board, and I could fly in the swing all the way up to the ceiling. I ran my small finger along the crack where the two halves of the table came together. And then, I heard a woman scream.

"Are you OK?" the voice asked me.

"No. I'm scared in this dark room. I'm running to see where my mama is."

"Can you tell me what you see?"

"The lady is on the floor next to her bed as mama holds her arms behind her. Daddy is hitting the man on the bed. There is something in his hand, and each time he hits, red stuff squirts out all over the man on Daddy."

"Can you see your mama's face?"

Why was Mama laughing while the lady screamed? She didn't laugh when I screamed. I think she knew when I was upset, but if I made her too mad, she would hold those smoky things over my arm. I didn't like that.

"She is laughing while the lady she holds cries. Why is she crying? I bet she loves the man that Daddy is hitting. He must have done something wrong."

"Is anyone talking to you?"

"The lady is asking me to help her. Mama keeps laughing and yells at me to go back to the kitchen, but Daddy orders me to watch."

I hoped I never did anything that bad. I didn't want Mama and Daddy to be that mad at me. I could be a good girl.

"Sara, don't be afraid. I'm here."

"Why are you calling me, Sara?" I asked.

"Isn't that your name?" the voice asked.

"No, my name is Prissy."

"Is that a nickname?"

Mama had told me many times who I was named after, and she loved playing that man's music in the house. She told me he died, but I didn't know what that meant. He must have gone away somewhere so people wouldn't make him sing anymore.

"I'm Priscilla, named after some lady that Mama liked. She was married to a king. We listen to his music."

"Sara, I want you to wake up when I count to three."

"Daddy threw the man down on the floor, and he ain't moving now. Daddy is walking toward the lady that Mama is holding."

"Wake up for me, Sara."

"My name is Prissy."

"Prissy, it's time to wake up."

"Daddy is holding the lady and giving Mama the shiny thing to use on the lady. She's looking at me right in my eyes and crying. I don't want Mama to hurt her like Daddy hurt the man. Please don't. Mama! Don't!"

"Prissy!" the voice called me.

"Don't hurt her, Mama!"

Mama looked so mad. I bet I was going to be in trouble when we got home. I was going to hide in my closet and not let them find me for five, eight days. Maybe they wouldn't care if they couldn't find me. I'd get hungry and not get any food.

"Prissy! Close your eyes, and come with me," the voice said. "When I count backwards – three, two, one."

I opened my eyes and tried to zero in on the pointed stars on the ceiling, but I felt sick to my stomach.

"Sara?"

"I'm gonna be sick."

I could barely get the words out before I jumped up to run out to the bathroom in his waiting room. I put my head over the toilet and threw up while holding on to the porcelain base. I couldn't believe what I had seen. It was something my brain couldn't even fathom. But it felt like I was right there witnessing it all. How I wished it were not true, but after the session with Samara and this, I knew it was.

"Sara, are you OK in there?" Dr. Pingleton asked from the other side of the door.

"I'll be right out."

I stood, flushed the toilet, trying to clear the memories, and ran water to splash on my face. I looked in the mirror to see if I could see what the small child looked like, one who had witnessed that horrible evening; but she was not looking back at me. I saw a woman who was completely overwhelmed by images that no one should see. I rinsed my face, dried it with a soft towel, and turned to open the bathroom door. Standing there, a giant Pingleton took me in his big bear arms and held me. For a moment, neither of us needed to speak or were able to, it seemed. The comfort of his arms was exactly what I needed. He made me calm down and took me back into his office. I sat back on the sofa, pulling my legs up underneath me like a small child. I grabbed the pillow at the end of the sofa and held it in my arms. I couldn't bring myself to look him in the eye.

"So?" he started.

"Completely drained."

"I'm sure. That was much heavier than you thought it was going to be."

"It's like a bad dream. Or something you'd see in a movie."

Yeah, a freakin' horror movie. You come from murderers.

"Take a moment to breathe, and then we can talk about it."

I noticed that I had been holding my breath. So I did some breathing exercises that I did in my cool-down at the gym and then spoke to the doctor, finally making eye contact with him.

"Why do you think parents would allow a child to witness something so horrible?"

"Some people are not meant to be parents, Sara. They don't know what raising a child is. Giving birth does not make someone a mother or father."

"I agree," I said. "Now, I definitely know that I don't ever want to have any. I could end up like them."

"That's not necessarily true … not at all."

I knew what he meant, but the fear of having my own child, to whom I could pass terrible traits through my genes was enough to make me think of having my tubes tied.

"The act itself was horrendous, but telling the child to stand there and watch..."

"That child was you," he reminded me.

I kept referring to her in third person, like she wasn't part of me. Because to me she wasn't. I didn't know that life and wasn't sure I even wanted to know it any further.

"I know," I said. "It's just easier for me to remove myself and think of her as someone else."

"I understand."

"And I know, deep down, I know that I wouldn't necessarily be the same kind of parent, but I would never want to risk putting someone through that."

"You have plenty of time to think about children and family later. For now, stick with what you unraveled."

Yeah, doesn't take a rocket scientist to figure out why you blocked that out, Sara.

"It's so crazy," I said. "I thought I wanted to know, and now look."

"In time, you'll see it's better to know than to live in ignorance."

"And what was that? Naming me after Priscilla Presley! Please."

We both smiled, needing to let some tension out of the room.

"I think we discovered why you have an issue connecting to people."

"You think?" I said sarcastically.

I wondered if Dr. Pingleton had ever dealt with something this bizarre before. I was sure he'd seen it all, though this had to be at the top of his psycho-meter.

"One thing I want you to think about, Sara. As you go down this road to discover your past, your future is so exceptionally bright. You have become an amazing woman, and you should always hang on to that."

"Thanks, doc. I know you're saying that because I seem to be the spawn of some sort of Manson clan."

"While it's important to get answers from our past, it doesn't change who you are now. It doesn't matter who gave birth to you."

"I understand."

I played with a loose thread dangling from the end of the pillow, trying to avert my eyes from meeting his.

"Filling in those pieces of the puzzle is good, necessary sometimes – just to have the answers – but what we do with those answers is really the true testament to our lives. So…"

Pingleton took a big pause.

"Tell me your thoughts," he said.

"I'm thinking I wish I had been adopted by whomever it was who took me away from those mad parents. I wonder how many acts of violence I witnessed. When it started? If anyone in their immediate family was aware of what was going on; and knew they were taking me on those outings."

"These are normal responses."

"I also wonder if they are dead. Or how many they continued killing after I was put into foster care. And how did I end up in New Mexico?"

I realized my mind was racing with questions.

"Why do you say that?"

"Because I think this must have happened in Maine. The dreams. Something tells me it was all there. But how could a three-year-old get all the way across the country?"

"These are answers I'm sure you can find in time," he said.

A sinking feeling suddenly came over me as I finally made eye contact with the doctor.

"How do I tell people?"

"You don't have to tell anyone, Sara. It's your past. This is only for you to come to terms with to assist you in your life now. It's not about others knowing."

I wasn't sure how much I wanted anyone to know, if at all. Maybe I'd talk to Erick about it. I was very confused. This was not the past I thought I'd uncover. Some people who couldn't handle having a child, that's what I expected, people who abused me with cigarettes and something else, but never in a million years did I expect a Michael Myers family from *Halloween*.

"Do you mind if we end now?" I asked.

"Under the circumstances, I think that would be apt."

"I really do thank you for being there with me, walking me through it."

I felt my eyes start to fill, but I held back.

"I'm here for you, Sara."

I stood to leave, dropping the pillow back on the sofa.

"Do you have plans for the holidays?" he asked.

It sounded as if the doc was trying to inject a sense of normalcy back into the session, but I still felt like a gazelle being circled by lions.

"I'm not sure what I'm going to do," I said in a fog. "Guess I'll play it by ear."

"Well, if you ever need me, please call the number on my card."

"Thank you, doctor."

I hugged him again before I left. I felt I needed to. We had just gone through something very emotional, and I wanted one more physical connection. And I swore he gave an extra squeeze, like a dad would do, knowing I had no one like that in my life at all. I left the office and got into my car, wondering about where to go, what to do. I was supposed to go to an office Christmas party that night, but I didn't feel like it. I picked up my phone to call Erick, and there were two more texts from Steve.

Don't do it.

I couldn't stop myself. I needed to feel safe in a man's arms that night. And in some strange way, being with Steve was just the thing I needed to feel that security. I instantly sent a text telling him to come over later.

CHAPTER EIGHTEEN

Once back in the refuge of my home, I made myself some hot tea, and sat down in front of my computer. Did I really want to go further down this road? I felt like I was stuck inside some strange CSI investigation. But this was about my own life; not a TV show. I knew the year. I think I knew the state. And thanks to Google, I should be able to get some information.

I decided to start with a few more of my yoga breathing exercises to try and put my mind in the best possible shape. I needed a clear head and steady hand to complete the task. Once I started plugging in phrases, I knew there was no going back. I typed in "murders" and the year in Maine and began to read. Up came cases about children who were murdered and DNA being used to solve crimes years after the fact. I read as quickly as I could, wanting to see some shred of evidence that pointed to this heinous crime I had witnessed in my subconscious. Crime rates popped in front of my eye. Something had to ring a bell in my brain. I knew there had to be something there.

I hit the "next" button at the bottom of the screen as fast as my eyes could scan the links. Missing people. Arrests made. I knew I couldn't give up simply because it wasn't resulting in instant gratification. I would pull my eyes away from the computer and look around my condo room ... just to ground myself back in reality before venturing into the world of the Internet again. The sun was going down outside and causing a glow through the window, but the illumination from the screen was stronger and sucked me back in. I knew that someone had to have scanned in an old story somewhere. So I kept digging deeper and deeper on pages, clicking on links that could lead me somewhere else like a detective scrutinizing a crime. Maybe it wasn't a huge case. Something small and local that no one knew about. But even a small morsel would have fed my longing.

And then ... it was there on the screen.

Holy crap, Sara. This is it.

Charles and Lois Reed were wanted for murders in the vicinity of Boothbay Harbor. Unsolved crimes. The two were never caught. This had to be the couple from the nightmares. I continued to read as the words came off the screen faster and faster. But there was no mention of a child. What?

It had to be there. Something about this baby named Priscilla. I wanted to see it, to tie me to these people.

Keep looking.

And in the midst of this, I just knew there would be a photo scanned in by some paper. That would help me ... put a face to the crime. See if they looked like me. But there were no photos of this Charles or Lois anywhere, my parents, I assumed. But how could I be sure? What if this was all just a coincidence?

No. It couldn't be. I was sure that these two had to be my parents. How many other couples were out killing people then? And the fact that it was an unsolved mystery added to my certainty. Where were they? Did they even know I was alive?

I traveled deeper into the Internet by hitting "next" over and over again. I found a book that had been written about the murders called *A Killing on the Bay* by Terrence Hightower. God love the Internet because I could go right over to Hightower's website where I found he was a professor at Emerson College in Boston, teaching creative writing. But there was no mention there of this book – only novels. Why had he left off his work of non-fiction from his early years? I decided to send him an email about the book and the couple to find out if he knew anything about a daughter. I included my email address as well as my cell phone number for him to reach me.

I had been sitting at the computer for hours, and the time had flown by when I heard a knock at the door. I went to answer it as quickly as I could.

"Hey, Red, long time no see," Steve said.

I pulled him into the house and fell into his arms. This was real. And it was happening to me in the here and now. Not a dream. Not something that happened 30 years ago, but a man who could use my body and allow me to use his in ways that only we understood.

The sane part of my mind said to send him home, end this. He had a girlfriend, and our last time together had been a mess of emotions that I didn't want to deal with again. But the crazy chick in me wanted to jump his bones and forget everything I'd just discovered and conjured up during my therapy.

The crazy chick beat out the sane woman that time around.

The sex with him was as incredible as ever. Either he had forgotten the uncomfortable ending we had previously, or he just didn't care. Because the passion that he displayed that night was so powerful. However, the speed at which he was going spoke volumes about how quickly he wanted to get out of my house. Come and go. That's all he cared for. And I was thinking about filling a void in my life, a void that was growing the more my past continued to haunt me.

Once he was gone, the emptiness returned. I felt isolated, with no one to turn to. But I knew that was not true, since I had someone I was turning to more and more in my life: Erick. The big brother who was a constant in my life. He was there in a flash holding up a bag with a late night snack, a sushi roll.

"Me love you long time," he said as he entered the door.

"Guess it's hard to get away from the comfort of food, huh?"

"At least we make good choices," he said, making his way into my kitchen and taking over as server.

"Not all of us do," I said, knowing I wasn't talking about food.

Erick came back into the living room with the food on two plates and sat next to me on the oversized sofa.

"You had sex," he said.

"Bingo."

"Thought I could smell that man's spunk."

"Stop," I said, chuckling.

"So tell me all about it," he said. "Think of me as a gay Dr. Phil and spill it."

So I did. The breakthrough of hypnosis earlier that evening. The online research in Maine. The people who gave birth to me. Saying the words out loud seemed to make it all that more real.

"Holy shit," he said.

"Yeah, right?"

"Honey, just remember – that does not make them your parents," he said.

"I know, Dr. Phil. Just sperm and an egg."

"You got that right," he said with a smile.

We sat in silence looking at each other.

"It's heavy, huh?" I said.

"I ain't gonna lie. It's got Movie of the Week written all over it," he said.

"I'm exhausted."

He stood me up, left the uneaten food on the coffee table, and led me to my bedroom.

"I'm sure you are," he said. "Traveling back in time like that, then traveling on Steve's dick for hours … and hours … describe that part again … just him, leave you out of it."

I gave him a smack on his head as we both laughed and crawled into my bed. We got under the big comforter where I had just had sex with Steve, and I thanked Erick for his support and for being non-judgmental. He stayed with me, holding me all night long. It was wonderful and felt so different from being held by Steve. That was because I could feel real affection from Erick. Something I never felt with booty text.

CHAPTER NINETEEN

"Middleton Industries," I said into my phone.

"Hey, I've been doing some online research," Erick said.

"What kind?"

"Trying to get information on you from your childhood, that sort of shit."

The man was so good to me. I wasn't used to allowing people into my life like this, and I was taking a huge step with Erick. But he had shared so much with me, and he was trying to take care of me in ways that he felt he could help solve this confusing situation.

"Look at you, Nancy Drew," I said.

"Do you wanna hear?" he teased.

"Of course."

"New Mexico Child Protective Services has Fed Ex'ed paper work to your condo that should be there by tomorrow. You fill it out, send it back, and perhaps some answers will come from that."

Erick was such a great guy. I didn't have the heart to tell him I had called them already. But maybe this time, I would actually fill out the papers and send them back. Especially now that so much more was coming out of my sessions with Pingleton. Someone had to know if I came from Maine or where the stork had taken me from.

"Thanks, sweetie. I really appreciate your help on this," I said.

"Just trying to do whatever I can ... these strange circumstances."

"That's putting it mildly," I said. "But so nice of you when you have your own issues to deal with."

"I'd rather deal with your issues than the crazy Botox man I share my home with."

"Thank you."

Erick didn't say anything for a moment, and I thought perhaps we had been disconnected.

"Sara, are you sure you want to go down this road?" he finally asked. "You really want to know the truth?"

I wanted to answer him straight out that, of course, I wanted to know, but the reality was, I wasn't sure. Part of me felt I needed to know the past so I would no longer be stuck where I was, but if I was really related to those horrible people, what would that make me? Something gnawed at my insides saying I needed to know.

"I think I need to know, Erick. For my own sanity. Even if I don't ever talk of it again," I said.

"Then, I'm in. I'm here to help you in any way I can."

My cell phone started to ring.

"Thanks, dude. Now, I have to go. Other line is ringing."

"As long as it's not the creepy boss wanting to feel you up," he said.

"Bye!"

I answered the call that had a blocked number on it.

"Hello."

"Is this Sara Butler who was asking about the book, *A Killing by the Bay*?"

"Yes."

I stepped away from my desk and went outside to take the call, my heart pounding.

"This is Professor Hightower. I was shocked that anyone knew about that book. It's been out of print for years."

"Well, professor, there is still a listing about it on the Internet."

"Damn," he said. "I didn't want anyone to know about my foray into the non-fiction world."

Didn't this guy ever do Internet searches to see what was out there? I found it a little odd but was still clinging to his every word in his thick Boston accent.

"I'm sorry for bringing up old wounds for you..." I started, but he interrupted.

"That was to be my *In Cold Blood*, but it never happened," he said.

Do you really want to walk down this man's memory path? Just get your answers.

"Since you obviously did research back then, I wondered what you knew about a child," I said.

The man got fairly flustered and excited all at the same time on the other end of the phone.

"That's why I called you, Ms. Butler," he said. "To find out what you knew."

What should I tell this man? That I had been having dreams and was hypnotized and believed I was there witnessing it all? That would come across as awfully strange, at least at first.

"I was doing some research on this very subject," I lied, "due to some family I have in Maine, and I was told there was a child that none of the papers knew about."

"I thought the same thing," the excited voice said. "But no one would share any of that with me during my investigation. It was as if the whole town was hiding this child, protecting her. Or at first, I thought they were protecting the killers, but to this day, I still think there was more to that case."

Obviously, I had awakened something in this literary scholar who felt a connection to my past.

"So you never found out what happened to the child?"

"No. My research was done, I wrote the book, and no one would even buy it. So there was only one printing. But 30 years later, I would still like to know why they did what they did. The killers would be my age by now … and that child is in her late twenties or early thirties … if still alive."

You believe the child is alive ... but who knows about the parents.

"Have you ever gone back to find out anything?" I asked.

"I went back a few times after that, but they were all on to me and knew I was a writer and eventually stopped talking to me. They wanted to forget it happened."

What if I went there to see if I could get any information? Would that be the stupidest thing in the world to travel across the country on a hunch?

"Well, professor, I appreciate you calling me."

"If you learn anything more through your investigation, please share it with me. This old brain needs an ending to that story," he said.

Yeah, so does this young brain.

"Will do," I said.

I promised to call if I found something. But I didn't know if I would want to share with a stranger the possibility of it being me. I wasn't sure if it were something I was even ready to know myself.

CHAPTER TWENTY

"Is this a special kind of Christmas drink?" Hahn asked.

"Do you feel jolly?" Matty asked.

"I feel fucking great!" she said.

"Then, it's working," Erick said. "Jolly ole St. Vodka-las. Lean your ear this way."

"I'll lean my ear your way," Matty said, shouting over the music.

"How many different versions of the same Christmas songs can they make?" I asked our group huddled around a very crowded table at Passions.

The place was packed as people were in town seeing families, and gay guys needed some place to escape to. Escaping families seemed to be a motif that went well beyond those of parents who might be murderers.

"It's the techno beat they put to them that cracks me up," Erick said.

"Well, since you've all been nice this year, except you, you've been naughty," Matty gestured to Erick, "I've gotten you a little something to celebrate."

All of us opened the cards from Matty, which had coupons to every fast food restaurant you could think of. We all broke out into laughter.

"So if you don't want to eat anything, you can always take me," he said.

"My turn, my turn," Erick said.

Erick made a big performance out of pulling presents from his bag like Santa and giving them to each of us. Some sort of computer game for Matty, a beautiful blouse for Hahn, and a season subscription to the theatre company in town for me.

"Thank you, Erick," I said.

"Well, you got us all those great seats for Kathy Griffin, so it was the least I could do," he said.

"I guess we saved the old bag for last," Hahn said, slightly inebriated.

We all looked around at each other.

"No, the oldest one just went," Erick said.

"You only think you're the oldest," she said.

The group sat in silence staring at Hahn as if she was about to make some huge proclamation.

"Let's just say there is a four in my age, and it's not the second number," she blurted out.

"Damn, girl," Erick said. "You look good."

"You've heard black don't crack? Well, Vietnamese don't squeeze," she said. "I'm as smooth as a baby's butt."

"Vietnamese! Now, we know," Matty said.

"Yes. I came over on one of the last boats to leave Saigon during the seventies. I was a mere child."

The alcohol had lowered Hahn's recalcitrance, and we were all amazed to hear her story about coming to America. She told us about the urgency to leave her home, the crowded conditions on the boats, what it was like to see her own cousin fall from the back of her uncle into the water and drown.

Damn, Sara, you think you had a rough life.

"Merry freaking Christmas, sunshine," Matty said.

Even though it was a serious subject, we couldn't help but laugh.

"Matty, you're terrible," I said.

"Leave him alone," Hahn said, grabbing him from behind. "He's right. What was I thinking, getting so maudlin?"

"Where are the gifts, bitch?" Erick said. "And if you have some thatched roof keepsake in there, I'm smacking you."

We all opened up individual boxes with a handmade scarf in each. Hahn had paid careful attention to us over the years to make sure she had each person's favorite color as the main color of their scarf. Matty's was red, Erick's was purple, and I had my bright orange woven through it.

"It's not a coat, but I still made them by my own hands," Hahn said. "When you wear them, think of the hundreds of thousands of Asian children who work all day long making those American clothes you love so much!"

"Yes, I'll be wearing this through the Arizona malls," Matty said.

"I know where I'll be wearing it," I said.

It was time to let my friends in on my impending adventure. I had sent the paperwork that Erick got for me back to the New Mexico office, but who knew how long that would take. I had spent many sleepless nights since my last therapy session pondering over all the information. Dr. Pingleton had asked me what I was doing for the holidays, and I had finally figured it out.

"Where will you be donning this gay apparel?" Hahn asked.

"I'm spending the holidays in Maine."

The initial shock on their faces made clear that I had never talked about this state with these folks, but then the questions started.

"That's not fair," Matty said. "You'll get a white Christmas. Who do you know in Maine?"

"You know they'll make you eat Christmas lobster instead of tofu turkey," Hahn said.

"I thought we knew you," Matty continued. "Are you hiding some other friends from us?"

So many questions to which I had no answers. Erick jumped to my rescue since he had already been privy to some information.

"Our dear friend has been dealing with some issues from her past, and she's going on a crusade of discovery," he said.

Everyone was silent for a moment. Then, Hahn spoke.

"I knew Samara had helped open up something within you." She took my hand.

"You had a reading with that chick?" Matty asked.

"Raise a glass to our gal," Hahn said. "Here! Here!"

The slightly drunk group made a toast to me, even though they weren't certain what it was about.

"You're going by yourself?" Matty asked.

"Can't expect anyone to run off during Christmas."

"Why not? My mother is," Matty said.

"Your mom? Mrs. 'Holidays are for Families'?" Erick said.

"She's taking a bus trip to Vegas, of all places," Matty said.

"That's the most un-Christmas thing." Erick said.

He stopped talking when his phone rang with a new text. He looked down and read the words from Ron. I just looked at him, waiting to see what it said.

"Spending the night with some real pros. Won't be home," he read aloud.

No one spoke. I knew more than the other two, but they weren't ignorant to what Ron was putting Erick through. I decided to break the silence.

"Pros are hoes," I joked.

"In this case, you are completely right," he said. "Yes, my friends, my boyfriend has decided to start paying for sex with his sick group of friends, and, oh yeah, he's fucking women. Any questions?"

The only sound heard was from the music and the crowds around us. No one in our group said a word. Matty and Hahn were thrown by the bombshell of information. Matty put his hand on top of Erick's, but all of a sudden, Erick was fired up.

"That's it," Erick said. "I'm done. Finished. And Sara, I'm joining you on your expedition."

"What?" I asked.

He looked as if he had a brand new lease on life; his entire face lit up.

"Yes. We'll make it a road trip. We'll see the Midwest and New England. It'll be great."

"I don't know if I can afford an entire road trip," I said.

"Oh ... don't worry. You're not paying. Ron is. All I have to do is go by the bank for a special withdrawal, and we can leave whenever you want."

"Now, I'm really pissed," Hahn said. "I can't get off work, and I'd love to join you all."

"Sara has days built up where she can get off, and I can't care less what they say to me at the spa. Someone else can take my clients," Erick said.

"Erick, you sure you wanna do this?" I asked.

Erick nodded and headed toward the bar. We had never seen him so ... well, butch and decisive. It was great.

"There goes my man," Matty said.

"Sounds like you'll have your chance now," Hahn said.

Matty took off after Erick to help him grab more drinks to bring back to us.

"Do you think I'm crazy, Hahn?"

"Not at all. Whatever you're dealing with, I think you're smart to confront it."

"Have you ever gone back to Vietnam?" I asked.

"There are times I wish I had, but we never know what we might uncover when dealing with the past. So I'm secretly glad our guy is going with you."

I was glad, too. Who better to go with me than someone I thought of as a brother?

"I just can't believe the amazing past you had," I said.

"Pay no mind to my past, girl – deal with yours. You think you're gonna find some family or something in Maine?"

"Or something."

"I'm glad I was able to play a small part in this by introducing you to Samara, even if you did cut me outta your life for a few weeks."

I squeezed her hand for emphasis, and the drink in her allowed it to stay.

"I really am sorry 'bout that."

"No sweat. Just bring me a big gift from Maine."

"What if I don't get the correct answers?" I asked.

"Better yet, what if you do? Are you prepared to deal with that?"

Suddenly, Hahn sounded like an older, wiser sage who knew and had seen so much. But I was ready. I couldn't rest or move forward until I knew for sure if I was Priscilla Reed.

"I'm ready" I said. "And tough."

"Don't I know it," she responded. "I've seen you kick the crap out of that punching bag at the gym."

The boys made their way toward us when Erick stopped Matty and pointed up at the mistletoe hanging above them. He kissed Matty right on the lips and then kept walking toward us with the drinks.

"More Christmas spirits. Merry, merry," Erick said, handing us our drinks.

Matty stumbled toward us, slightly stunned.

"Guess I'll get to use my new scarf, too," Matty said.

"As long as Sara doesn't care," Erick told him.

"What?" I asked.

"Matty is off for the Christmas break and doesn't want to sit alone while his mother hits the penny slots in Vegas, so…"

"So he should go with us," I almost shouted.

I was thrilled that my two favorite men would be making this journey with me.

"Now, I'm fucking pissed," Hahn said dejectedly.

"Call in sick," I told her.

"I can't. You three will have to play Thelma and Louise … and Louise without me."

"But think what a great time we'll have on the road," I said.

"I like having job security in this economy," Hahn said.

"Then, it's set," Erick said again with that tone of authority. "Tomorrow, I go to the bank and take out the money. And as soon as Matty's done with school, we hit the road."

"This is gonna be a freakin' sweet trip," Matty said.

"And we'll all think of you while we wear our scarves in that cold winter air up there," I said, giving Hahn a hug, knowing the alcohol lowered the part of her defenses that would usually push me away.

"You better," she said. "And I want postcards and big ass gifts."

"Oh, Ron will buy you very nice gifts," Erick said. "I promise."

CHAPTER TWENTY-ONE

We decided to take my Acura I had purchased for a great steal the year before. Erick's convertible didn't seem practical for the New England winter; and no one thought Matty's old car would even make it. I picked everyone up. Bags were thrown into the trunk – with Erick bringing enough for a transatlantic cruise – and I took the first leg driving, with Erick calling shotgun.

"OK, what music do we want for the road trip?" he asked. "I brought my entire collection."

"Oh, Lord, it's gonna be a gay adventure all right," I said.

"We don't have to play ABBA," he said. "I have music from this decade."

"Let me see what else you have," Matty said.

"Let's discuss the difference between Matty's small bag and Erick's mammoth set of luggage," I said.

"Will someone just pick some music," Erick said, ignoring the comment.

"Fine, fine. Put in some Beatles to start with," I said.

"The choice of excellence," came Matty's voice from the back seat.

"Who has the map?" Erick said.

"I have GPS," I said. "Welcome to the 21st century."

We started out toward New Mexico, a state that held so much of my childhood memories. All that isolation, fear, and anger of being a foster kid– but I had come to believe that was nothing compared to my earlier years. We headed north in Arizona first, toward the Petrified Forest National Park.

"I was here as a kid," Matty said. "Probably the first time I thought about wanting to study science."

In all the time knowing Matty, I had never thought to ask him what drove him to become a teacher. I was so bad at asking questions of people. I always just took whatever they told me. With that kind of track record, I was probably in for a really bad experience trying to find answers in Maine.

"So rocks and earth excited you even then?" I asked.

"Are you kidding?" he said. "I couldn't learn enough about geology. The age of the earth. The composition of each type of rock and how you can decode the age from…"

"I remember being here, too, professor," Erick added quickly.

"Never made it here myself," I said.

Why didn't any foster families take you anywhere? Were you a bad child?

"Do you wanna stop?" Matty asked.

"Too soon. We're still in Arizona," I said.

We passed a Navajo Indian reservation. All those things that made our state what it was. But I noticed my body starting to tremble the closer we got to New Mexico. I didn't quite understand the reaction I was having to the state. It had been 15 years since I moved, and that part of my life was left on that land. I tried to recall the good moments and forget about the ones that involved taunting and jeers.

"Are we there yet?" Matty teased from the backseat.

"Did you go on lots of road trips as a child?" Erick asked Matty.

"We went to the Grand Canyon once. That was pretty cool. And sometimes we'd go camping. I was always the pain in the ass when traveling, though."

"Great, now you tell us," I said.

"Only child, so I could usually rule the car," he said.

"Interesting," Erick said. "We are a car load full of 'only childs' here. So who will rule?"

"Well, Oprah, why don't you dig a little, and maybe we can find this out," Matty said. "Or we could just draw straws."

The guys laughed and continued talking while I thought about what Erick had said. I assumed I was an only child, but for all I knew, there was a sibling I never knew. Every foster family had other kids, so there were always plenty of people around. Funny that I still felt so alone during that time in foster care.

The Beatles CD was on repeat, *Yesterday* playing again. I thought about the time prior to my hypnosis when I desperately wanted to know about yesterday. I had spent my twenties trying to run from it. Moving to Phoenix. Dating a married man.

Immersing myself into a world to try and become someone other than "that foster kid." But nothing I tried then seemed to work. That was a troubling time in my life, but I felt as if my troubles grew even larger with the new knowledge that I was seeking. Would my thirties turn out to be any better than the previous decade?

"Is someone going to put on a new CD, or are we just going to be listening to this one the whole trip?" I asked, feeling a little hostile.

"Chill, Miss Priss," Matty said grabbing another CD.

I stared out the windows to take my mind off it all. The desert landscape that came up to the very side of the road, rocky and brown, was all I'd known as an adult. Soon, signs appeared for the New Mexico border.

"Time to switch. I've been driving for hours now," I said.

"Pull over, and I'll take a turn," Erick said, looking deeply at me to figure out my malevolence.

God love Matty. He had to make a big deal about getting out of the car and stretching his legs, but I was glad we stopped to change drivers so that Erick could take us across that border. Driving through it, images flashed constantly of the families I had grown up with, while my two new brothers talked back and forth, reminding me of how far I had actually come in my life. I tried to place my head against the window and rest a while, barely listening to them talk and sing with the CDs. Surprisingly, I was able to calm myself down, and breathing the same air I had inhaled from my childhood through my teen years invigorated me. We got to some small town outside of Albuquerque and decided to stop for food, since we had been travelling for seven hours. As soon as Erick pulled in, Matty opened the door and flew out of the car.

"Man, you guys are intense," Matty said. "I've been dying to take a leak for miles."

"Then, speak up, guy," Erick said.

"I was starving, too."

"Of course you are," I said.

We found a purportedly authentic Mexican restaurant. Matty was thrilled – he could pour cheese all over his meal, and Erick and I could survive on rice and beans and an avocado salad. There was mindless chatter going on, and then Matty came out with it.

"So, is anyone gonna tell me what this trip is all about?" he asked. "Or am the child that Mama and Daddy are afraid to tell anything to?"

Go ahead and share. What do you have to lose?

I looked at Erick, and he nodded. Matty was a good friend. There was no reason not to fill him in.

"You know how I told you I grew up in foster care without any parents?" I said.

"Yeah, but you know we're your family, right?" he said.

"Right ... but I think I got some information on my real family back in Maine, and I just wanted to check it out in person."

Your family of killers.

"Nothing crazy about that," Matty said, as he bit into his burrito.

He acted as if he were fine with that piece of info, so I figured that was enough for the time being. But I knew I'd give him the rest of the story before the trip was done.

Just not yet, Sara. Not until you have more answers.

When we got back in the car, the guys started playing the license plate game. All these road trip games I never played as a child. I seemed to get into it a little too much, pointing out plates from every different state I saw. I couldn't believe that most people on the road were out doing things like that, and I had missed out on it growing up. I'd do anything to take my mind off of the true reason for our ride: the journey into a gruesome past.

As soon as we entered the Texas panhandle, Erick started something new ... showtunes.

"Texas has a whorehouse in it," he sang.

We laughed, and the guys gave me a lesson on Broadway shows. Then, it grew into a game about how many shows used states in them. Not a game I was going to win at all. Matty took over driving as we got into Oklahoma.

"Oooooklahoma where the wind comes sweeping down the plains," Erick sang again.

"You're good," I said.

The place was flat and dusty. Not in the same way as Arizona. It's amazing how our country's landscape changes just a few states from each other. Arizona had rock beds and uneven terrain, while Oklahoma had land as far as the eye could see. We had been driving all day long when Matty decided we should stop and sleep in Tulsa.

"Shouldn't we push on?" I asked with a definite edge in my voice.

"It's okay, Sara," Erick said. "We don't want to kill ourselves on day one."

You just want us to get there.

I begrudgingly gave in.

"Now, just take a look around, boys," I said. "Let's not put out the gay flag here. I don't need to be visiting a hospital with you guys."

"I can butch it up," Erick said.

"I'm a teacher; I do it every day."

We found some motel that was just a few steps up on the freaky-meter from the Bates Motel, and Erick went in to get us rooms.

This is right where your crazy ass belongs.

Matty was getting our bags out of the back of the car when Erick came running back toward us.

"It's already feeling chilly out there," he said.

"You scared me when I saw you running," I said, noticing the one key in his hand.

"What? Safety in numbers," he said.

We went into the tiny room that smelled of mold covered up by spray disinfectant. There were generic photos of Indians above each bed and faded blue bedspreads that draped down to matted pink carpet. I looked at the two beds and the three of us.

"Erick can sleep with me," I quickly said.

I didn't need to give the two of them a reason to do anything. Not tonight.

Erick looked around the shabby room.

"We can keep driving to find something else," he said.

I felt guilty about pushing earlier.

"I'm not a princess," I asserted. "This is … perfect."

"Speak for yourself," Matty said, standing behind Erick like something was going to reach out and bite him.

"It's too late to keep driving," Erick said. "Get used to it, guys; this is part of the adventure."

Matty realized we weren't going to give in, so he turned on the ten-year-old TV and pulled out his iTouch, looking for an Internet connection as he cautiously lay down on his bed.

"Pull the comforter off the bed," I yelled. "That's where all the gross stuff is, and they don't wash 'em."

"I saw that TV special, too," Erick said, laughing.

Matty inspected his sheets thoroughly and then pulled his own pillow from home out of his bag. My mind jolted back to carrying a pillowcase from foster home to foster home.

"I love seeing local news people," Matty said. "It makes me think I'm in a foreign land."

Guess you ain't the only freak, Sara.

"We need ice; hand me that bucket," I said.

"I can go get it," Matty offered.

"What do I look like, a scared invalid?" I said, walking out the door.

I went down the outside corridor to the foot of a staircase where there were ice and vending machines. Sitting on the bottom of the stairs was an elderly Indian man. Native American, I should say. Not sure why he was just sitting there, slumped over and smoking a hand-rolled cigarette. I gave him an impish smile and opened the ice machine looking for the scoop.

"They keep it on top," he said, pointing.

"Thank you."

I reached up to grab it to fill my bucket with some ice.

"Nice night for it, isn't it?" he said.

Nice night for what? Killing women at the ice machine?

"I guess," I said.

"Damn wife won't let me enjoy this in our room," he said as he sucked in on his cigarette. "Like I really need to worry about death at this stage."

He seemed to be so content sitting there enjoying his nicotine. He had to have been in his eighties, a face wrinkled like leather and deep set eyes that had witnessed more of a life than I could imagine. I felt bad for the bit of fear that had slipped into my mind when I first saw him.

"Life is too short," I said. "Might as well do what you like."

Why can't you give yourself advice like that?

"And to get a few moments of peace without the wife nagging at me? Well, that's worth gold," he said.

"Enjoy your evening and your holiday," I said as I started walking away.

"Good luck to you on your road trip," he said.

I turned and looked at him with a hint of fear returning in my eyes.

"I saw you and the two guys come in and heard you talking," he said. "Don't worry, girlie. I ain't some psycho Indian."

The man let out a strange laugh with his final puff of smoke and slowly stood and walked the opposite direction down the corridor. I wanted to make sure he was actually a guest and not some apparition I was talking to, so I made sure I saw him go into a room.

That will be you someday. You're always on the outside looking in.

I got back into the room and passed the ice to Erick, who had pulled out his stash of vodka and Sprite to make a cocktail.

"Took you long enough," he said.

"I was rapping about life with an Oklahoma Indian," I said.

I went into the bathroom and turned on the lights, illuminating the cracked dingy tiles and cobwebs in the upper corners. I wished I had my own room to escape to, but I could understand Erick's reasoning. I just needed some alone time … to breathe. I let the hot water run to brush my teeth while I changed for bed. I couldn't wait to fall asleep. We still had such a long way to go. I hoped we could get there before the town shut down for Christmas. I took my blood pressure medicine, chuckling as I swallowed it down. A health conscious chick like me who worked out daily and ate right still having to fight high blood pressure.

Must be another hereditary trait from the crazy people who brought you into this world.

I wasn't sure how much a trip like this would help with keeping my blood pressure down. I had fought dredging up the past in therapy, and suddenly, I was purposely seeking it out. My, how times had changed.

I went back into the room where Erick had changed into some short stylish nightwear ensemble – I was sure Matty enjoyed watching that – and crawled into bed.

"Honey, I'll be right back," Erick said jokingly.

He went into the bathroom, and I watched Matty so intently staring at that technical thing in his hand. I swear he looked like a little boy in his dirty night shirt (which I'm sure he thought was clean when he pulled it from his drawer) and some baggy boxer shorts.

"You having fun, Matty?"

"This is great. Being with two of my favorite people going across the country. Yup, having fun. But tomorrow, we have to stop and do something."

"We will."

That hurt to say, didn't it?

I had to remind myself the guys needed to enjoy this trip as much as I needed to find my answers. They were here for me, but it was hard for me to take my mind off the real reason for the expedition. They saw it as a cross-country holiday jaunt, while I saw it as being sucked up by a black hole.

Erick was back in the room and not happy to see me getting ready to go to bed.

"We're not going to sleep yet," he announced, taking a sip of his drink. "Slumber party!"

Before I knew it, the 36-year-old was beating me with a pillow, and Matty was right over on top of us, too. It was a great way to get some of the pent-up exhaustion from a road trip out.

"You boys are too much," I said leaning against the headboard.

"Boys will be boys," Matty said, as he rested his hand on my thigh.

"Are you going straight on me now, too?" Erick said with a half smile.

"Hell, no," he said, stroking Erick's bare leg.

"Did you even tell Ron you were leaving?" I asked.

"I don't think he'd give a shit, but I did leave a note that I was getting away for the holidays."

"I know this has to be hard on you," Matty said.

"Matty, don't ever fall for an older guy," Erick said. "He'll fuck you in the end."

"All men are pigs," I said. "Present company excluded."

"We've all had heartache at one time or another," Matty said.

The room had somberness in it as we lay there; me combing my fingers through Matty's head as he rested it on my leg.

"You've never talked of yours," I said to him.

"It's the past. I prefer to leave it there and move on."

Wow. I was so locked up into my past, I could never think of doing that.

"Ten years of my past I gave to that plastic ass. Ten years! My youth stolen from me," Erick said.

"You still look great to me," Matty said. "And you're an older man in my eyes."

Erick smiled and leaned his head on Matty's shoulder. I wasn't sure if these two could ever go somewhere, but I was glad I had introduced them and that they had formed such a great friendship.

"Do you know how infectious your smile is when you allow it to take over your face?" Erick asked me. "You need to show it more often."

I patted his head and hid under my blanket.

"Goodnight, guys, it's time for me to go to sleep."

"No, wait! I have Travel Scrabble," Matty said.

"What are we? *The Golden Girls?*" Erick asked.

"You two can play. I'm turning in," I said.

I pushed them both off my bed, and instantly, they were over on Matty's bed playing a game like two small kids. I don't know how much time passed, and I barely heard Erick crawl back into bed with me. But I did feel him grab me and spoon me as I fell back asleep.

The next morning, we went to the small restaurant attached to the motel and had breakfast served to us by a woman who seemed to be missing half her teeth along with huge clumps of hair from her head.

"Some sort of alien experiment," Matty whispered to me.

As Erick paid the bill, I looked around the room and noticed the previous evening's Indian sitting across from his wife. He gave me a small wave goodbye. His face was pleading to be saved from the non-stop talking of his wife, but I gave a cheesy "How" salute – so un-PC – and followed the guys out to the car. It was time to start off toward Missouri.

CHAPTER TWENTY-TWO

The air felt like what I thought winter should be. Crisp and clean, and the smell I had become used to in the Arizona heat was gone, replaced with a freshness that I wanted to bottle up and take home with me to enjoy whenever I wanted. The landscape was that of countryside with leaves that had changed for winter. Browns, red, and orange layered the hillside, creating a beautiful postcard image. The three of us were happy to have sweatshirts on. Matty rolled down his window in the passenger seat and stuck his head out.

"Hello, Missouri!" he yelled.

"So what's the Broadway song for this state?" I asked.

"Meet me in St, Louiy, Louiy ... meet me at the fair," Erick sang.

We got to St. Louis and stopped to admire the Gateway Arch and get a tourist to take a picture of the three of us in front of it. I had seen it in photos, but everything is always so different when you see it for yourself. It was the gateway to the West, and we were heading east into unchartered territory. It was beautiful with the city on one side and the water on the other. An amazing man-made structure that should stop everyone in their tracks as they go past it. Yet, there were not many people around. They were probably all getting ready for Christmas in five days and crowding the stores. The guys wanted to go up inside, but I figured it would take too long. They decided to get Hahn a souvenir from the place instead. I chose to call our girlfriend to check in on her.

"Greetings from the arch," I said.

"You bitches are making good time," she said.

"What are you doing? Tracking our moves?"

"Yes. I have you on radar like Santa."

"Wish I had your smart-ass remarks in the car," I said.

"The gay quota getting to you?"

"Not at all. I'm just a little impatient to get to Maine, and the boys want to see everything."

"You'll be fine. If I could offer advice…"

"Please do," I interrupted.

"Plan out what you want to do when you arrive. You'll feel overwhelmed, and I'm sure time will be precious … so use it wisely."

"You are a smart chick."

"Comes with age," she said.

"You'll never live down telling us your age. Though I'm pissed we missed celebrating your 40th birthday."

"Make it up to me by bringing me a chunk out of that big arch."

I laughed and said goodbye as the guys walked back out of the souvenir shop.

"Back in the car, kids," I said, sounding impatient again.

"Ahhhh, Ma!" Matty teased.

I took over driving as we headed toward Indiana. The temperature was definitely dropping the more north we headed, but I found that I loved the Midwest. There was something so bewitching about this part of the country. I even loved the cold weather. As we drove, I pictured myself living in each section of the country – wondering which was the state where I should put down my stake. Other than my mafia, there was nothing keeping me in Arizona. I could live wherever I wanted, wherever it felt like home.

Erick's phone rang from the back seat, and I didn't think he was expecting this particular call.

"It's Ron," he said to us and answered.

"Hello."

We continued to hear a one-sided conversation, evidently inquiring where Erick was and when he was coming home.

"I never thought you would even care about me being away for Christmas," Erick said.

I could tell Erick's blood was starting to simmer. I'm sure he felt trapped in the backseat.

"Do you want me to pull over?" I asked.

He motioned for me to keep driving.

"Ron, this hasn't been working for a long time. You pretty much do whatever you want when you want."

I felt bad that he had to do this over the phone and with us listening.

"Call a spade a spade. You haven't loved me in a long time, so don't give me any shit about this."

I could only imagine what Ron was saying.

"Tough shit. You do what you want and I'll do…"

He must have been cut off.

"No, Ron! I'm done. This is it. I don't care how long it's been. I don't deserve the crap you dish out to me. I deserve to be happy just as much as you do. And if those people make you happy – fine. Go. Whenever you want! As a matter of fact, a lot is going to change when I get home."

He had said the "home" word, and I was sure Ron would use that against him.

"Yeah, well, I'm not a child, and I'm sure I can do fine out on my own," Erick said. "You best just be worried about who all finds out about your drug problem. And I'd keep stuff out of that house if I were you."

I knew Ron had a drug problem, but it sounded as if Erick was threatening to turn Ron into the cops. I didn't think he had that in him, but perhaps people can get pushed just so far before they snap.

Wonder what made Charles and Lois snap.

"No. Don't worry about me," Erick continued. "My shit will be out of there soon enough. I'll make sure you're not around when I come get it."

Ron's voice got a little loud, as if pleading for something, but I couldn't make out what he was saying.

"Goodbye, Ron. Have a fucking great Christmas!"

Erick shut his cell phone, and I checked in the rearview mirror to see how he was. I thought I'd see pain, but all I saw was someone who had finally had enough.

"Sara, is that unit in your building still for sale?" he asked.

"I think so."

"I'll have to look at it we get home," he said.

Matty put his arm over the backseat to hold Erick's hand. We all sat in silence for a while, unsure what to say.

"Gary, Indiana, Gary, Indiana, Gary Indiana, let me say it once again," Erick sang.

The tension left the backseat as if someone had exhaled, and things were back to normal with the showtune queen playing her game again. We all knew there was no need to discuss Ron or what had just happened.

"Car rides are all about the food," Matty said.

This meant he was hungry, and it was time for us to stop, although I really wasn't ready to give in. At the rate we were stopping, we would never see Maine.

"I thought you bought snacks at the last gas station?" Erick asked.

"Those things don't last forever," Matty answered.

It seemed hard to find places that would match both Matty's and our culinary sensibilities. And we knew we wanted to try and stay true to the flavor of each particular area. (Something the teacher had already dictated guess he did rule the car.) Matty would sometimes go from science teacher to history teacher – filling us in on each important fact about a city or state. He really was a wealth of knowledge, though my brain was stuck on the history of Maine and the history of the family I did not know.

From the confines of the car, I reminded myself of the advice I had told the Indian as fears crept into my mind about the road trip. I really didn't know what I expected to find. Was I completely an idiot for heading across the country based on a therapy session and something I read on the Internet?

I can answer that for you.

But life was too short, and I wanted to learn as much as I could. And just possibly, whatever I learned would help me with decisions for my future.

CHAPTER TWENTY-THREE

We decided to stop in Columbus, Ohio for the night. According to Matty's search in his technical toy, there was a great part of the city with a bar scene, night life, and the guys were chomping at the bit to get out there and see what the town had to offer for gay men. Erick was especially antsy after his long-distance breakup with Ron. He found us an expensive, luxury high-rise hotel this time – to really stick it to his "now ex" – with a room on one of the upper floors. He opted for a single room again, which I think he did more for me than for the two of them. He wanted us all to be in the same room together and not put me, as the only girl, alone.

I was starting to get fidgety myself from all the *togetherness*. I lived alone at home and was not used to spending so much time with other people. I loved the guys and had to constantly remind myself they were doing it for me, they were doing it for me.

But you really want to scream, don't ya?

We got settled in, showered, changed into some fabulous clothes, and headed over to High Street in Short North, which was the area full of gay bars, art galleries, and everything one would expect in a big city. I had protested, trying to send them out alone so that I could just sit quietly in the room, but they were having none of it and insisted that I accompany them.

"Hello, boys!" Erick exclaimed as we made an entrance into their gayborhood. "I'm single, willing, and available."

"So am I," Matty added.

I cracked up at the two on the prowl for new men in a strange city. The air was bitter as we dashed into a bar that had the rainbow flag in the corner of the window. You would think my guys felt they had hit Mecca. Cute men all dancing to holiday songs mixed to a disco beat. Erick went straight to the bar and ordered us martinis and brought them back to the table that Matty grabbed for us.

Maybe a drink this evening will calm you down, Sara.

"College town," Erick said. "So drinks are cheaper here."

There was something festive about watching all these strangers smiling and having such a great time for the holidays – but I still was not in the party mood. My brain was eating at me about what I might find once we hit Maine. Who was Gracie? What had become of the terrible people who had borne me?

My thoughts were stopped by two cute men who found their way to our table – or should I say to Erick.

"Hello, strangers," one said. "Welcome to Columbus."

"Do we look that out of place?" Erick asked, in a tone that said he was up for flirting.

"You're much too tan to be from here," the other said as he placed his hand on Erick's shoulder.

I watched Matty's face completely drop at the overt attention Erick was getting, and I felt for the guy. People were always going to approach Erick first. Matty's dingy Polo shirt and khakis couldn't compete with Erick's tight jeans and tighter shirt that caused his muscles to bulge.

"We're just passing through for the night," Erick said as he flexed. "These are my friends, Matt and Sara."

After appropriate greetings, we found out the guys worked at the university. It was great to watch Matty go into teacher talk, and before you knew it, one kept touching Matty's arm while they talked. I found myself sort of beaming as I witnessed the transformation in my boy.

"I taught in Pennsylvania before I moved here," one said. "You should think about making a move from Arizona."

This guy seemed to really be into Matty's brain. Then, don't you know it, Erick made his way in between the guy and Matty and kept touching Matty to lay some sort of claim on him.

You little bitch.

"Matty is one of Arizona's best. We can't give him up," Erick said.

Erick was back to calling him Matty again, to show how familiar they were, I guess.

"Anyone want another drink?" the one ogling Matty asked.

"Would love one," Matty replied.

I raised my glass to gesture to Matty that I'd like another as he made his way with the guy to the bar. Erick kept staring at him the whole time.

Down, boy.

"So, cutie, do you teach also?" the other asked Erick.

"Yeah."

What?

"I'm an English teacher in the high school," Erick lied.

"What the hell," I said. "You are a masseur."

It came out before I even knew I had said it. Perhaps it was the drink or just my brain ready to explode, but I had outted my friend.

"A masseur … cool," the guy said. "Maybe I can get a freebie."

Erick glared at me with contempt in his eyes that I had never seen.

Don't glare at me.

"I was a masseur to put myself through school and still do it on the side … once in a while," he said.

"Yeah, a teacher's salary isn't that great," the guy said.

I was getting pissed at Erick for shooting daggers my way.

Is he challenging you?

"Erick is always looking for new ways to make money, aren't you, Erick? Didn't you just lose a bunch in the stock market or some other hit to your account?" I asked, thinking about Ron.

The next thing I knew, Erick was dragging the tall cute man to the dance floor.

That's your friend, idiot! Why are you being such a bitch?

I wanted to tell the voice in my head to shut the hell up. I wanted everyone to leave me alone. How I wished I had stayed at the hotel. I didn't need to be there playing a fag hag. I knew the guys needed to release some steam, but damn it, I had my needs as well. Just then, I caught the steam that Erick was releasing on the floor as the tall man wrapped his arms around him and tried to suck his face off.

"We're back," Matty said, handing me a drink.

My eyes shifted back and forth from Matty to Erick on the dance floor, wondering what was going to happen if Matty saw that. I was tired, irritable, and didn't feel it was my place to worry about their problems.

"Where did they go?" he asked.

I pointed to the center of the room. Erick looked up, caught Matty's eye, and winked at him.

What was his deal?

Matty's face looked crestfallen. He turned back to the guy he was with and was just about to lay one on him when Erick stepped right in between them, grabbing Matty by the arm and yanking him to the dance floor.

"Matty! We love this song," he said.

The four of them danced up a storm with quick kisses stolen from each other. I felt like some twisted babysitter with four grown men. Erick's shirt came off, and he was allowing all around him to worship his muscles. Suddenly, my phone started buzzing with a text.

Fucking Steve was on the prowl and thinking he could find me back in Phoenix.

I was watching the boys on the floor going at it and thinking about what I could be doing back home with Steve. My mind was on overdrive, and I needed to get out of that space. I was tired of men – surrounded by gay men – and I just wanted to be alone. The one thing I had been fighting my whole life, and I was suddenly thirsting for it: solitude. Just for a couple of hours even. I went to the floor, said goodbye to the locals, and told the guys I was leaving.

Erick wouldn't talk to me.

"Don't go, Sara," Matty pleaded.

"You guys can come later. I'll get a cab."

I grabbed my jacket and headed out the door. I was walking down the street looking for a cab when a light snow began to fall around me, adding to the piles of snow that had been left from a snow storm we had just missed. My phone was buzzing with another text.

Leave us alone, Steve.

Christmas lights were twinkling on the buildings, and it should have been a picture perfect night. But my brain was working overtime. I needed to get to Maine and discover whatever the hell it was I needed to discover.

You're never going to get your answers.

That negative voice didn't help with anything. I knew I had dragged my two best friends on a road trip that was going nowhere.

Those guys don't view this the same as you. They have no investment in your past.

"Shut the hell up!" I yelled aloud.

Shit. I was speaking back to myself. Someone on the street would surely think I was a crazy nut walking and talking in the snow.

There were no cabs stopping as the guys came up behind me. All of us had had a few too many cocktails.

"What the hell was that, Sara?" Erick said.

"Go back inside, go-go boy, and play with your new friends," I said, not looking at him.

"No, I want to know why you didn't have my back," he said.

"Have your back?" I yelled still looking for a cab.

"Erick, leave it alone," Matty said.

"We're on this damn trip for you. Are you pissed that we wanted to have a little fun and forget the bullshit seriousness for one night?" he asked.

"What's so serious?" Matty asked.

This is it.

"I just snapped," I said. "Forgive me."

I knew I hadn't used the right tone, and I still had a fight building inside of me. So I tried to walk down the street away from them.

"I can't believe you'd be jealous of me," Erick said as he followed.

"Right. If anyone should be jealous, it should be Matty watching you make out with other guys while you lead him on," I yelled.

"Sara, please," Matty said.

"God, Matty, grow a pair," I yelled again. "Why do you let him do that?"

Now, they'll both be pissed at you.

"I don't let him do anything," Matty said. "I can take care of myself, thank you!"

"So I wanted to be someone else tonight," Erick said. "Sue me! You should understand wanting to be someone different."

"I don't lie, teacher, to get in some guy's pants," I said.

The only guy whose pants you get in has a girlfriend, you freak.

"No, you're just busy trying to find out who the fuck you are," he yelled. "You don't even know."

"What the hell are you two talking about?" Matty said.

You're screwed, Sara. You're losing everyone now.

"We can't all have such cushiony lives being kept by another man," I said, crossing the street to get a cab on the other side.

"You can't even hold on to a man," Erick said. "But you have no problem using my man's money on this trip."

"You know what, fuck you," I said stopping to confront him. "I was going to fly to Maine. You're the one who wanted this road trip."

Done.

"Guys, stop!" Matty pleaded.

"So I'll just go on to Maine alone, and you guys can fly home or stay here or whatever the hell you want to do. I don't give a fuck," I said as I jumped into a cab.

I told the driver the name of the hotel and slumped down in the back seat. What had just happened? I had no idea where it all had come from, but there was some pent-up shit that we were all dealing with, for sure.

Watch it all come crumbling down.

I got to the hotel, paid the cabbie, and ran right up to the room. It was quiet, and I looked out over the city from our huge upper window. It looked beautiful all lit up as the snow fell outside – and my world was falling apart on the inside. The view out the window had a feeling of Main Street, but it was as foreign as could be. And I felt like a lost child.

How did you even get here?

I grabbed my bag and started to pack, to move to another room for the night. I had messed up everything. Pushed away the two people who cared the most for me and who I cared about. And all the while fighting with them, I was fighting with the voice in my own head, too. God, I wished I had Pingleton around to help me through this mess. I saw no way of getting out of it. I'd have to get my stuff and move on away from them. My instincts from my youth were coming right back out, and a wall was going up.

The guys came through the door. We were all still tipsy, but coming down some from our drunken craze. The only noise was me throwing stuff in my suitcase.

"Sara," Matty said, walking toward me.

"I'm going to go downstairs and get another room," I said, continuing to pack.

Packing the mortar on that brick wall.

"Erick!" Matty said. "Say something!"

"Stop," Erick said. "Just stop. This is nuts."

No, you're nuts, Sara.

"It's not us," Erick continued. "What are we doing?"

"I'm packing to give you guys space," I said, trying to hide my guilt.

"Matty and I discussed this on the cab ride here. We don't act like this," Erick said. "We tease and play, but we never get nasty."

Erick was right. We didn't do the nasty "gay man and his hag" thing. This was not the family we had created. But they didn't really know the negative, crazy Sara in my head. She was trying hard to get out tonight.

"It's been a long road trip," Matty said. "We all needed to blow off steam ... in our different ways."

I turned and looked at the guys. These were my two best friends. They knew me as well as anyone, as much as I'd let them. I didn't want to leave them. And I certainly didn't want them to leave me.

"I'm sorry, guys ... I really am," I said.

I dropped my bag and sat down on the edge of the bed and started to cry. They were both right by my side.

"Hey, I'm sorry, too," Erick said. "I said some pretty stupid things. It was just the alcohol talking. It wasn't me. I couldn't care less how much of Ron's money we spend on this trip. And I wanted to take this trip with you ... for you. I want to help you through anything you need."

He was holding me in his arms, while Matty was rubbing my back.

"You guys are so good to me," I said. "And I go and crap on you both."

"I was dishing out just as much crap," Erick said. "Acting like I was some big shot teacher instead of my stupid job."

"Your job isn't stupid," Matty said.

"But you have a real job – helping kids learn. That's special, Matty."

I had never seen Erick so down on himself and talking Matty up in that way. I really loved the person I was seeing. It made me feel so much worse.

"It was a strange night all around," I said.

"Tell me about it," Matty said. "When has a guy ever paid attention to me?"

"No, that was a great part of the night," I said. "I just knew I shouldn't have gone out tonight. I'm not used to spending this much time with others. I'm always so alone."

"Try living with my mother," Matty teased.

"Or Ron," Erick said.

I started to laugh.

"I'd rather live alone, thanks," I said.

"I should have been getting us separate rooms," Erick said. "I thought I was being helpful."

"I had no right to say those things."

"We were all saying things," Erick said.

"Actually, I didn't say much," Matty teased.

"No. You are a good person, Matty. You, too," I said rubbing Erick's arm. "I'm the bitch."

"You are not a bitch," Erick said. "You are under so much stress. And you just released some tonight."

"On us!" Matty joked.

"Usually, I release it through Steve ... who was texting me all night."

"Well, I'm sure that didn't help matters," Matty said.

"Now, go wash your face, and put on your bed clothes so you can get a good night's sleep," Erick said.

"You're gonna need it for the drive in the morning," Matty said.

"Yeah, I drank less," I said. "Guess I'll be driving first."

"We'll be fine once we have breakfast," Erick said.

"Yum, breakfast. I could go for that now," Matty said.

We all laughed, and I grabbed my sleep stuff and went toward the bathroom to change. I stopped at the door and looked back at them.

"Are we okay, then?" I asked.

"We're fine," Erick said, trying to sound convincing.

"What? Did something happen?" Matty joked.

I went in the bathroom and sat for a while. What a mess I was. The smallest thing could set me off, and that wasn't like me at all. I just couldn't wait to get to Maine and get an answer … some answer. I could hear the guys talking in the next room and tried to hear if what they had said to me was true, that they forgave my outburst. Guess I would have to trust them on that. I brushed my teeth, washed my face, popped my pill, and went back into the room. The lights were off, and I could hear snoring. I tiptoed over to a bed and touched two sets of legs. Looked like they wanted to give me room with an entire bed to myself that night.

I got into the empty bed and prayed I heard no sounds coming from the other bed during the night. I was tired but couldn't go to sleep. My eyes had adjusted to the darkness, and I watched the snow gently falling outside. I wasn't even sure if it was sticking, but it looked beautiful. Just as I was thinking I was in some sort of fairytale, I heard rustling in the other bed – small, deliberate moves of drunk people trying to do God knows what under those sheets and thinking I was asleep. I closed my eyes and counted vibrators in my head so that I could fall asleep thinking about female pleasure and not whatever was happening in the other bed ... though part of me knew it served me right if they were getting theirs while I was left alone.

CHAPTER TWENTY-FOUR

The next morning, I was out of the room and went down stairs to get a local paper, check the temperature outside, and make a call back home.

"Aren't you done with that workout yet?" I said into the phone.

"It's not the same without you," Hahn said. "How's the drive?"

"Not bad. We miss you, though."

"Are you having any fun … and think carefully before you answer because I can hunt you down, skin you alive, and hide the body parts in a homemade soup."

It was actually great to hear Hahn's warped sense of humor coming through my phone that morning.

"We're trying to make the road-trip part fun, but I'd enjoy it much more if you were here."

"Good answer," she said.

"The guys are having a good time," I said.

"Don't tell me those horny freaks hooked up."

I thought before saying any more since I didn't think it was my place to let her in on that.

"We were at a gay bar last night, and they met some locals," I said. "You should have seen our little Matty hitting it off with a college professor."

"I've taught him everything he knows."

"We had a bit of a blow-up, too, something that we've never done before. Weird," I said.

"That happens, girl. Three people traveling who are not used to spending that much time together, and you're bound to have some bumps in the road."

"I hope we got it out of our system."

"Always remember to go to your separate corners to regroup, and you'll be fine."

"At least we're getting some nice cold weather," I said.

"Hey, it dropped into the 30s here at night," Hahn said.

Oh sure, now that we're not in town.

"Well, enjoy your work week," I said.

"Fuck you," she said in that way that meant "I love you" coming from Hahn.

"We'll check in."

I hung up and went into the restaurant in the lobby, where I read the morning paper, finished my breakfast, and waited for the guys to come downstairs. I was just finishing up my coffee when the two of them walked up to the table.

"Hungry?" I asked.

"Starving," Matty said.

"I bet."

"I don't even remember what happened last night," Erick said.

"Me either," Matty added.

"We went to some bar where some locals showed you both a nice time," I smirked, flipping through the paper.

It looked as if we were all going to forget the horrible part of the evening and just concentrate on the pleasantries. That's what real friends did, wasn't it?

Erick downed the coffee the waitress poured in his cup.

"Oh, yeah. The university guys," Matty said.

"I think I remember them," Erick said.

The waitress came to our table to find out what the guys wanted.

"The toast of French," Matty said in that odd way of speaking that I had come to adore.

"He wants French toast," Erick said as he went on to place his own order.

I informed the two that the snow had stopped outside for our final days of driving.

"Thank God," Erick said. "I didn't want to drive in that. Never done it."

"None of us have," I said.

"Did you go outside?" Matty asked.

"Yup. It's so nice to be out in crisp winter air. I love it," I said. "And I called Hahn to fill her in on our trip."

The guys stopped and looked at each other.

"I said the trip. Not the sleeping arrangements."

"I slept like a baby," Matty said.

"Yeah, with that pillow you brought from home," Erick teased.

I suddenly noticed a mark on Matty's neck.

"Mr. Reiner, is that a love bite on your neck?"

The guys looked at each other like deer caught in headlights.

"If only you knew who the culprit was … so many men last night," I teased.

The guys laughed, and Erick tried to rub away the mark on Matty's neck.

"You guys are good friends, you know that?" I said, patting each of their hands.

"You ain't so bad yourself, for a chick," Erick joked.

"Enjoy your breakfast," I said. "I'm gonna go pack up."

"We're aiming toward New York State," Matty said.

"Don't you dare start singing in this restaurant," I said, and kissed them both on the forehead.

We were heading north toward Cleveland, driving on Route 90 along Lake Erie where the winter wind off the water made the air frigid. The sides of the roads were all piled with snow, which looked completely unfamiliar to the three of us. The guys were back to being their regular selves, talking, singing songs, discussing the old Drew Carey show in Cleveland. The moment we saw signs for Buffalo, New York, all was back to normal.

"Shuffle off to Buffalo," Erick sang.

"You missed one," Matty said.

"What?"

"Why oh why, oh why-o. Why did I ever leave Ohio?" Matty sang.

"You go, boy," I said. "I wouldn't know a showtune if it bit me in the ass."

"You don't have the gene," Erick said.

"I figured all my years with you guys, I should know something," I said.

Heading toward Syracuse, it grew very cold, but not as bad as near the lake. The highway signs made us feel like we were back in Arizona as we noticed the Native American names that were indigenous to the area. Matty took over driving, and I got in the back seat as we continued toward the state capital. The more north we drove, the more I noticed it was harder for me to breathe. Not because of the cold air, but because of the impending end of the trip.

After stopping for a mid-afternoon lunch once we got into Massachusetts (where Erick and I were able to eat a large salad from local farm vegetable gardens and Matty indulged in an all-you-can-eat buffet), I could feel we were in the area of where our great country had started. The towns in the state were charming – like something from another time with picturesque villages we passed through. The fact that everything was decorated for Christmas was an added bonus. Night fell quickly, and visibility on the unlit highway was minimal. Erick had taken over the drive, and the guys talked as if they were on some great expedition. They were the gay Lewis and Clark, and my history was their Louisiana Purchase. We were in some small town around Springfield and stopped again for the night. Our third night away from home and even closer to my true roots.

"We'll be there by tomorrow," I said.

"Just in time for a white Christmas, perhaps," Matty added.

Just in time for you to find your crazy past.

"Haven't you seen enough snow yet?" Erick asked.

"I want to see it on Christ's birthday," he said.

The place we had stopped was one of those nice suites hotels with adjoining rooms. You had to hand it to Erick for spending Ron's money in such a crazy way.

"Figured it was time for the woman to have her own space," Erick said as he handed me a key and kissed my forehead. Matty took his bag and was headed into their room.

"Goodnight, Sara," he said as he disappeared into his room.

"You OK?" I asked Erick.

"Of course," he said. "Sleep well."

He made sure I made it into my room, and I heard him go into his. I found the door that connected the two, and I knocked. Matty answered.

"Yes, Mother?" he said.

I marched past him to see in their bedroom. There were two beds.

"Just making sure you didn't get a better room than me," I said and kissed his cheek.

"Did you hear the strange voices on the news channel here?" Matty asked me. "What an accent!"

"Matty, Matty, Matty. I'm so glad you find things that amuse you," I said as I went back into my room.

I couldn't quite figure out my aversion to the two of them being a couple. Maybe I would feel left out. Or maybe I was concerned how it would change the dynamics of our friendship. They were obviously getting closer on this trip but still trying hard to not make me feel squeezed out in the process.

One more day and we'd be in the state where I was born. I was trying hard not to call Dr. Pingleton during this trip, but something told me I might need to make that call. I decided to charge my cell phone, and I looked down at the missed text. There was another one from Steve. "Hey, Red ... Where are you? *Need* to see you." I couldn't imagine what his poor girlfriend must have thought when he disappeared at night, especially during a holiday week.

You're no better for having that kind of relationship with him all this time.

I decided to not respond again – to Steve or the voice in my head. Steve deserved to be left holding his own dick, and crazy voice would go on chatting whether I answered her or not.

I'm sure he finds someone else when you don't answer.

I plugged in the phone, heard the boys laughing next door, and turned my TV on for background noise. Who knew what was going to happen since they had their own space. When sleep didn't coming easily to me, I decided to venture down to the hotel bar.

It was the Monday of Christmas week, and the bar had a few people who looked like business travelers and a couple who looked as if they had returned home but chose to stay at the hotel instead. *It's a Wonderful Life* was playing on the TV above the bar. I ordered Bailey's on the rocks, and next thing I knew, I had two yutzes in business suits on either side of me.

"Well, hello, Miss Christmas Eve," one said, staring at my chest.

"Too soon; it's not Christmas Eve yet," I said.

"Shitty to be working this week, huh?" the other said.

"I'm not working. I wouldn't know."

If these men thought they were getting lucky, they were out of their freaking minds. I tried to stare at the television, while the man behind the bar played clean-up and disappeared into the back room.

"I sure would love to blow off some steam while being away from home, if you know what I mean," one said.

"That's what a bar is for, I guess," I said.

The other had his arm around me, trying to reach for breast number one.

"How about a Christmas party up in our room?" he said through breath that smelled like a brewery.

And these lines have worked before on women sitting in a hotel bar? Really?

I watched the couple of people I assumed were not business travelers get up and leave the bar. So I was left with Tweedle drunk and Tweedle drunker.

"I'm not in a party mood," I finally said, trying to dismiss them.

"We sure as hell are," one said as he leaned in toward me. "And we've got the Christmas balls and canes all ready to be unwrapped."

I pulled them close to me, somehow pulled some guts from within, and spoke.

"Then, why don't you tell me the room number, go on up there to get those presents opened, and I'll send along someone who enjoys penny candy right away."

I pushed the guy's arm off of me and turned to walk out when I noticed an older gentleman standing there smiling. Some women may have felt they were in some sort of trap with the three men, but there was nothing threatening about the older one. It was obvious that he loved the show he had just witnessed.

He said, "Bravo! Now, you two nimrods get on up to your room and either take a cold shower or jerk each other off. I'll see you bright and early for our meeting tomorrow."

The two men looked like they had been caught with their hands in the cookie jar and grunted a goodbye to the older gentleman as they left the bar.

"They work for you?" I asked.

"They're very good at what they do – but very bad at being single and alone on the road," he said.

"Men think that gives them an excuse to act like assholes."

"You're right, but you handled them beautifully. I do apologize."

"You're their boss, not their keeper," I said, walking back to the bar. "Can I get you one of these?"

"I'm not too chauvinistic to allow a woman to buy me a drink, thank you," he said.

I ordered him a drink and looked him over. He had to be in his late sixties, attractive for his age like one of those Wall Street suit-types on CNN, and exuded the confidence of someone I would want to talk to.

"So what did I do right that they did wrong to get a drink from you?" he said with a laugh.

"You haven't looked at my breasts once," I said, handing him his Bailey's.

"My wife would claw my eyes out," he said.

"I like a woman who can keep her husband in line."

"Men are out on the road, traveling for work, doing these meetings – but no one can say they are running anything. It's women who do it all. Either in the boardroom or at home; women rule."

"Tell that to the people who wouldn't elect a female president," I said.

"Someday, this country will wake up to see who actually gets the job done."

"I'll drink to that," I said, thinking of my own boss back in Phoenix and wondering who was doing his Christmas shopping for him while I was away.

"So let me guess, a woman in a hotel during a holiday week who already said she isn't working means traveling home to the family or getting away from all the craziness of the family down the street," he said.

"On my way to Maine for Christmas," I said. "And where are you spending Christmas?"

"Well, actually ... I just finished my holiday. Hanukkah was early."

"I'm sorry for assuming..."

"Most people assume in this country."

"Guess I'm not around many Jewish people in Arizona."

"Nah ... we head to Florida," he teased.

I found myself speaking so freely with him. Much as I had started doing with Pingleton.

"Where is home?"

"New York City," he said.

I was never one of those people who gave much thought to New York, Los Angeles, or the other big cities our country had to offer. I'm sure I looked unimpressed, though our trek across country had opened my eyes to possible places to live.

"I've never been there," I said. "I've actually never even been to this part of New England, but it's beautiful."

"There's something very nice about this part of the country, but I've traveled so much – it all starts to bleed together."

"The road trip we've been onI'm traveling with two friends – I've seen parts of the country that I never imagined."

"I was a very young child when we got to America, but I've heard so many stories from my mother from her days in Poland during the Holocaust, God rest her soul, that I know this is the place for me."

I couldn't talk for a moment.

"I'm sorry. I said the dreaded H word and I've scared you," he said.

"I've just never talked to anyone who was there."

"I was so young that I don't really think of it as being 'there.' I can't really recall all that much. I was four when it was declared over, but that following year, there were still pogroms happening against the Jews in Poland, so my mother brought me and my older sister to America. She worked hard to give us a life here, and I've worked just as hard to make something of that life."

"What an amazing woman to make that journey with two children," I said as I finished up my drink.

"She had no choice. Our father had been taken away…"

"Why did you cut yourself off?" I asked.

"Because this is not the kind of talk for a nice woman who is going to visit her family on Christmas week," he said as he winked at me.

I wanted to talk to the man some more about his past – to learn something about someone else's life on this journey of self discovery – but I sensed he had put the ending on that topic.

"Well, thank you for your support with your two workers," I said.

"They won't even remember it tomorrow. Thank you for the drink."

The man stood to leave the bar.

"Guess you gotta turn in for your early morning meeting, huh?" I said.

"And I need to make sure those two stay put in their rooms," he chuckled.

I started to go back to my room and gave the man with the warm eyes the type of hug you would give a grandfather. I wondered about what kind of life the man must have had as a child. The atrocities he had probably seen with his young eyes. And I realized there are so many people out in the world who have gone through so much more than I have, other children who have witnessed horrible things. I could only imagine the stories he had shared with his family and grandchildren. And I had no intentions of sharing any stories of my past, or even having those grandkids to pass along information. But talking to him for just a little while made me long for a grandfather.

I lay in bed thinking of the Jewish man's mother. What balls she had to travel around the world to this country with two kids. The thought of her abilities made me feel weak.

But you're taking your own journey, Sara. Different time and place – but just as scary for you.

That felt like the first time my inner voice had actually paid me a compliment. I tried to hold on to that feeling while I drifted off to sleep.

CHAPTER TWENTY-FIVE

The following morning, we took Route 90 across the state toward Boston, winding through so many small towns as strong winds pounded the car. The countdown in my head continued to tick ... getting louder and louder. At times, I thought it was going to burst right out of my brain.

"It's been years since I was in this state," Erick said.

"You've been here?" Matty asked.

"Back when Ron and I were in love," he said. "We flew to Boston one summer and took the ferry over to Provincetown, a gay Mecca, Matty. You'd love it."

"Well, maybe I'll have to check it out with a proper tour guide," he said.

"That might just be able to be arranged next summer," Erick said.

I listened to the guys talking about future plans and thought about how much you learn about people when traveling with them, like the fact that Erick loves to take control of a situation, sometimes talking right over you to the people at a restaurant or store. He also spends more time primping in the bathroom than any woman. And Matty has these quirks such as bringing his own pillow from home, and he bites his fingernails and spits them everywhere when people are not looking. Lord knows what things they had learned about me that I didn't even know I did. But all in all, we remained friendly.

One blow-up excluded.

Negative Nancy voice was back.

We hit Route 95 North which took us to the top of the country. Each town was quainter than the next. The word that came to mind was "history." You couldn't find much older places in our country ... well, outside the lands of the Native Americans near my home. But this was Founding Father shit, stuff we read about in school. Seeing it with my own eyes made it all that more real, churches that were so old you could just imagine Washington and Franklin walking down the front steps, or visions of Puritans running through dirt roads in this state, looking for those who disagreed with what they were doing and calling them witches. Oh, the irony that this state was one of the first to offer same-sex marriage. Surely, my boys would have burned at a stake.

"You can see where that Nor'easter storm passed through here over the weekend," Matty said, pointing out fallen debris and signs that were still up diverting traffic around flooded areas.

"I'm in awe of what Mother Nature can do in just…"

Erick stopped the science lesson with one sentence.

"Welcome to Vacationland," he said as we crossed the border into Maine.

I had been so stuck in my daydreams that I hadn't even noticed how close we had actually gotten to Maine. This was the place. I half expected to see "Wanted" signs of Charles and Lois posted on a tree as we entered the state, something reminding all of the horror that had occurred here. But nothing about it looked evil. Instead, it was the kind of place one would imagine older couples would want to live out the latter part of their days. Well, that is, if they could stand the cold and the snow. I'm sure the state hadn't thought twice about what happened all those years ago. But that date – this place – it was all very important to me. Part of me hoped that I would make a connection to the place like I was never able to in New Mexico or Arizona. A beautiful place that personified a true winter wonderland. The roads were clear, but there was snow packed along the sides that obviously had fallen recently. It was white and peaceful, and I could tell why Stephen King loved it here so much.

"I can't wait to have a big bowl of chowder," Matty said. "But I bet you two won't even touch it."

"When in Rome," Erick said.

"Get out – not you!" Matty said.

"Sometimes, I can surprise even myself," Erick said from the back seat.

"Do you want me to drive?" I asked Matty.

"No, I think I got it," he said. "Besides, the roads don't feel slick at all."

"Wait until we get off the highway," Erick said.

"Excuse me, sir. I think I'm the science teacher here. I'll be the one making those sorts of remarks, not you," Matty said, looking into the rearview mirror.

"Keep your eyes on the road, Teach," Erick quipped.

"I bet this place is amazing in summer, the boats, the water," Matty said.

"I think it looks pretty amazing right now," I said almost to myself from the passenger seat.

I was mesmerized by what I saw outside the window. Sights I had never seen in my lifetime – well, sights I didn't recall ever seeing. Trees with snow sprinkled on them like perfectly poured powdered sugar. Deer slowly walking in the fields at the side of the road with the peek of a red barn standing out in the snow meadow in the distance. Signs for cranberry bogs which were frozen over with winter's thick blanket. I was sure they were all beautiful with the bright red color that we had missed during fall harvest.

"I am so glad we came on this trip," Erick said, hugging me from behind.

"I'm very glad you guys are here," I said. "Even if it doesn't seem that way when I get nuts and scream stupid stuff."

"It's ancient history," he said.

It was the 22nd, and I would have two days before Christmas to hopefully get some answers on my "ancient history" at a library somewhere. I'd been trying to do as Hahn suggested and plan out for the last few days what my move would be once we got into Boothbay Harbor. It had kept me up at night. But once I was there, I wasn't sure what to do first.

We passed Portland (which looked like a pretty decent size city), but once we hit Route 1, the road became narrower. I felt like we were crawling to the end of the earth – crossing over bridges and driving further into the tunnel where I believed my findings would be. This particular day had been the shortest time we spent on the actual road, but it had felt the longest by far. But I knew I could endure it. I had my stamina tested on that damn bike ride to Sedona, and I'd have to recount that moment to get through the next few days as well.

At times, a truck would go around us and throw up loose snow onto our windshield, creating a wintry hurricane that only seemed to encompass us. The sun had not gone completely down as we pulled into Boothbay Harbor, a winter gloom over the town. Even with the grey sky mixed with streaks of sunshine peering through the clouds, one could get a true sense of this small community. It was a beautiful place, nonetheless. A fishing village, with bells attached to boats dinging in the winter air, signs for lobster everywhere, adorable historic homes, and beautiful bed & breakfast places. Icicles dripped from the eaves of homes, and bushes were covered in white blankets of snow. Homes were a mix of Victorian and cottages that reminded me of images on a postcard or an old-time magazine. The Christmas decorations and lights twinkled on the snow, adding color wherever we looked. As beautiful as it was, an eerie feeling crept over my body due to the paradox of how it looked and what this town represented to me.

Horror. Atrocities. Murder.

"Trivia. Did you know the movie version of *Carousel* was filmed here?" Erick asked.

"I don't even remember that movie," I said.

"Girl – don't even. *You'll Never Walk Alone?*" he said.

"Oh, really?" I said.

"No. That's the song."

"Maybe this will help," Matty said. "Jerry Lewis telethon."

"Oh … yes … the song he did at the end!" I said, as excited as a little kid.

"Blanche, you are hopeless," Erick said.

We drove past gazebos that were covered in snow and meadows filled with pine trees that we knew were glorious when they were green and flourishing.

"Where should I stop?" Matty asked.

"Let's stay at one of these B&Bs," Erick said.

"Whatever you want," I said. "You're paying."

"Ron is," he said.

The problem was that each bed & breakfast we pulled up to had a "Closed" sign out front. So many of them were seasonal. I hadn't thought about calling ahead, as there was not a lot of time in the planning phase. I started to feel a little panicky, so we decided to stop at a restaurant and get some food while we thought about lodging.

"Why didn't we bring boots?" Erick asked.

"Like we own any," I said.

We trudged through the piles of snow in our sneakers and non-winter clothes, looking completely out of place, and into the warm eatery. Three tan visitors missing boots and wearing flimsy jackets stood out like mink coats in the Arizona summer. As we opened the door to enter, a big lumberjack of a guy was walking out the door with a young girl.

"Stay warm, Brent!" the woman inside called out to him.

"Will do," he replied. "Excuse me, folks," he said to us as he walked past.

I swore the little girl was looking at us like three oddballs, but my two oddballs' eyes were fixed on the big guy leaving.

"If all the men look like that in this town, I've found a new home away from home," Erick said as he fended off a punch from Matty.

"Butch it up," I whispered.

"Can I help you?" the nice elderly woman asked.

"Three for a late lunch or early dinner," I said.

She took us to a table by a fireplace, and the glow from it felt wonderful. The smells of homemade cooking from the kitchen gave the place the aroma of a grandparents' house – if I had grandparents.

"OK, I'm thinking it's time to eat real food," I said to Erick.

"Sweet baby Jesus boy," Matty said. "You said the magic words. I feel like I've died and gone to culinary heaven."

The woman came back over to us.

"We don't have everything on the menu right now, but we have great chowdah and turkey sandwiches," she said.

"Sounds great," Erick said.

"Told you we'd be eating chowdah," Matty said in the woman's accent with a grin.

The woman brought us some drinks, asked us where we were from, and why we ended up in Boothbay, as if there was nowhere else to go from there. I gave some lame answer about visiting family for the holidays, which made no sense since we needed a place to stay. Erick mentioned that none of the B&Bs were open.

"Let me see if I can find one open for you," she said, smiling, and went on her way back into the kitchen.

"Where is this family?" Matty asked.

I looked at Erick and knew it was time to fill Matty in. We were here, and he needed to know why. I told him everything. Even the horrible parts of my past. He held my hand across the table as I shared the more gruesome details.

"This is like some *Cold Case* episode," he said.

"Hey, it's my life," I said with a smile.

"You really are a woman of strength," he said. "I'm more impressed by you than I thought I could be."

"Guess now, you see why I lost it out on the road," I said.

"Let it go. We have," he said.

You can't let anything go, girl.

"We've got quite a gal here, Matty," Erick said. "And now, we have to help her."

"Whatever you need, we're here for you, Sara," Matty said.

"I know," I said. "It's just to figure out a plan of attack."

"Poor choice of words," Erick said.

"Bi-otch," I said.

By the end of the incredible meal, the nice lady at the restaurant had called one of the owners of a bed & breakfast and gotten us a place to stay. I couldn't believe how kind she was. We said our goodbyes and headed up the road to the Quail & Dove Bed & Breakfast.

"Am I a quail or a dove?" Matty asked.

"If you have to ask, then you really have problems," Erick said.

The place was beautiful. An old white Victorian home with a huge wraparound porch that had garland and holly hanging around it. The smell of evergreen and cedar was mesmerizing. Standing in the door was an older couple who were waiting for us to arrive – very American Gothic. The woman's white hair was up in a bun, and her sweater was pulled all the way up to her chin. She looked at us over her glasses. She was a skinny, elderly woman, only she had a sweet smile and disposition unlike the woman from the famous painting. The man looked like a farmer more than a Maine fisherman, wearing a cap to keep what appeared to be a bald head warm.

"Eileen said you three were desperate for a place, and no one should be homeless on Christmas," the woman said.

"This is too kind of you," I said, walking up on the porch.

"Come on inside," the man told us.

We walked into the living room, and I thought I had stepped back into time. The décor was that of an old French country house with Toile paper on the walls, ornate moldings, and furniture that had been collected for years. A hand-carved banister went up a long staircase. The roaring fireplace was an invitation to sit at its hearth and feel the warmth with gorgeous old-time stockings hanging from the mantle. It was cozy and warm – everything you would assume of an old country house, including the smell of delicious cooking in the oven from a nearby kitchen.

"I'm Ida, and this is my husband, Samuel."

"We can't thank you enough," Erick said, pulling money from his wallet.

"As long as you all don't mind taking over the third floor," she said. "We have family coming into town, and they'll be using the rooms on the second floor."

"Not at all. We will stay out of your way," I said.

"You're not in our way," she said. "Not at all."

Erick was busy filling out the guest card and giving all our information to Samuel.

"Are either of you married?" Ida asked.

I knew the boys wanted to make a joke, but I cut in.

"No, ma'am," I said.

"Well, there are three rooms upstairs, so you can take all of them," she said.

I winked at Matty, who was definitely pouting. I half expected him to retrieve some sort of food from his pocket to turn to.

"But you'll have to share the water closet in the hallway," she said.

"Not a problem," I said.

"There are water basins in each room, though," Samuel added.

Ida looked at the card Erick had filled out.

"Arizona? My, you are a ways from home," she said with what appeared to me to be a suspicious look.

"We wanted a true white Christmas," Matty added.

"Well, you're getting one," she said. "But you should get over to Parson's before he closes to get some warmer clothes. We're getting more snow tomorrow."

"We'll just get settled in and do that," I said.

"I have the credit card," Erick said with a smile.

Ida looked at the names Erick had written down, "Well, Erick, Matt, and Sara…"

The woman paused and looked at me a little too long.

She knows you.

My heart stopped for a moment.

"If there is anything we can do, let us know," she finished.

"Come on up, and I'll show you to your rooms," Samuel said.

"We can handle that," Erick said. "No need for you to climb up the stairs when you're supposed to be closed."

"Very well then. Top of the stairs. Here are your three keys," he said.

We thanked the couple profusely, almost falling over ourselves in gratitude, and made our way up the stairs. I swore to myself the woman was on to me, but I knew I was just being foolish. You could tell the old house had been closed up for the season. There was stillness on the second floor, showing no sign of recent activity.

"Now, I really feel like Nancy Drew," Erick said as he led us up the second flight of stairs.

We got to the top and opened doors to the three rooms so that we could see all of them from the hallway. A little musty smelling, as if closed up for a while, but warm and cozy just the same. The boys took the two that were closest to each other, and mine was on the other side of the bathroom across the hall.

"I don't want to hear any tippy-tippy-paws in this hallway at night," I said.

The guys just looked at each other and smiled.

"I think we should get to that store," Erick said.

"I just want to wash my face first," I said.

"Fine, I need to see if I can get an Internet connection for my game," Matty added as he walked into his room.

My room had the slanted ceiling from the pitch of the roof, making it obvious that we were in the attic of the house. The walls were covered in an old paper of roses and vines. On the double bed was a crocheted bedspread that someone had obviously put some major time into. There was a window seat underneath a lace-covered window with a water basin and pitcher next to it. I had stepped into an episode of *The Waltons.*

I put my bag on top of a trunk instead of putting any clothes into the provided drawer, washed my face, and sat down on the window seat looking out the window. The place was up on a huge hill that overlooked the harbor. There was snow-covered land that led right up to the water's edge. Boats were drifting in the water, and a dinging bell was a constant chime in the distance, creating a soundtrack for the landscape. I watched a light systematically beaming every few moments as it turned from a lighthouse in the distance. Those lights were to warn ships of the coastline or to welcome others home.

Which is it doing for you?

I almost couldn't believe I was there. Only a few short days prior, I had been safe in my condo wondering what I'd be doing for the holidays, never thinking this excursion would or could ever transpire. But I had made it. Much like my recent friend's mother from Poland when she arrived in this new land all those years ago. It had been an actual lifetime since I was in this place … if I had been here … and it was my chance to get to the bottom of my horrid past. What was I going to find in this town?

And would there be enough time to find it before the holiday was upon us? I had traveled 2,800 miles to find out, and I needed to. Somewhere out there, someone knew about Charles and Lois Reed, and I was ready to find them.

CHAPTER TWENTY-SIX

We didn't have the time to really look at the town since I was there on a mission. The guys drove me right to the small library with its big white pillar columns and old-timey arched windows. They dropped me off to trudge my way up the snow-covered path while they went to the store to get us some warm clothes. I didn't care what they bought me. I just had my mind set on Charles and Lois and wanted to see what I could find in some old files.

The wonderful woman at the front desk did not play into the librarian stereotype at all. She was dressed from this decade, and her silver hair was streaming down over her shoulders. No glasses and bun … leaving that for the sweet women who ran the bed & breakfasts in town. She took me right back to an area where they kept newspapers and one single microfilm machine – even though it was very near to closing time, and the place was empty.

"We're still working on transferring items to the Internet, so we have hung on to this machine," she told me.

"There was a time this was cutting edge," I said, smacking the machine.

"Don't I know it," she said. "What kind of research paper are you writing?"

I knew she was just making small talk, and I wasn't sure how much I wanted to share.

"It's not a very Christmas-y thing to discuss, but there was a horrible murder case 30 years ago, and I'm trying to get information on that."

That's it, Sara. Sound as journalistic as possible.

I swore for a moment the lady looked at me strangely. As if she knew something.

"Well, if you need anything, just let me know," she said. "I'll just be up front preparing to close."

"I'll move fast," I said.

I thought she was trying to get away from me quickly as she tossed her silver mane over her shoulders and dashed back to the front of the library.

I wasn't sure where to begin, but I knew I needed to move quickly. I decided to go straight for the newspapers and found some from the eighties and kept scouring them to find what I was looking for. I put in microfilm from decades past and read the same article I had read online. At least this connection took me back to the excitement I felt in my own condo when I first discovered the clipping on the worldwide web. But there, in the local paper, I found more. Stories about the victims. Names. Faces. The people whose lives were taken that I had witnessed as a small child. But what if none of this was real? I continued to read the information I found but hoped that it was not true. Even though years had passed and people's lives had moved on, for me it felt as new as when I woke that very morning. I couldn't help but think about each event as if it were occurring right in that moment. What if these victims had children who were still living in Boothbay Harbor? What if I ended up passing them on the street and never even knew it? Too many "what ifs" plagued my mind.

I looked at my watch and knew the woman would want to close up soon. I needed more. I had traveled so far, and my heart was pounding. As hard as it was to see the words in print, believing these were my parents, I still wanted to get more details, to be able to get inside their minds and what might have set them off.

And then I found it.

A picture of Charles and Lois staring back at me. The photo frightened me more than anything I had experienced to date. There in Lois' features was my own reflection looking at me. The bent nose, the tiny lips – it was me. I could see myself hidden inside of that monster's face. I suddenly felt sick again and tried hard to continue thinking like a fake journalist, divorcing myself from the event and looking for facts. Someone local – some family member – had to have given the paper that photo. So someone didn't mind turning them in. Not everyone had covered it up as Hightower had mentioned to me. Would I be able to find those same people on my trip?

I wished the guys were there with me. What was taking them so long? I'd kill them if they were having a quickie while I was going through the worst hell of my life.

I read the story as quickly as possible. It said the two of them were wanted for seven different murders.

My God!

They hadn't even robbed the homes of the people they had killed. Like it was all just for fun. What sick people. They had lived on Pearl Street, it said. Maybe the family that had given the photo to the paper was still in town, but surely not. The article went on to state that they had left town and were never heard from again. More stomach pains shot through my body. No mention of the baby Priscilla. Where was I?

I noticed the machine was hooked up to a copier, so I printed out the article and photo. Lights were starting to be turned off in the library. I shoved the photocopy into my pocket, cleaned up the mess I had made, and returned to the front.

"Did you find what you were looking for?" the woman offered, only a politely inquisitive look on her face.

I was certain she had heard the copier running and knew I was walking out with evidence.

"I'm not sure," I said. "Thanks for your help. Merry Christmas."

I ran out the door before she could get a good look at me and connect me to the Reed family.

Now, you're just being stupid ... again.

I stood in front of the library in the dark night, breathing in the cold, crisp air to calm the queasiness and shock. The article may not have mentioned me, but Lois' photo said it all. I had the answer – at least part of it – even if I had hoped perhaps it would all be wrong. But why had they done it? How did I get to New Mexico? When I noticed my Acura pulling up in front, I ran to the guys.

"What took you so long?" I jumped in the backseat.

"His highness couldn't find the right color jacket," Matty said.

"I want to look good for Christmas," Erick said. "Oh ... and we saw that God of a man from the place we ate earlier. Big earthy stud."

"Mountain men are way hotter than the ones back home," Matty said.

"But you have a hot brain, Matty," Erick said, tousling Matty's hair.

I was trapped in an old episode of *Will & Grace* ... and they were Jack and Karen.

"Oh ... and get this, there is a bed & breakfast run by two gay men," Erick said. "We're at the wrong place *and* they do accept our kind in this state."

"Are you OK?" Matty finally asked me.

Hello! The whole reason we're on this trip!

"I know I'm the child of these two sickos," I said, handing him the newspaper article.

"Holy shit, she does look like you, I have to say."

"Yup. But there is no mention of me in any of the papers."

"How do you feel?" Matty asked, taking my hand over the headrest.

"Emotional, to say the least. Glad to know. Upset it's true and that I didn't read anything about Priscilla."

"Maybe someone was trying to keep you out of the stories to protect you," Erick said.

"That's what that author I talked to said he thought when he came to interview people."

"That has to be it. The cop on the scene or a child advocacy group ... or something," Erick said. "Someone didn't want it out there that these people had a child."

Erick made as much sense as Professor Hightower had. Either a grandparent or the cop or someone else was protecting an innocent child. A pretty rational explanation. Maybe I could find that person and get some answers on the why and how of the situation.

"What's the name of the sheriff in the article?" I asked Matty.

Matty did his speed reading best and said, "Timothy Gibbons."

"We need to look up Timothy Gibbons and this Reed family, too," Erick said.

Matty brandished his iTouch as if it were a magic wand. "This town has Internet service, right?"

CHAPTER TWENTY-SEVEN

We were sitting in a pub, drinking beer and going through our list of things to accomplish the next morning. The guys were great, supporting me in every detail of my crazy endeavors while peppering the conversation with just enough wit and sarcasm to keep me from going insane. I finally noticed Erick's new outfit from his shopping spree.

"You look like you walked out of an L.L. Bean catalog," I said.

"That's what they're known for here," he said. "But of course, I'm sure it looks much more fashionable on me."

We laughed and ordered another round of beers.

Matty kept putting his hand over one eye and studying my face, comparing it to the photocopy of Lois.

"Stop that," I said, swatting his hand. "You're freaking me out."

"I just find it so bizarre," he said. "To be able to look like someone and not even know them."

"That is a stupid statement, mister teacher," Erick said. "You think you only look like your mom 'cause you grew up with her? God help the children of Arizona in your school. I take back my 'hot brain' comment."

"I didn't mean ... oh hell, you know what I meant," he said, taking out his iTouch.

"Sara, it's been 30 years. Do we really think Sheriff Gibbons will still be around?" Erick asked. "And even if he is, he won't be senile or something?"

God love Erick for trying to be a voice of reason, but at that moment, I wasn't sure what other leads I had.

"One can hope," I said.

"Stop hoping," Matty said, reading his gadget. "He died three years ago at the age of 75. Pneumonia. It's so odd to think people still die from that."

"Matty," Erick said in a parental sort of way.

"I'm just saying," he said.

"OK, try Reed," I said, sort of hoping he wouldn't find any of the Reeds, but there had to be a ton in this town.

"That's a pretty common name," Erick said.

What would I say, even if we found the right one?

Hello. I'm your long lost relative from the psycho couple?

Matty found over 25 Reeds, as I expected, but some were at the same address. That cut the list down some. Still, could it be that any of them were related to Charles Reed's family? Matty went into his teacher mode, using a paper napkin and creating a chart by area, deducting possibilities of families based on location, and before we knew it, he had a list of people we could reach out to.

"So, genius, what are we supposed to say when we get to these people?" Erick asked.

"Hey, I did my part," he said as he gulped a beer. "You have to think of something, Sherlock."

"We can't just walk up and ask for Charles and Lois Reed, two criminals who have been missing for all these years," I said.

"How do you know they are still missing?" Erick asked.

The thought gave me the creeps. What if they were living in this town still, hiding in some way so that people would never recognize them?

They would be so far away after so much time. Maybe they had been committing a string of murders across the country, like Bonnie and Clyde going from state to state performing horrific crimes. They would be in their sixties, I guessed, so I couldn't imagine they were still out there doing the same heinous things they had done. But who knew?

"I don't think they are still in town if that's what you mean," Matty said.

"No. They could be dead," Erick said.

He was right. They could have been wiped from the face of this earth, and I would never even see them again. Not that I really wanted to. I wasn't sure what I wanted any more, actually.

"Sara, what do you hope to find from this trip?" Matty asked.

"I want to find out the truth about who I am," I said.

"Don't you think you know that by now?" he asked.

"I think I'm close. I think I'm really close."

There could be a Reed in the town who would be so happy to see the young Priscilla all grown up. Or perhaps I would just be opening old wounds for them. I wasn't really sure what to do.

I noticed Matty staring at me again.

"Stop it!"

"You don't look like a Priscilla. You're a Sara," he said.

"I hereby christen this budget Barbie camper ... Priscilla. Queen of the desert!" Erick exclaimed.

We all cracked up thinking about the gay Australian movie we had watched together.

"I'm disappointed neither of you thought of that while we were on our road trip," I said.

"What?" Erick said doe-eyed. "I was just waiting for a bleak moment in conversation to declare it."

"Sara is a bus," Matty teased.

"There is a tacky sex joke in that statement, but I'm staying away from it," Erick said.

We finished our beers and headed back to the Q&D as Erick was already calling the Quail & Dove Bed & Breakfast. Snow had started falling, and I prayed it would not keep us from our search the following day. We quietly went inside the front door, and there was a note from Ida with a thermos of hot chocolate and some homemade muffins. How I wished I had had a grandmother who did things like that for me. Not once in my life had someone taken time to show me kindness of that nature.

We crept up the stairs with our loot and gravitated toward Erick's room, which had a fireplace that someone had lit.

"I swear to God, this place feels like something from a Scooby Doo episode," Matty said.

"I wanna try on my long-johns," Erick said, ripping through the bags from the store.

"I'll help you get into them," Matty said.

"Pour me some hot chocolate, and keep your hands to yourself, please," I said. "I'll be right back after I go change."

"I'm going to give Hahn a buzz," Erick said.

I left the boys and went to my room where the small lamp on the bureau had been turned on, and my bed turned down. The couple running the B&B was too much. We were there off-season, invading their home, and they were being as nice as if we were royalty, visiting smack in the middle of Christmas. I felt bad for taking them away from what they needed to be doing to prepare for their family arriving on Thursday. I noticed a rocking chair in the corner with a handmade doll sitting in it. How could someone have the kind of time to sew something like that? It had been patched together by pieces of different quilts, and I could feel the years of love wrapped in the smile of the doll's eyes.

I decided I needed a shower and took the new, warm clothes the guys had bought me down the hall to the bathroom and turned on the water. It took a while for the hot water to make it to the third floor, but once it did, it felt wonderful on my chilled body. I lathered up the lilac-smelling soap and washed it over my breasts, arms, and stomach. As I reached down further, I thought of Steve and how he could probably have made me feel so much better at that point. But I was sure he was with his girlfriend, and the thought of that made any possible sexual feelings vanish. He was a user, and I allowed him to be a crutch for way too long.

A crutch that you enjoyed leaning on.

But it was time to stop thinking of what Steve could do or how he made me feel. He was someone who kept me from ever thinking I deserved something more – or from trying to find it. Steve was Mandy's problem to deal with and one I needed to forget.

As I washed my body, I couldn't help but think of the following morning and what kind of shock or joy I might bring to someone in Boothbay Harbor. A long-lost kin that had always wondered what happened to me. Family. Real family.

I hadn't washed my hair in a few days, and it felt so good to get myself completely wet and scrub the long car ride out of my hair. As I ran the soft washcloth over my skin, I saw the fragile skin of Gracie from my dream. I still had no idea who she was or what she had to do with any of it. But hopefully, some things would begin to make sense to me soon.

CHAPTER TWENTY-EIGHT

It was December 23rd, and I felt that the clock was ticking toward a conclusion that I had no control over, as if the entire world were going to shut down on Friday – and I guess that maybe for me, it was. Celebrating "the birth of Christ" was a much bigger happening than Sara Butler finding out who she was and where she came from.

The guys were waiting for me downstairs in Ida's kitchen, where she had made a wonderful breakfast of pancakes and homemade maple syrup. Even Erick had a pile on his plate.

"I'm in complete shock," I said as I looked at the plate in front of him.

"Leave him alone," Matty said. "I'm thrilled to see him eat for real … finally."

"I forgot what it tasted like," Erick said. "This is wonderful, Ida."

"Come on, Sara," Ida said from the stove. "Let me make you a plate."

"Thank you, ma'am. But just one."

I didn't want to offend the kindness of the woman, and the smell was incredible. I would probably be the size of a house if I lived there and ate that way all the time.

"How did you sleep?" Ida asked.

"Surprisingly, like a baby," I said.

Though my brain was going non-stop as I tried to drift off, once I hit that part of sleep where you feel there is no return – I was out for good. Peaceful. Content. Completely forgetting why I was even in Maine.

"Are those fresh blueberries?" I asked.

"You betcha," Matty said, pouring more of the syrup on top of his stack. "From local bushes."

"Listen to the Mainer here talking as if he knows," Erick said.

"I teach, I learn," Matty replied.

"Are you all going to be out in the snow today?" Ida asked as she continuously moved about the room doing things.

"We have some running around to do," I said.

"Bundle up. I don't want you catching a cold. You're probably not used to this weather," she said.

I loved how the old woman showed such care and concern for us.

Why is she being so nice to you?

"Do you need any help before we head out, with your family arriving tomorrow and all?" Erick asked.

"Samuel and I can take care of it, dear, but thank you," she said.

"Where are they coming from?" I asked, cutting into the delicious breakfast in front of me.

Look at you asking real questions.

"Veronica and her clan are coming up from Boston. Jeffrey and his wife from Vermont," she said as she filled my coffee cup.

Boston. That author is from there.

"Just the two kids?" Matty asked.

"Oh, no. Veronica has two grown children, and her daughter Emily has two kids of her own. It'll be a full house."

"We are very appreciative of you allowing us to stay," I said.

"Not a problem at all," she said. "It'll be a wonderful Christmas Day."

Ida went into the back room as we finished up our breakfast.

"So did you guys do any exploring last night in the old house?" I asked with a smile.

"Once you left the room after the chocolate of hot, we turned in," Matty said.

"Turned in? My ass!"

"Don't take that obscene tone with us, young lady," Erick said, mimicking Ida's voice. "So what's the game plan for today?"

Nice change of subject.

"Well, Shaggy, you and Scooby need to keep old man Wilson busy while I sneak into his office to get the keys to the mineshaft," I said, chortling.

"Hahn would be so proud of your smart-assiness," Erick said.

"Speaking of Hahn, we need to get her a present today," I said.

I caught the guys making eyes at each other, but I wasn't able to read their minds.

Must be using their gay telepathy.

"You mean Ron needs to buy her a present," Erick corrected.

I decided it was time to tell the boys what I had concluded during the night while I tossed and turned in my bed before sleep hit me like a Mack truck.

"Honestly, guys, I'm not sure going to any of those Reed homes is going to do any good," I said.

The guys looked crushed.

"But, honey, you want to find out if you were their baby, don't you?" Matty said, with a look of concern.

"I know, but I thought about it all night," I said. "Can you imagine someone coming to your door at Christmas-time with news of this nature?"

"Not exactly a trio of wise men looking for the virgin-birthed child," Erick said.

"I could completely shatter someone's holiday."

"But they could also be happy about finding you," Matty said.

"But would the chance be worth it?" I said. "I put myself through this, and I've pulled you in as well. Do I really want to ruin someone's life just so I can have some sort of Kodak moment?"

"You didn't pull us," Erick said. "We came willingly."

I suddenly felt stupid for dragging my friends halfway across the country on a wild goose chase. Who just up and leaves home to go after something with no concrete evidence about it?

"I don't know what I was expecting to find here," I said, a sad note of truth in my tone.

"We're having a great trip, and we're getting a white Christmas," Matty said, as he grabbed my hand in support. "What more can you ask for?"

"Don't give up yet," Erick said.

"Do you guys want to leave?" I asked as I pushed the plate of food away from me.

"Hell no! We're staying until Christmas," Erick said. "We want to see snow on the actual day."

"Then, let's do something fun today," Matty said, digging into the food left on my plate.

Erick and I focused our attention on his eating.

"What?" he asked. "We shouldn't waste Ida's food."

I swore I caught Erick glance at Matty again, but I couldn't figure out what was behind it. Did he want to steal Matty so that they could go off by themselves?

I sure could use some time on my own.

"Why don't you two go off and do something and give me a little time to be alone?" I said.

"Are you sure?" Erick asked, almost eagerly.

"I'll be fine. You take my car and have fun – but be careful."

"I thought my mother was in Vegas," Matty quipped.

The guys were done with their food and got up to head out. Erick kissed my head as Matty took their dishes to the sink. Erick went into the other room and asked Ida about the distance back to Portland, but I couldn't hear what else he wanted to know. I finished my breakfast and carried my coffee out on the porch to wave goodbye to the guys as they drove down the long hill to the street and out of sight. I turned and looked out toward the water where the snow was beginning to fall harder.

I stepped in the house to grab a parka that Ida had hanging by the door, zipped it up, and headed down to the jetty that stuck out over the harbor. The rocks were all jagged and covered in white-capped snow with freezing, frothy water lapping against them. Pieces of ice floated across the top, and I thought what a different scene it was to the one outside my condo window in Phoenix. I looked out on the land where the wind had blown snow into gorgeous, pristine drifts that looked like God had plopped a huge dollop of ice cream down from the sky. Those were my favorite parts, where no cars or footprints had disturbed the fallen snow. And while I watched, the wind continued to pick up the soft snow on the top and move it to another place, as if it were playing a favorite winter game with itself. The seagulls circled above, looking for food hidden beneath snow and ice. I lifted the coffee mug to my cheek to let it warm my whole face. What a different life from my life back in Arizona. It was beautiful and peaceful and cold and exhilarating.

"What would my life have been like if I had stayed in this town?" I thought. "Grown up as a Reed? Had normal parents? What kind of child would I have been?" That child – Priscilla – she was dead and gone. Sara had taken her place at three years old and grown into a different woman.

And then a flood of realization came over me.

This was the location I had stood during my dream. These were the very rocks I would go to as I thought about Gracie. This was the embankment where I had taught her to fish. These were the seagulls that taunted me at night. Or were they calling me to return? How in the world could I have been drawn to this exact place after all these years? How could I have seen it as a child well enough to register it in my dreams into adulthood? Maybe Samara was right about destiny. Our past leads us to places we're not even aware of.

I thought I would be frightened, but I was comforted by the realization. Knowing it was real and not a dream for the first time. Maybe the dreams were meant to reassure me in a way as well, but they just confused me. Dreaming about the death of a child.

It was you. You had died.

That had to be what the dream meant. The death of my innocence. And Lord knows that I could never have remained innocent after everything that I had witnessed. Perhaps Gracie was really grace … the grace that God or some Higher Power had shown me by getting me away from that horrible family. Or maybe I was just reaching for answers, but it made sense to me – and that was all that mattered at that moment. It gave me a peace to think I had some kind of answer about who that dream-child might have been.

I drank my coffee, listened to the birds and the dingy boats, and watched the snow falling harder and stronger around me. I loved it.

I wasn't sure why I was a man in the dream, unless I was meant to never have a child, but I didn't care. No child was coming out of my loins, not after what I had gone through with my miscarriage from years past. And at that moment, I felt a calm I had not felt in a very long time. I wanted to stay on that jetty all day.

I turned to look across the white sheath that canvassed the lawn of the B&B and how beautiful the house looked all lit up for Christmas time in the snow. What an amazing place. I saw my window up at the top of the house and noticed the light on. Had I left it on when I came down for breakfast? Just then, a figure passed by the window. Someone must have been in my room.

I looked once more out over the water toward the horizon to take in the place that had filled my dreams for so long. Then, I trudged through the gathering snow back up to the house. Walking inside and removing the parka, I was instantly filled with the warmth of the home and the smell of fresh bread baking in the oven. I went up the long staircase to the second floor where all the doors were open, being prepared for the family to arrive. Going up the final staircase to the third floor, I noticed my door open with the light on. When I went in, Ida was busy changing my bed.

"I'm sorry, Sara. I was trying to do this quickly while you were out."

"Ida, you don't need to climb all those stairs to do this. We can handle it."

"I used to do it all the time, but now, during our season, I have workers come up here."

I noticed the photo of Charles and Lois I had copied from the library out on top of my suitcase. I thought I had put it away, but I guess I was too busy staring at it all night. I made my way to it and tried to casually shove it inside the suitcase, but Ida didn't miss a beat.

"Did you know them?" she asked me as she tucked a fresh sheet under the corner of the bed.

I walked toward the bed to help her.

"No, but I was doing some research."

"That was a rough time for Boothbay Harbor," Ida said without looking me in the eye.

"I'm sure it was."

"We had our kids at home then, and the entire town was so nervous about the murders."

I couldn't believe I was standing in the room with someone who had lived through all of it.

"I knew Lois and Charles. Normal people. Nothing odd about them at all. I met Lois when I was a nurse, and we bonded during one of her visits over blood pressure medication, of all things."

My heart skipped from this shared trait we all three had as Ida actually smiled recalling a good memory of Lois.

Ida continued, but her smile dissipated.

"No one ever suspected. They had us all fooled. But … I also knew some of the victims."

This was a tough conversation to be having with this sweet older woman. I was very uncomfortable but also hanging on her every word.

"I … I was working on a paper about serial killers, and we came to this town because…"

"It's you, isn't it?"

Ida didn't seem scared or upset. She never lost a bit of the sweet look in her eyes.

"What … what do you mean?" I asked.

"Oh, dear, I see it in your face. You are Priscilla."

CHAPTER TWENTY-NINE

I slumped down on the bed and began to sob. It felt as if a huge weight flew off my shoulders. I wasn't sure why I was crying so hard, but Ida was right there by me, holding and rocking me.

"There, there, shhhhh ... it's all past," Ida said.

She smelled like rosemary and lilac as I buried my face in her chest. I had never been coddled in such a way, and I felt very sheltered.

"Ida, I don't know what to say."

"It's all right. Your secret is safe. So this is why you are here, isn't it?"

I looked up at the woman and studied the lines on her face marking all those years, the many things she must have experienced in her life, the children she raised, her love of her husband and family.

"Yes. I've been having nightmares, and I worked with a therapist back home who unleashed some horrible memories."

"You mean you knew about it?"

"I was there. They took me."

The woman's eyes teared up as she continued rocking me.

"That is just terrible, dear. How anyone could do such a thing."

She began humming a lullaby. It was one of the most beautiful moments I had ever shared with anyone. I was very nervous to ask her about it, but perhaps she could give me some details.

"Can you tell me anything?" I asked.

"You mean about what actually happened?"

"No. About me as a child ... what happened to me."

"Well, those who were local knew that there was a daughter. But nothing was ever in the papers about you. You were kept out of everything dealing with ... you know ... the murders. But then, when they left town – you were all of a sudden gone. Vanished. We didn't know if you had gone with them or what happened."

"Did anyone look for me?"

"The people in the town began to question the remaining Reeds, and then I found out a few years later that your next of kin ..."

"What?"

"They signed papers to release you to the state."

"I know. I ended up in the foster care system in New Mexico."

"I'm so glad," she said as her eyes moistened with tears. "I mean, I was happy to know you were not out in the world with Lois and Charles."

"Why didn't their parents keep me?" I asked.

Ida paused for a moment as she fiddled with the glasses hanging from the string around her neck.

"I'm sorry, dear. This is all so long ago. It's strange to be recalling it now."

"You don't have to," I said, taking her hand in mine. "It's not right of me to ask you for such personal things."

"No ... no. Not at all. How else will you learn if you don't ask? Lois wasn't from here originally, but Charles was. His parents – your grandparents – loved you. But they were older and tried to think what was best for a young girl. They really believed getting you away from Maine was best and only agreed to sign the papers if it was promised you would move away."

"They got their wish. New Mexico is pretty far."

"Did you have a nice family out there?"

I stood and walked over to the rocking chair and lifted the patchwork doll in my arms. I'm sure I looked like a child to the elderly woman.

"I was never adopted. I stayed in the system until I was 18."

"I'm sorry about that, dear."

"Made me stronger," I said with a small smile. "I guess they were doing what they felt was right."

"They had a rough time for a while with how they were treated by the rest of the town. But they stuck it out; they both passed away in Boothbay. They never allowed it to tear them away from this town they loved so dearly."

"Is there any ... other kin ... still in town?"

"Yes. There are still some Reeds, but no one blames them. And it's never discussed anymore."

I wrestled with the thought that people here had loved me, but still gave me away. Was it truly best for me, or were they thinking about themselves? I supposed it didn't matter. I was very happy I had not knocked on any doors belonging to the Reed family that morning.

I took the doll in my arms, walked back to Ida, and sat by her again on the bed.

"You knew them, but does anyone know what ... what made them do it?"

"No, dear. We were all stunned. They seemed like such normal people. Really. No one would have ever guessed they could do such a thing."

Ida kept using the word "normal," and I thought about my definition of the word and what normal was in my own life.

People would never guess that they were abusing their child behind everyone's back either.

But I couldn't say that aloud. It seemed the poor old woman was suffering enough already. That part of the history would stay with me.

"Was it obvious that it was Charles and Lois?" I asked.

"Actually, at first, some people didn't believe it was them," she said. "They thought it had to have been people traveling through town and that they were wrongly accused. But then,

Victoria Silvers survived and identified them. They had left town while the police were looking for them, and we discovered the amount of murders that had happened in other areas. It was all so awful."

"I read in the paper there were seven murders," I said.

"Victoria would have made eight. It was a miracle she lived. All the others each taken by a knife. Some of the victims knew their attackers, some didn't. Absolutely no rhyme or reason to…"

I knew it was hurting Ida to relive it, since she obviously knew some of the people. I couldn't image what it was like to carry the knowledge that a person you knew could be capable of such a thing. And no motive. No taking of money or anything. Just for sheer enjoyment.

"I can't believe they took a child with them to the houses. The things I must have witnessed … I understand why my mind blocked it out."

"You know, I could sense you were here for a reason," she said as she swabbed the corner of her eye with a tissue pulled from her sleeve. "On a kind of mission. I could just tell. That's why we offered you the upper floor. I just couldn't put my finger on what it was, though I knew it wasn't simply for a 'white Christmas.'"

"You see why I couldn't be completely honest," I said, smiling.

"Absolutely. And I'm telling no one."

I suddenly felt dirty for my connection to my past. I stood to move away from the old woman again and placed the doll back on the chair.

"The guys and I can leave today."

Ida rose from the bedside and walked to me.

"No, you're not. You're staying here for Christmas on Friday," she said.

I couldn't have been more thrilled that she responded in the same kind way that I had grown to love during the past day.

"I know this will sound completely sick, but you gave me the best Christmas present ever. The truth of who I was."

"We all want to know where we come from; nothing sick about that."

"Sometimes I think it would be best to leave it all buried in the past."

Ida placed her sweet, soft hands on my shoulders and looked me in the eyes.

"You can do that. You got what you came for. You have two wonderful friends who took the trip with you. You must have a nice life out there." She signaled with a hand as if Arizona were a universe away.

"I do."

"Then, be thankful for that. And leave Priscilla Reed back here where she belongs."

I hugged Ida again, as hard as I thought I could without breaking the old woman. What an amazing lady she was.

Strangers had continually shown me such compassion and care, from Dr. Pingleton to Samara to the Jewish man in the hotel, and Ida. They had all helped me in one way or another.

"Why don't you wash off your face, dear, and come down and visit with me in the kitchen while your friends are out."

"I'd love to help you cook," I said.

"I have plenty to do and would appreciate your help," she said.

I watched her walk out of the room and heard her slowly going down the creaking stairs. I picked up the patchwork doll again and held her tightly while I looked out toward the jetty. I couldn't help but wonder what sent Charles and Lois off the deep end and caused them to do what they did. Was there a mad murderous gene that ran in our family? If Ida and people in the town knew them, that meant they must have led double lives. No one in town would have suspected them as parents who would treat a child the way they treated me – like a human ashtray – or worse yet, of the crimes they had committed against people they probably knew, and knew well. They kept that side of them successfully hidden. Something they had obviously passed to their daughter. I was such a master at compartmentalizing my life so different people only saw what I wanted them to see. I was just happy the desire to do what they had done never came into my mind. I would walk in front of a moving bus before I allowed myself to ever do something like that. I was thankful that trait was not passed down to me.

Still, I finally knew, and something felt brand new to me – the discovery of the truth, which felt like a warm blanket wrapped around me. I had a kind of peace. I felt settled. I wasn't sure how I had wound up in New Mexico, but I thought I could deduct the story from what Ida shared and the gnawing feeling of wonder had left my mind.

I went into the bathroom to wash the tears from my eyes and let my nose lead me to the kitchen where I could assist in cooking with this woman who had just helped me tremendously. Doing something with my holiday-adopted grandmother that I could never recall doing in my life.

CHAPTER THIRTY

The snow had piled up in town in a way my Arizona eyes were unused to. After assisting Ida, I had gotten a ride from Samuel into town so that I could do some shopping. Inside the warmth of a local store, I had written out a Maine Christmas card to Hahn and was finishing a second one.

Your hunch was correct. There was a child, and 30 years later, she is doing very well since she did not have to stay with her birth parents.
Wishing you a Merry Christmas.
Priscilla Reed

I addressed it to Professor Terrence Hightower at Emerson College in Boston. It seemed like the right thing to do, and I was suddenly feeling very generous that Christmas season. Must have been the atmosphere in the town. And though I'd be leaving Prissy behind, signing her name was cathartic. I stamped both cards and gave them to the nice man behind the counter to mail for me. Next, I had to find the perfect gift for the couple who had become our Christmas family, and I knew that wasn't going to be easy – not in this town in which they had lived forever. But there I was in a gift shop trying to find a token that would make sense. There were locals all running around town, doing last minute shopping, and I felt like one of them in my borrowed parka and boots.

I heard the store bell ring as the door opened, and in walked a big guy with a handsome face hidden by a scarf and strands of dark hair peeking out from under a toboggan. I realized I hadn't looked at a man since the beginning of our trip; it had been Erick and Matty doing all the male-window-shopping.

"Hey, Brent, whatcha looking for?" the worker behind the counter asked.

"Need to grab something for my babysitter," he said.

What a great husband to be out looking for gifts.

"How's that daughter of yours doing?" the man asked him.

"She's trying to run the house. Thinks she's supposed to be the lady or something," the attractively tall man said.

Don't even look at the married men, girl. Does the name Robert Michelson the third ring a bell?

"Must be hard on her at this time of year," the clerk said in a hushed tone.

"She's getting better, each holiday that passes without her mother – but thanks, Nick."

A widower. A hunky widower. He must be the catch of the town.

It suddenly occurred to me that I had seen him before. He was the lumberjack guy that Erick went nutty for at the restaurant the day we arrived into town. I must have been really preoccupied not to notice him that day, as the man was stunning.

We both went about our business doing our shopping, but I kept an eye on him because he was so damned rugged and cute and had such an imposing presence. You had to pay attention to him, as he towered over everything. He was humming along to *I'll Be Home for Christmas*, which was playing on the loudspeaker radio, while he shopped for the babysitter.

I saw a beautiful angel that caught my eye – made of hand-blown glass that sparkled underneath the lights twinkling in the store. Ida had been like an angel to me. I knew this was what I wanted to get her as a thank you for these wonderful days. It was placed up higher on the display, and I was afraid of the sleeve on my parka knocking something else over while I reached up for it.

"Let me get that for you," came his voice from right behind me.

"Thank you," I said, as his eyes twinkled with a smile, which I liked to imagine was meant only for me.

The man smelled of woods and nature, and I thought he had walked right out of a freaking romance novel. This crap doesn't happen; or it had never happened to me. He handed me the angel, placing it carefully in my hands.

"You got it?" he asked.

"Yup … long as it doesn't slip out of my hands."

"It's beautiful," he said.

"Just needed to get something for the nice couple at the Quail & Dove B&B who have been great to me this week," I said.

"Ida and Sam are wonderful people."

"You know them?"

Of course he knows them, Sara. This is Mayberry.

"I've lived here my whole life," he said, as if I were a Martian. "Everyone sort of knows everyone."

The store owner was at my side taking the angel from me.

"Let me just wrap that up for you in a box so we make sure it doesn't break," he said as he took it to the counter.

"Well, yours was easy. Now, I still have to find something," the lumberjack said.

In my fantasy narrative, I was sticking with my initial thought of him being a lumberjack.

"I overheard you stating it's for a babysitter. Is she older or younger?" I asked.

"Older."

Good. Don't want some young babysitter intruding into my fantasy world.

"Women love perfume. Or bath beads. Something to make them think of a luxury spa," I said.

He smiled at me.

"You're good at this."

"I'm a woman."

"Yes, you certainly are," he said.

I swore I heard the store owner give a snort of laughter. Was my lumberjack flirting with me?

It's been so long, you wouldn't even know.

"I'm Brent, by the way," he said.

"Sara."

My phone buzzed in my purse.

"You need to get that?" he asked.

I grabbed the phone and saw it was a text from Steve.

("B*ch! R U F-ing ignoring me?")

Steve had never sent a message like that to me before.

"Not important," I said.

"You've been quite a help to me," he said. "How's this?"

He held up one of those pre-packaged sets of soaps, lotions, bubbles that seemed perfect as a "thank you" to someone.

"I think that would do nicely for the person who is looking after your child."

"Sometimes, I think Britney is the one watching her. She's a very old six-year-old," he said.

"You're a family that likes that "Br" sound, huh?" I said with a laugh.

Stupid, Sara.

"Cheesy, huh?" he laughed back.

"Not at all."

"You visiting family?" he asked me.

I wasn't sure what to tell the cute stranger about my reason for being in town.

"I'm here with friends. We came from Arizona to get a taste of a real white Christmas."

"Arizona. Dang. This must seem like a brand new world," he said.

"It's a bit of culture shock but something very soothing about the pace of this small town, the people, the festive setting."

"We can be very cordial to our visitors. It is vacationland after all," he said.

My gift was all wrapped and ready to go, so I paid the man at the counter and started to walk out the door to call Samuel to pick me back up.

"Do you have to hurry off?" Brent asked as he was paying for his gift.

Did I? The boys were off doing God knows what, and my CSI investigation had come to a close. So I was officially on vacation.

"I can wait for your gift to be wrapped ... if you want to walk out together," I boldly said.

"That's exactly what I was hoping for," he said with that rugged smile that already felt familiar.

Walking outside led to a tour of the waterfront which was amazing to walk through as the snow fell and holiday music played, blasting from stores, art galleries, and restaurants – so different from walking through a warm mall in Phoenix. The hustle and bustle in the town felt ... well, organic in some way. I learned Brent was not a lumberjack, but instead was on the police force, as was his wife before she had died from ovarian cancer. It seemed he needed to share that information with me, and I was happy to receive it- to be the ear that he needed to bend. Lord knows I had been using strangers to get me along on my journey. If I could help this man get beyond his grief by talking, I would gladly oblige.

He took me to a coffee shop where we chattered and gabbed. I didn't even notice anyone else around us. It had been so long since I had been out with a straight man in public. But it felt wonderful. With Steve, there had never been any dates, only sex. And I had allowed that to happen for much too long. Oh, I'll admit Brent got me buzzing with his chiseled jaw, unshaven face, dark unkempt hair, and green eyes. I wondered what that body must look like underneath the layers of winter clothes he wore – but more and more – I was enjoying his company and his sense of humor and the great time we were having. The thought of sex drifted out of my mind.

"So being a cop must be a really exciting job," I said.

"It has its moments, but not much goes on here."

Not like in the olden days, huh, Prissy?

Don't call me that!

"Are you ever nervous?" I asked. "Things like that horrible Midwest cop-slaying I read about last month. Does it make you question your choice of jobs?"

"Everyone has questions about what they do, no?" he said smiling. "But I knew ever since I lost my dad at an early age that I wanted to be a cop. It just made sense to me."

"It's a wonderful thing to know your passion."

"Protect and defend, that's me."

"Now, I'm a little nervous," I said.

Brent laughed.

"Ah, Sara. I'm just a big ole pussy-cat," he said.

"Well, this Arizona Cardinal has loved spending time with the Maine pussycat."

Stop flirting, Sara.

"Crap," he said looking at his watch. "It's almost 5:00. I have to get home to let my sitter go."

"I'm sorry I've kept you for so long. It is Christmas after all."

"Not at all. This has been a great afternoon," he said.

"It was really nice to meet you," I said, as he helped me get that oversized parka back on.

"I noticed you a few days ago as I was leaving Rosemary's restaurant and hoped I'd get to see you again."

I couldn't believe this guy actually remembered … me. I never thought I could make an impression on someone from a glance. Other women do that, not Sara Butler. I couldn't help but beam when he said it.

"Yeah, I remember you, too," I finally said.

"Let me drive you back to Ida's place," he said. "I just need to stop and get Britney."

"You don't need to."

"No trouble. Besides, I don't especially want to let you go, not yet."

We walked out to his truck as his last words played over and over in my head. I tried to think back to those times that I did actually date and what it was like. But I couldn't remember. All that I could recall was Steve's urgency to leave my condo each time he was done. And Brent was a man who didn't want me to leave him. And yet, it was already heartbreaking, for I knew I'd be leaving in just two days.

We pulled up to his house, and he was out his door and around to open mine and help me down from the cab of his truck so quickly. His house was one of those cottage types with the screened-in side porch and dark green cedar shingle siding that you only see when watching *House Hunters* on HGTV. Nothing like what you see in Phoenix, but an adorable home with a small child's face looking out the window. We walked through the front door, and his six-year-old wrapped herself around his waist.

"I saw you looking out that window," he said as he kissed his daughter.

Britney was a cute little girl with long blonde curls. I was sure he saw his wife every time he looked at her.

Just like you look like your mom, Prissy.

"She is getting very excited for Christmas," the babysitter said.

Both of them stared at me, the stranger in the kitchen.

"Oh, where are my manners," Brent said. "This is Sara. She's visiting Boothbay for the holidays and helped me pick out this for you, Mrs. Reed."

As Brent handed her the gift, the name he had spoken reverberated in my head like a loud cymbal that had just clanged.

Mrs. Reed.

A possible family member ... my own blood ... standing there in his home only eight feet away from me. But how could I find out? How could I be sure? My knees buckled.

"Hello, Sara," Britney said.

"Hello," I responded.

"It's nice to meet you, dear," Mrs. Reed giggled. "And glad he had someone to help him choose a gift this year."

The two of them laughed as she put on her coat.

"Open it!" Britney said.

"I can't, sweetie. It's not Christmas yet. But I'm sure I'll love it."

I was in a complete fog as the two of them spoke. My mind was racing over ways to make a move toward the woman. A signal to let her know who I was. While I was thinking, I swore she was looking at me. Did I remind her of a family member from her past perhaps?

She was down at Britney's level to give her a hug goodbye.

"Merry Christmas, Mrs. Reed," Britney said.

The name pounded in my head again.

"You, too, love. Have a wonderful time with your father."

She wrapped herself up nice and warm to head out into the cold air. So many thoughts were flying through my head. Pull her aside and say something. Let her know who I was. Everything else in the room disappeared, and all I could see was that woman. She stopped and looked at me once more. Was she sizing me up as a female who came in with Brent, or was she remembering something?

"I hope you have a Merry Christmas in Boothbay as well, Sara," she said, and she was out the door.

So much for a family reunion.

"Let me just get Britney all settled, and we'll be ready to go," Brent said as he walked into the other room with the young girl.

I looked around the old country kitchen as I let out a huge breath. It looked as if Brent was not one who was into modernizing an old fashioned house. The place had dark wood moldings everywhere with huge wooden beams across the ceiling. The walls were a faded yellow that seemed as if they had been that way for years. I wondered if this house had been handed down to him by family. People without families think that way sometimes – that things must be passed from generation to generation. I could picture him standing at that old stove making food for Britney.

And then, I had a flash.

I had been in that house.

CHAPTER THIRTY-ONE

How was it possible that I had been in Brent's home? Something about staring up at that ceiling sent me back. I was a small child sitting at the kitchen table waiting for my parents in the next room. This was one of the houses! One of the horrible places where a murder had occurred! My stomach started to churn, and I felt the coffee I had sipped rising up in my throat.

Calm down, Priscilla.

What could I do? I had to get out of that room. I wanted to run out the door, but what would I say to Brent?

He and Britney were laughing in the next room as she was looking for her scarf and gloves. Such sounds of happiness bounced off the walls.

And then I heard the screams, the woman pleading for her life, asking my parents not to do it. But they taunted her and made it into a game – a game that I had been forced to play as a young child.

Brent was playing his own game with his daughter, and I could sense true love in his home. It had taken over whatever had happened there in the past. But still, flashes of a Formica table and chrome chairs blurred in my vision as if they were there in the room trying to fade in from the past. I recalled the fear I felt as a child waiting in that room for my parents. Trying to think of other things in my mind to not be afraid but that small child didn't understand what was going on. But suddenly, I knew what had happened. I knew it was not a game being played but someone's life coming to an end. A woman witnessing her husband dying in the arms of my father while she waited for a blade to be plunged into her own gut. The jeers and taunts of Charles and Lois, who had been friends with their victims. Her reaching out to me to help her. The entire thing was sickening, and I suddenly felt so scared.

I walked to the doorway, unsure if I'd see Brent and his daughter or Lois and Charles killing someone. But there was a father and daughter oozing with the joy of the Christmas season. My entire body felt warm as perspiration beaded around my temples. I tried to zero in on the young child in the room. She must have missed her mother terribly, but you could tell how much she loved her dad. It must have been better to have one parent than none at all. And the sight of those two overshadowed any horror that I had sensed in the house before. There was something wonderful there – love. Brent was tickling his daughter as he put on her coat and looked up to see me standing there.

"You all right?" he asked when he saw me.

You must look a mess, girl.

"Just a little warm," I said, dabbing the sweat on my head.

"We do keep it toasty in here," he said. "Britney had a good idea."

"You want to join us for dinner?" she asked.

"Why, I…"

"I know you have friends here with you, but it'll be an early dinner," Brent said. "And then, I'll take you right back to the B&B."

"Come on, Sara. Please," Britney said.

I was nervous about what I had just remembered, but I wasn't ready to walk away from Brent's warm family.

"I would just be waiting for my friends to return from Portland or wherever they went," I said.

"Great! That answers that. Now, have you had a lobster yet since you arrived?" Brent said.

"Can't say as I have."

"What? That's a sin! Isn't it Britney?"

Britney grabbed me to pull me down to her level.

"I don't really like lobster," she whispered.

"You have to eat lobster when in Maine," Brent said. "I know exactly where we're going."

The three of us trekked out into the snow and got into the truck. (I personally wished for a delicious vegan or organic meal, but I knew that was not in the cards that evening.) Britney was talking all about Christmas, what she had asked Santa for, as well as filling me in on all the things that the young girls of the day were into. At the restaurant, Brent made them do the entire bib thing on me with the big picture of a lobster on it, and he took a photo of me and Britney with his phone. He then sent it to my phone so that I could share it with the guys later. I secretly liked the fact that he had a photo of me to keep with him.

"Now, you hold up your lobster so I can take a photo, too," I said like a silly girl.

The hunk of a guy held up his lobster that looked so small in his big hands. I snapped the photo that captured his huge smile.

Way to go, Sara. Now, you have a photo of him, too.

I was having a wonderful time, and any thought of a vegan dinner floated right out of my mind. This was so much better! It sort of reminded me of my dream with Carol and the man and their daughter, Gracie. Only my dream was always overshadowed with sadness, and this particular evening was amazingly wonderful. It felt ... right. And for the first time, I could see myself as a mother.

Someday.

I wondered how different my life would have been had I given birth ten years earlier. Raising a child alone. How that child would have changed me. Would it have tied me to the absentee father? Or would the loneliness I'd felt as an adult diminish with the addition of a child?

"Do they have boats in Arizona?" Britney asked.

"Some people have boats on the lake, but nothing like what you have here in the harbor," I said.

The little girl used a French fry to draw fish made of ketchup on her plate as she spoke.

"It's an important part of the Maine economy," she said. "Without boats, we'd never be able to catch all the fish people love to eat."

Brent and I laughed at the smart child who obviously paid attention to what was being said around her. I rubbed her arm in a way I'd noticed older women do when a child said something cute. Spending time with Britney was an eye-opening experience, and I found that I did have that motherly gene in me after all. I had almost completely forgotten about everything that had brought me to Maine. If I could have bottled up that one moment in time and kept it, I would have. But I'd always have the memories of it … and the photos on my phone.

CHAPTER THIRTY-TWO

We were back in the truck, heading to the well-lit Q&D house when neither of us knew how to end the evening.

"Well," he said, pulling the truck up the drive to the house.

"Quite a day," I said.

"Yes, it has been."

"Britney, it was wonderful to meet you," I said to the girl strapped in the small seat in the back of the truck cab.

"You, too," she said. "I had fun."

"Are your friends and you coming out tomorrow evening for the town gathering at the gazebo?" Brent asked.

"If that's what they do here, then we probably should," I said.

"Good," Britney said.

"Good," her dad echoed.

"Then I'll see you both tomorrow night," I said, starting to get out of the truck.

Brent was out of his door and walking around to open mine for me again, reaching toward the floorboard to get the present I had purchased.

"I'm sure Ida will love this angel," he said, shutting the door behind me.

"Sometimes, it's nice to have angels watching over us," I said.

You are so freaking corny.

"I couldn't agree more," Brent said, leaning into me.

I wanted to kiss this man. I really wanted to kiss him so badly. The afternoon and evening had felt like a lifetime, and I could have sworn I'd known him forever. But kissing him didn't feel right. Not here. Not yet. Not with me leaving town. Not with his daughter peering out of the truck window watching us. And I noticed someone inside the house looking out a window at us, too.

You are on display, Sara. Nothing happening here.

"Goodnight, Brent, and thank you for a wonderful time," I said.

I kissed his cheek and started to walk up to the front porch.

"I'll see you tomorrow night. Look for us," he shouted.

"Oh, I will. I'll be the one with the two guys. You won't be able to miss me," I said. "The three tan westerners sticking out."

I stood on the porch as they pulled down the drive and out to the street. I noticed that my car covered in dirty snow was in the drive, so the guys were already back. I couldn't wait to tell them about my day. I also enjoyed the fact that Ida was being so protective, watching me out the window as she had. I went straight up to the third floor to find my boys waiting for me.

"Girl, where have you been?" Erick said.

"We've been worried sick," Matty added.

I was excited, but decided to play coy.

"Out of my way," I said, as I went into my room to put the gift away.

The boys followed eagerly.

"Oh no, you are up to something. You're glowing!" Erick said.

"You had sex!" Matty said.

"No. Did you?" I said to them.

The guys looked at me and at each other, both seeming a little awkward. Had I hit a nerve?

"We had a great drive up to Portland," Matty said.

"Why would you go up there?" I asked, plopping down on my bed.

"We had to pick up a Christmas present for you," Matty said.

"Waiting at the airport," Erick continued.

And then Hahn came pushing her way between them into my room toward me.

"I travel all this way to be with you, and you're not even here waiting for me when I arrive," she said.

"Hahn!"

I grabbed my friend and hugged her harder than I ever had. And she didn't even push me away.

"I should spend more time away from you to know how appreciated I am," she said.

"But how? What…" I started.

"I called her last night and told her to get her butt on a plane to Portland so we could spend Christmas together," Erick said.

"I do get some time off … not as much as you guys."

"So she's riding cross country back with us," Matty exclaimed.

"*If* I can put up with you three that long," she said.

"I am so glad you're here," I said looking at my little Asian all dressed for winter like an Eskimo. "Now, we feel complete."

"The gay mafia takes on Maine," she said.

"Now, I'll have to tell you what this trip was really all about," I said.

"We filled her in," Matty said.

"Girl! You have some heavy shit going on," she said. "Maybe meeting Samara wasn't a good idea after all."

"No," I said. "It was wonderful. She started me on this journey, and it's been an eye-opener."

"So that was one reason we went to Portland, but there was another," Matty said.

"Don't get mad," Erick said.

"It was all for you," Matty said.

"Spill it," I said, pulling Hahn down to sit next to me on my bed.

"We went to the child advocacy office of Maine and talked about your case," Erick said. "It was really difficult, and before you get your hopes up, they couldn't give us any information."

"But we left them your cell phone number and everything, hoping someone would want to help out," Matty said.

My initial reaction was to lash out at them for doing this without me. But then, I realized what a kind thing they had done – knowing I had been upset thinking this trip was for naught. I realized I had the best friends any child born of a homicidal team could possibly ask for.

"That's so great of you guys."

"We wanted information about baby Priscilla," Matty said.

"You know I'm gonna start calling you Prissy," Hahn teased. "And you can call me Miss Scarlett."

The guys cracked up at Hahn.

"Put a knife under the bed to cut the pain," Erick said in his best Butterfly McQueen voice.

"Laugh all you want," I said with a smile. "But I got some information on that little baby."

And I told them about the amazing moment I shared with Ida and all I had learned, how well Ida knew about the entire ordeal. The three of them sat there like kids with their mouths open.

"Holy fucking shit," Erick said. "I can't believe of all the places we could have gone, we end up where someone knew them."

"And you wanted to go to the gay-owned B&B," Matty said.

"Well, in this town, that's not too hard. Everyone knows everyone, I've been told," I said.

"I got to talk with that old lady while waiting for you, and she is one smart cookie," Hahn said. "She puts this broad to shame with her knowledge."

"So that's why you're smiling from ear to ear," Matty said.

"That and…"

"You had sex!" Matty said again.

"Bitch! Am I the only one not getting it on this trip?" Hahn said.

"No! But I did meet someone. And I had the best afternoon and evening that I've had in a long, long time."

"Good for you," Erick said.

"You've seen him by the way," I said. "The first restaurant we went to when we arrived."

"That big hunk leaving the place?" Erick said. "How could I forget?"

"Yeah, except he lives here and I'm so far away."

"Long distance romances are great," Erick said. "Then, you have none of the day-to-day crap to deal with."

"You ass," Matty said.

"What about my ass?" Erick asked as he gave Matty a peck on the cheek.

There was no alcohol involved, and the kiss seemed genuine. Maybe he really did care for Matty.

"Wait a minute," I said. "What did Hahn mean about the only one not getting any?"

"Focus," Matty said. "This is about you."

"So details, we want 'em," Erick said. "Describe him to Hahn, as I have a picture ingrained in my mind."

I told them everything. From Brent and his daughter to the house and Mrs. Reed. The gang was fascinated by the day I had experienced. It was really more than I ever thought it could be.

"Do you think you're getting enough answers here?" Matty asked.

"I do. I'd never have been able to do this staying in Phoenix. And look at the great trip we got to take? And now, it's complete with Hahn here!"

"Yeah, it's been pretty wonderful," Erick said, taking Matty's hand.

"All I know is this doesn't mean I'm not expecting to see gifts that were purchased for me along the way," Hahn said.

"Hey, Ron paid for your trip out here on that plane, so I think you win," Erick joked.

"So what's on the agenda for tonight?" Matty asked.

"I went out and bought Ida and Samuel a gift, and their family arrives in the morning. And then, after lunch on Christmas, we'll head out," I said hesitantly.

"Someone doesn't want to leave her Maine man," Hahn said, nudging me with her elbow.

The thought did cross my mind that I could send the three of them back in my car on Christmas, and I could fly back later. But I wouldn't share that possibility ... just yet.

"I asked what we were doing tonight," Matty asked again.

"Snippy little bitch," Hahn said, swatting Matty.

"Let's go out," Erick said.

"I saw this sign in a store today about a sleigh ride," I said.

"Now, how much more of a New England Christmas can you get?" Erick asked.

"I just want to make a call to Phoenix, and then, we can head out," I said.

"I'm here, so you ain't calling me. And I sure as hell don't think you're texting that male slut," Hahn said.

"Not on your life. Just want to reach out to the doc back home."

"We'll run down and ask Ida about where this ride is," Matty said.

"Wait. Where is Hahn sleeping?" I asked.

"It's all worked out," Matty said. "She took my room."

The three left my room before I could comment, and I finally let out a huge breath from the dramatic intensity of the day. It had been a rollercoaster of emotions, but all worth it. When I thought back to greeting the morning from that very bed, I had had no idea what was in store for me. But it had been a day of enlightenment. Not only about finding out the past, but looking at how I was in the present. A man like Brent. He opened my eyes to a new side of me that I only hoped I could hold onto and not return to my old ways when I got back to Phoenix.

CHAPTER THIRTY-THREE

I dialed the phone, and he answered.
"Hello?"
"Dr. Pingleton, it's Sara Butler."
"Sara. It's great to hear your voice. Is everything all right?"
I told him about the road trip and what had happened, trying to keep it to only the main points so as not to waste too much of his time.
"What an incredible journey you've been on," he said.
"I thank you for it. For pointing me in the right direction."
"It's all about discovering who you are now. It's not really about the past. That only helps you to be who you are meant to be."
"I understand that. I do. I even think I realize the dreams have been about me losing that child that I was at three years old when I became Sara."
"You are doing some great work."
"But, doctor, I'm still stuck on who the man is in the dream. Why I'm a man."
"Sometimes a dream is just a dream and requires no interpretation."
"I hope you have a Merry Christmas, doctor."

"You, too. And I want to see you when you return from your trip."

"Absolutely. I'll be there."

And I meant it. I wasn't skipping out on him again.

"Thank you for everything," I said. "Take care."

I hung up and felt good about life, about myself. I went to grab a sweater from my drawer so that I could spend a cold country evening with the gang. I was so excited that Hahn had made it out to join us. There on the bureau was a small envelope with my name on it. I opened it up, and inside was a folded piece of paper with a black and white photo of a baby. Someone had cut out the people holding the baby, leaving the child alone. I read the note.

I know I told you to leave baby Priscilla in Maine, but I thought you might want one old baby photo of yourself.
Love, Ida.

Ida knew my parents. She knew me as a baby. And she gave me something no one else in the world would ever be able to supply for me. I didn't know why she had a photo or how she came to have it, but I didn't care. I studied it. I was a cute baby, if I said so myself. I came to Maine to discover, and I'd been able to do so much more than that.

I went down the stairs to meet the others to go off on our sleigh ride adventure when Ida stopped me and asked me to come in the kitchen for a moment before I joined them in the parlor. I was so excited about the photo.

"I just opened…"

"Sara, I saw Brent Silvers' truck out front when you came home."

Home? That was sweet.

"I met him in town today, and he gave me a ride back here. What a great guy and a wonderful little girl."

Ida seemed pensive, as if she wanted to share something with me.

"He is a wonderful guy. Everyone has looked after him since his wife passed."

"I hope you're not worried about me doing anything."

"No, child. That's not it at all. I think you're a lovely person, and it's so nice that you spent time with someone around your age in town here."

She stopped talking and walked over to her stove.

"Ida? What is it?"

"Did he tell you anything about his family?" she asked, her back to me.

I was starting to get nervous. I loved spending the day with Brent, but I had also experienced a horrible flashback. What was Ida intimating?

"Not really," I said.

"Sara, his mother was Victoria Silvers. She was … she was the one victim who survived the Reed murders."

I sat down in the chair at her kitchen table. I was in that house that evening when his mother was attacked. That was the one I had witnessed – the woman who cried out for me to help her. But she lived! That was wonderful. Brent said he knew he wanted to be a cop when he lost his dad. I saw his dad. Oh, my God. The man on the floor. Of course. It was all coming at me so quickly, and I was having problems processing it, suddenly putting faces to the stories that I had only been acquainted with for the past month. I could see in my mind the man who lay there dying, but now, he had Brent's face. That poor family.

"Sara, are you all right?" she asked.

It suddenly occurred to me that the man I had spent that amazing day with could have shared the exact same memories that I had on that night. For all I knew, he was asleep in his bedroom – just steps away from me as I waited in his kitchen. But how could he have slept through all the noise?

"Brent said he knew he wanted to be a cop when he lost his dad. Was he there that night?"

"No. For some reason, God had seen to it that Brent was staying at a friend's house that night."

I felt a sense of relief, even though the story I was hearing was awful. I needed just one more piece of the puzzle– though I was already certain I knew the answer. I just needed to hear it from Ida's mouth.

"Ida, I was in Brent's home today. Is that the same house?"

Ida looked as if she didn't want to share any more information with me, but the woman understood that this had been my quest to come to this town. She wasn't going to hold back on me.

"Victoria moved Brent out of that house as soon as she recuperated and was out of the hospital. But once Brent was grown, he bought the house back. He wanted to start over there and raise his family in love to create new memories, until his own wife died."

I could never have done what he did. This man was more incredible than I had known. If I knew a loved one had died somewhere, I'd burn that place to the ground.

But you are back. You're right here looking to see where a part of you died.

"Thank you for telling me, Ida."

"I wanted to give you full disclosure on all of this. It was so strange to see his truck in front of the house and to know he had been with you today."

"Yes," I nodded, agreeing, "very strange."

"Maybe that's the wrong word, dear. Who knows? Perhaps it's some sort of fate."

Ida walked over and started wrapping my scarf around my neck. She handed me a thermos full of coffee she had made for us and some brownies.

"Now, you have a wonderful time with your friends tonight," she said. "It makes me warm all over that your other friend joined you, and a sleigh ride is such a fun thing to do. Forget about everything else, and enjoy the night and the season."

"Thank you," I said as I hugged her.

I went into the parlor where the gang was waiting, and they snatched up the brownies and thermos to take to the car.

"Come on, girl," Erick said. "We're getting tired of this waiting game."

"That's what men do for women," Matty teased.

"Oh God, I'm so glad we're gay," Erick said.

"Let's all go see how well an Asian can take snow," Hahn said as we all walked outside.

The words "destiny" and "fate" ran through my mind like a news ticker on the bottom of the television screen. I knew I was supposed to be there learning all I was learning. But the wonderful feelings I had felt about the day with Brent and Britney were replaced by a melancholy feeling. I was sad for him, but I was also bewildered by the strange way that we were connected. I just wasn't sure if it was a connection I was willing to share with him.

CHAPTER THIRTY-FOUR

The dinner table seemed complete with the three of us sitting there. Carol was no longer somber and sad. She was alive and smiling and had a rugged, chiseled face. When she said my name, it sent shudders through my body. And we took Gracie out for a sleigh ride where she snuggled up under the crook of my arm, between Carol and me. The three of us. A happy family. The way it once had been. Carol placed her big strong arm on the back of the sleigh to pull me over to her and leaned in for a kiss. The stubble on her face pricked at my own as she kissed me over the child we had made. She looked into my eyes and said my name again, which caused my heart to skip a beat.

"Sara," she said.

I sat up in my bed and looked out the window to the fresh blanket of snow that had fallen during the night.

That dream!

Gracie was there. And I finally had a name in it. And Carol … Carol was Brent. It was all so mixed up with the old dreams I had and the new life I was living. But should I question it? Was the universe telling me to enjoy what was happening in the quaint village by the water, or did I need to come clean to Brent in order to enjoy my time with him?

I looked at my watch, which said 11:00 a.m., and I realized I had slept longer than I had in forever. I put on a robe and went out my door to Erick's room. I opened the door, and there were Erick and Matty snuggling in bed.

"Am I interrupting?" I asked.

"No. Come on in. We finished breakfast and came back up, waiting for your sleepy butt to wake up," Erick said, his arm gently around Matty. "Hahn is in her room reading."

"Why didn't you get me up?" I asked.

"With the day you had yesterday? We figured you needed the sleep, girl," Matty said.

I crawled under the blanket and squeezed next to Matty on his other side so that we were both holding him.

"Wasn't last night beautiful?" I said.

The sleigh ride had been the ultimate winter thing to do. A big horse pulling us across snow-covered terrain in a sled right out of *A Christmas Carol* or something. And spending it with my favorite people was the cherry on the sundae.

"We were just discussing it," Erick said. "We should come back here every Christmas. Or at least for another winter break."

"I had never done a sleigh ride, and the fact that they gave us a hot toddy also ... yum," Matty said.

"I know, but I'm sure Sara wished she had Brent wrapped around her under that blanket last night," Erick said.

I had decided to not share the last piece of information from Ida with the boys. There are some things we need to keep to ourselves ... unless I eventually decided to share it with Brent.

"No, I actually loved being with you all," I said.

"I think I want to get a bed shaped like a sleigh just so I can pretend I'm on it again," Matty said.

"You are too gay even for me," Erick said.

"What if I ride *you* on that sleigh bed?" Matty asked.

"Hello ... I'm right here! Do I need to leave?" I asked, starting to get up.

"Get back here," Matty said, pulling me back down to his side.

The three of us just lay there, not wanting to move from the warmth of the old quilt on the third floor of the bewitching B&B.

"It will be strange with Ida's family here today," Erick said. "We've gotten used to having her to ourselves."

"I think she'll treat us the same," I said. "She's really taken with us."

"At least with you," Matty said.

"Jealous, bi-otch?" I asked.

"Hey, I'm just happy to get a real homemade meal tomorrow, which I know is gonna be amazing. Wait until you smell her kitchen today," he said.

"This boy and his belly," Erick said as he patted Matty. "What am I gonna do?"

"Take me for what I am," Matty sang.

"OK ... that's an old show," Erick said.

"Then we should go to New York and see a new Broadway show," Matty said.

"Maybe we'll just have to do that," Erick said, as he got up to head to the bathroom.

I watched him walk out, and I sat stroking Matty's hair as if he were a little boy.

"How do you feel, Matty?"

"Good. I know what you're thinking."

"No, you don't."

"You think Erick is upset over Ron and just turning to me for comfort."

"I never said…"

"And if that's all it is, I'm fine with it. We have gotten close on this trip, and I'm more grateful to have him in my life than I was before. I'm not looking for a ring, a husband, to settle down. I'm just enjoying this Christmas."

"That sounds like a plan. And I'll be right here with you," I said, hugging him from behind and resting my head on his shoulders.

Hahn appeared in the door.

"Well, look at Miss Thing finally awake from her beauty sleep and trying to get Matty to switch teams."

"That ain't even possible," Matty said. "Even if I do love this girl."

I gave him a peck on the cheek.

"You ain't my type either," I said.

"But we do get to meet your type tonight, right?" Hahn asked.

"Yes, you will."

Erick walked back in the room and sat down to put on his shoes.

"There's movement on the second floor," he said. "Guess family is arriving."

"And I guess I missed breakfast," I said.

"I'm sure Ida will have something down there you can nibble on," Matty said.

"What do you guys wanna do today?" I asked.

"I'd like to stay out of the way here as much as possible," Erick said. "To just give them room as a family."

"Let me get dressed, and we can head into town," I said.

"Don't take so long," Hahn said. "I didn't come here so I could read books all day. My time in this town is less than what you guys had."

"Let's make Hahn eat something really fattening today," Matty said.

"I notice Erick has put on a few pounds," she said.

"The place is known for cream soups and blackberries," he said. "You do the math."

I went back into my room to find some layers of warm clothes to put on as the three kept chatting. While there was sun shining through clouds outside, it was still a cold Maine morning. Or by then, it was probably closer to noon. December 24th, and all was right with the world – at least my world. Even with screwed up dreams and strange paths crossing, I didn't mind. I was spending a great day with my friends, and I'd be seeing Brent again that night before I left town.

My cell phone started vibrating. My mind expected a text, but when I picked up the phone, it was a call from a number I didn't recognize.

"Hello."

"Is this Sara Butler of Phoenix, Arizona?"

"Yes."

"You don't know me, but I'm calling from the Child Advocacy Group of Maine."

The guys had said they passed along my number, but surely, no one would be calling me back that quickly.

"There was a case 30 years ago in this state. I know you're well aware of it. The two young men who came to see me yesterday told me all about your story."

"Yes, that's right."

I started to breathe a little heavy.

"I did an investigation on you to be certain who I would be calling, ran the report from that year on the Sara Butler case, and I have to tell you, Ms. Butler, I could be fired for doing this…"

"It stays between us, I promise," I said quickly.

"You were the child who was given a new name and sent to New Mexico, but you were never adopted. Priscilla Reed is your birth name."

I had known it. I had known it since the hypnosis and the investigation online and with Ida telling me. But here was someone who read some file – a file marked "confidential" in some office that had stories about my name switch and sending me off across the country. About not telling whatever family I had left – to protect me, I assumed.

"Ms. Butler, are you still there?"

Sara, say something.

"Yes, sorry. My mind…"

"I'm sure it's a shock to you, but the guys told me how you traveled all the way here for answers. And I thought you'd want to know before tomorrow."

It wasn't a shock. It was just confirmation. It was a part of my past that I'd definitely be discussing with Pingleton when I returned home.

"Absolutely. Thank you, thank you. You have no idea what this means to me," I said.

"I'm sure that I don't, but it's the closest thing to a Christmas present the CAM could give you."

She had that right. That group just helped to seal the entire envelope on my past.

"Thank you so much, Mrs.?"

"Honey, I ain't giving out my name – just in case – but have a blessed Christmas."

I laughed at the candor of the woman.

"Same to you. And thank you again … so much."

"Thank those friends of yours for being so persistent. They got to me."

"I will."

I hung up and waited for the rush of questions to start in my head. For the negative voice to begin beating me up over this new knowledge. But it didn't happen. She didn't speak. I actually had an overwhelming calm feeling settle over my entire body, which shocked me more than the news the case worker had just shared. I knew there was the hustle and bustle of the start of Christmas on the floors below me, but there in my small room in the attic of that amazing place in Maine, my world was still, free of any anxiety. The buzzing and nagging that had been in me for the past few months had ceased. The constant wonder and search for something was over. I had my truth. Someone in that state saw to it that I was given a chance in this world. They did it by giving me a new name and setting me on a new path. For that, I had to be grateful. And I had to really make something of my life so that what they did was not in vain. Someone wanted me to go out in the world and be something different from Priscilla Reed, and I was going to do just that.

CHAPTER THIRTY-FIVE

The gay mafia had a great day together walking along a snowy rock cliff, drinking coffee, pontificating about life and what all four of us wanted to do when we got back home. I wanted to wrap Brent up and take him with me – or simply stay and see in the new year with him but that seemed too movie-like even for me. We had met Ida and Samuel's family, and they were as warm as the older generation, all which made me feel like I was having the best Christmas I'd ever had. And then, snow lightly fell again, and we headed into town to meet around the gazebo in the park for the Christmas festival.

"OK … it's beautiful and all, but this boy is getting cold," Erick complained.

"Shut up, Mary. When will you ever get a chance to experience this on Christmas again?" Hahn asked.

"Have I mentioned how warm your scarf is?" Matty asked.

"That is an original "made in Vietnam," and don't you forget it," Hahn said.

We all laughed, wrapped our scarves she had made around our necks, and got out of the car, following the crowd. There was a live reenactment of the Nativity. People passing out hot apple cider and popcorn balls. Matty thought he had died and gone to food heaven. In the middle of all the noise, Hahn's Blackberry beeped, announcing she had an email.

"You are not doing work on Christmas Eve," Erick said.

"Let me just check the damn thing."

"Come on," I said.

We stood while Hahn read, and her body started to shake.

"What the hell is wrong with you, girl?" Matty said.

"You have got to be shitting me," she said, reading her email.

"What is it?" Matty said.

"I got an email from that reality show, *People Like Us,* and they want me to fly to L.A. for an audition," she said.

"That's amazing!" I said.

"'Bout freakin' time," Erick said.

"I had given up on hearing from any of these folks," she said.

"L.A. doesn't know what they have in store with you," Erick said. "Earthquake Hahn hits Hollywood!"

We were all laughing, but I was really looking through the crowds, trying to spot Brent.

"You gonna take more time off from work for that?" Matty asked.

"Screw work," she said. "This is a dream I've been waiting for."

"What happened to 'keeping a job in bad economic times'?" Erick teased.

"E&Y will love the publicity I'll bring 'em," she joked.

We caught up with Ida and Samuel and their clan. I thought about all the people we had met in her family and all the people who were in her house. We were just the age between her kids and her granddaughter Emily, so many decades were covered through the adults in that house. I thought Ida even caught on to the guys being gay, but it didn't seem to faze her.

"We got separated leaving the house," Ida said. "Isn't this a great way to spend Christmas Eve?"

"Absolutely," I said, giving her a small hug.

I whispered in her ear, "I love the photo, by the way. Thank you."

"Lobster-fest was written on the back of it," she whispered back. "Figured you'd like a Maine photo of your younger self."

How I appreciated that woman and the thought she took to remove everyone around me from the photo.

Ida smiled, and Emily's youngest pulled on her hand to go look at the live animals they had.

"Rachel, leave Great-Gam alone," Emily said.

"She's fine. Honey, yes … we can go see the sheep," Ida responded.

I saw Erick was just about to make some sort of lewd remark about sheep, so I put my hand over his mouth.

"My kids love to drive Grandma crazy," Emily said.

"At least it gives us a chance to be kid-free for a moment," her husband said.

"I knew there was a reason I had no kids," I joked.

"Me, too," Erick said.

"You guys could always adopt," Emily said looking at the boys. "Gay couples are doing it all the time."

"I'll be Auntie Hahn – the one they come to when they want to escape the parental units," Hahn said.

The boys looked each other in the eyes and at the same time said "Mame."

We all started laughing, and then, I heard the scream.

"Sara!"

It was Britney. I felt my heart skip.

"You made it," Brent said.

"A regular local already," I said.

I looked at him as he walked up but saw a boy who would have been six or seven when I had sat at his kitchen table all those years ago.

"I think you could fit right into Boothbay Harbor with no problem," he said.

"I'd need to see what the summers are like."

"Then you might just have to check it out," he said with a grin.

"We might do that," Erick said, extending his hand to Brent.

"You must be Erick, the attentive brother," Brent said with a smile.

I was very curious how Brent was going to take my "family." But misfits though we were, we belonged to each other.

"I don't even want to know what you called me," Matty said, as he shook Brent's hand.

"You're the science teacher," Brent said.

"Hey, I'm impressed," Matty said. "I didn't get thrown under a bus after all."

"Do you think I'd do that, Matty?" I teased.

"You have to be Hahn," Brent said. "She didn't tell me you were here, but she did talk about you ... a lot."

"My Christmas present flew in to meet us," I said.

"Who is she kidding?" Hahn said. "I just came to meet you."

Brent laughed and said "hello" to Ida's family. He apparently hadn't seen them in a while. Then, we all started to move around the festival as a herd. But I didn't care. I was happy spending the holiday with this huge extended Maine family that I had adopted over the past few days. Ida and Rachel were back, and Brent gave her a warm hug.

"It's great to see you, Brent," she said.

"Merry Christmas," he said.

Why is this man still single? Everyone adores him.

Ida looked at me and smiled, sharing the secret that I was keeping inside.

"We have quite a gal staying at the Quail & Dove, don'tcha think?" Ida said.

"Ida," I blushed.

"I couldn't agree with you more," Brent said.

Brent took my hand as we walked around, and I enjoyed how our hands fit together. I noticed how some people looked out of the corners of their eyes at us, only because they were used to seeing Brent alone with his daughter. But I didn't mind. I was floating on cloud nine. And leave it to my boys to run into the gay guys who owned another B&B in town. It was like their gay radar was on or something, and the next thing I knew, the four of them were talking with Hahn. You'd think that Erick was planning on opening his own place there.

"Thought you didn't like the cold," I joked.

"I never said that," he said as he made a snowball and threw it at me.

"That is freezing!" I said.

"There is more where that came from," Erick said as he packed up another ball.

"Watch it there," Brent said. "I'm a master at a snowball fight."

I liked how Brent went into protective mode. It made me feel safe even in the midst of a silly game.

"I'll just roll over and play dead," Erick teased.

"He can turn into a big ole girl," Matty whispered toward Brent so that Britney didn't overhear.

I saw Brent's mother in my mind. She must have played dead in order for Charles and Lois to leave, praying for the three of us to get out of her house, so she could crawl to a phone and get help. Only it was too late for her husband. Brent grew up with no father.

I pulled Brent aside while the others were playing and talking and found myself up next to a huge pine tree. The smell was wonderful as I took in his entire face. The man had gone through so much in his life. I looked deep into his eyes to try and peer behind them. Where was the pain and hurt? He always had a twinkle and a nice word for everyone. I wish I could learn to look at the world like he did.

"You amaze me," I said.

"Why?" He seemed befuddled. "Because of my snowball skills?"

"No," I laughed. "You seem so full of joy. And you told me so much about things in your life yesterday…"

"I'm sorry if I shared too much. You seem easy to talk to. Plus, you're not a local. Everyone from around here always has that 'poor him' look when they see me."

But I was from "around here" – and it was time Brent knew. But how? How to say it?

"You didn't share too much at all," I said as I touched his broad arm. "I felt … honored … that you wanted to talk to me."

"Are you kidding? You have this smile that lights up, and it makes me want to smile and pulls me right in. I wanted to be with you all day today."

Erick had told me that about my smile. What a great thing to hear from a straight man, though.

"Brent, you never mentioned your mother. You said you lost your father early on."

"Mom passed away before my wife ... before Jennie did. She was a smoker her entire life, and lung cancer took her. She died right after Britney was born."

My mind flashed to the cancer bike ride I had done. If only I had known his mother, I could have biked in her memory.

"So much sorrow," I said.

"No more than anyone else."

I knew I needed to tell him. I couldn't keep it from him.

"Brent, I found out something that I believe I really have to tell you, as much as I hate it. Only, I'm not sure how to do it."

He looked at me with that same twinkle in the eye, but there was also a puzzled expression.

"I know we just met," I continued, "and you have been very open with me. I need to do the same."

"Sara, you can tell me as much or as little as you want. I'm enjoying the short time I have with you – even if it's just for one Christmas Eve."

"I was in Boothbay Harbor before," I said quickly. "This is all going to sound strange, and all these pieces have just come together for me in the last day or so ... but I was here as a little girl. Only, I didn't remember it. I was taken away when I was three years old."

"When was that?"

"Thirty years ago."

"I was living here then," he said. "I was older than you, but..."

"Brent."

I could feel tears forming in my eyes.

"I was a part of the Reed murders. I was the daughter of those two ... monsters ... the people who took your father."

Brent grabbed me in his arms and held me close to his warm wool coat. I wasn't sure if he wanted to snap me like a twig or if he could feel the pain and embarrassment that I was feeling.

"Hey ... don't cry," he said. "You're not to blame for anything. You were a three-year-old child. Shhhhhh!"

He was right. I didn't even know the people who had done it, who had given me life, yet taken so many other lives.

"I had no idea. Then, Ida saw your truck last night and told me about your mother and father ... and ..."

"Sara, that was such a long time ago," he took my face in his hands and looked at me. "People in this town have moved on. Didn't you notice my babysitter is Mrs. Reed? A cousin of Charles Reed. I let go of any rage I had over losing my dad. And I decided to do something positive with my life."

"I heard," I said smiling and wiping away tears. "You are the poster child for all things good in this town."

"Well, I don't know if I would go that far," he teased.

"Ida told me about you buying your parents' house back, just to put good memories into it ... and I saw you creating those yesterday. You and Britney. So much love."

"I love that child with all my heart, and there's nothing I wouldn't do for her. But if, God forbid, I was taken from this earth from her ... I hope I'm teaching her to stand on her own. Keep her head high. And to not hate everyone in her wake."

Wow. This guy is amazing.

I had spent a lifetime being angry and upset as I moved from home to home as a child. And then, I carried that same self-loathing into all of my relationships with men. If only I had the same coping skills that Brent possessed.

"I wish I could do that. I've had a very tough life with no parents," I said. "I just found out recently about the Reed family and that I was a part of it."

"You should hold no guilt for what they did," he said. "And they are dead and gone now."

My eyes jerked up to meet his. How did Brent know about them? Where did he get the information that I was unable to find? He made his proclamation in that same easygoing way as he had talked to me about so much in his life. He had no idea what kind of news he had just shared.

"What?" I asked.

"That case pushed me to become a cop, and one of the first things I did was to track down what happened to them."

I waited to hear more about the outcome of their lives. But he stopped speaking and just looked at me.

"I've been trying to find out ever since I discovered I was their daughter."

"Well, they can never hurt anyone again … including you."

"We're connected to our past," I said.

"But we make our future," he reminded me.

"I thought you would want to run away from me."

"Are you kidding? I have the most amazing woman here tonight."

"Tonight."

We both knew I was leaving the next day and that many miles would separate us.

"Thank you for sharing that, though," he said. "What a burden for you to carry home with you. I feel an even stronger connection to you … if that's possible."

"And I'm so happy that you were the one to tell me they are not out there … somewhere."

I wanted to ask him how they died, what happened. But it didn't feel right. Not then. Maybe that was a reason to stay a few more days – to get that information out of him. Plus, I couldn't tell him the horror that I had been in his house as a child.

Brent took me his arms and gave me the strongest hug that I think I've ever felt from a man. It was powerful and warm and full of a sort of kindness that I don't think I had ever experienced before.

"Are we going to go celebrate Christmas Eve together now?" he asked. "The birth of Christ? A season of peace?"

"And all that is good about the world," I said. "I'm with you."

We made our way toward the gazebo to join the others for a sing-a-long of Christmas tunes. Britney and Ida's great grandkids maneuvered themselves down to the front with the other children. I looked around at that group, and for the first time felt like I was part of a real family. There were grandparents and siblings and even a male partner who made me feel special.

But it's only been one day.

My negative inner voice had not been as vocal. She had been somewhat quieted by Brent who was pointing over my head.

"Look what you're standing under," he said.

I looked up, and sure enough, real mistletoe was hanging down from the gazebo.

"It's an unwritten law or something," he said.

"Well, officer, I know you don't like people to break any laws."

I grabbed him to pull his head down to meet mine. The kiss was soft and wonderful. As he backed away from me, he looked into my eyes, and I saw such warmth and sincerity there.

"Sara, I know that it's crazy nuts, but this has been the best 24 hours I've had since … well … in a long time."

"I agree," I said. "And it has felt like so much longer than just a day. I feel I've known you for…"

"I thought about you all day today," he said. "Wondering what you were doing, where you were."

"I have to admit, I kept looking at my watch hoping tonight would get here."

"Oh ... I got you something," he said, reaching into his coat pocket.

"No. Why?"

"Just a small present to remember this one special Christmas."

"I didn't get you anything." I felt like such a heel.

"Don't worry. I know I'm going to remember it for a long time," he said.

"So who helped you pick it out?" I teased.

"I did this on my own."

I took the gift and placed it in my pocket.

"For tomorrow. I'll save it for Christmas," I said.

"It shouldn't be any other way," he said.

We turned back with the group and continued singing *Silent Night* and *We Wish You a Merry Christmas* and all the other standards. All the other times in my life, singing these holiday songs left me hollow. But not that night. Each word I sang felt genuine and carried the weight of happiness and peace. By the end of the night, we were making our way back to our cars so that everyone could get home and prepare for visits from Santa. Brent and Britney walked us back to my car, where the others said goodbye to them.

"If you ever wanna see what real warm weather is like, just come visit us in Phoenix," Erick said.

"Be careful what you offer because Britney and I might just show up," Brent said. "I could easily become a Cardinals fan."

"I think I know a certain red-headed chick who would love that," Hahn said.

"Oh, really?" Brent said as he put his arm around me.

They each shook hands with him and got inside the car to turn on the heater.

"Those three really care about you," he said.

"They're my family," I shrugged.

"It's important to have them. You can make your own family. Remember that."

"I've learned so much about family on this road trip," I told him.

"Well, remember you have some people back here who would always love to see you if you ever care to make this journey again," he said.

"Count me in on that," Britney said from her dad's side.

"Well, Britney, I hope you come out to visit me, too," I said, leaning down to hug her goodbye.

"It was nice meeting you, Sara," she said.

"You, too. Take care of your dad."

"I always do."

I stood back up to look at Brent in his eyes. I wasn't sure what I should say or if anything more needed to be said. This man had helped me come out of my shell in more ways than he would ever know … or perhaps he did know what he had done for me.

I paused, trying to think of a way to ask him if I could stay longer. If I should stay longer. The evening had been perfect, though, and I didn't want to ruin it. But if for some reason, I was meant to see him again in my life, I could open up more and let him know what I witnessed in his home. Dig deeper into how he learned about my parents' demise ... but not yet.

"So here is a paper with my numbers and address, in case you ever get out my way," I said. "Not that I had pre-planned and had it all written out or anything."

"Ditto," he said as he pulled a piece of paper from his pocket and gave it to me.

"You better get this girl to your truck before she freezes," I said.

"I can't believe this is all the time we get," he said. "I'm losing you as I just..."

I didn't let him say another word. I kissed him goodbye and watched him walk away. I was stuck in my moment when my own car horn blew, and the guys waved to me to get in. I jumped in the back seat and watched my lumberjack turned cop walk away in the falling snow.

"That hot cop could have helped us in our investigation," Matty said.

"He helped in many, many ways," I said.

"It's nice to see you with a man," Erick said.

"It's nice to see you with a man, too," Matty said, as he put his arm up behind Erick on his headrest.

"Yeah … well … that man lives a little far away for me to be able to date," I said from the backseat, as I tried to look back to where Brent had walked.

Hahn pulled my head over onto her shoulder and didn't say a word to me. Her actions were kinder than any smart-ass remark she could make to lighten the somber mood I was in.

CHAPTER THIRTY-SIX

We drove back to the Q&D and walked in on Ida's family in the main parlor around their Christmas tree. The family was walking down memory lane, reliving their past, and it was a sweet moment. We said goodnight and made our way up to the third floor. I thanked the three again for all they had done for me and went into my room for the night. I got into my bed clothes, did my nightly routine of teeth brushing and pill taking (actually feeling as if my blood pressure had stopped boiling so perhaps a change in prescription could be in my future), grabbed my phone, and lay down on my bed. I took the paper that Brent had given me and programmed "Brent Silvers" and his number into my phone. Then, I deleted all the texts that Steve had ever sent me and decided to block his calls once I got home. There was no need for me to return to that part of my life. Even if I never saw Brent again, he had taught me that I was worth so much more.

There was a knock at my door, and Erick came in.

"Silver balls, silver balls … Sara wants to unwrap those for Christmas," he sang.

"Ha ha! Making fun of my Brent Silvers, huh?"

"Just his balls."

"Stop it," I laughed. "So what's up?"

"I saw your light on under the door." he said.

"And…"

"I just wanted to thank you for introducing me to Matty back when you did."

"Erick…"

Erick sat next to me on my bed and took my hand.

"And I wanted you to know what a great guy he is. Most guys talk to me because of my looks, I know that. And yes, Matty makes his comments, but we've had the best trip getting to know each other better. And no, I'm not going to make any fast moves with him. We've discussed it. I've spent ten years in a relationship, and it's gonna take time to get over that. But I have him there, he has me … and we both have you."

"You are such a great guy, Erick. You know I feel that way. And whatever happens between you two is fine with me. I love you both so much."

I had finally let go of trying to dictate the lives of those two boys. Finding someone, falling in love, and sometimes … even getting hurt are all part of the process. Pingleton would be proud.

Erick saw the phone in my hand.

"What are you doing?"

"Getting rid of my past. All booty texts … gone."

"Good girl! That Brent is something, huh?"

"Yeah. He is."

"He beats Steve out in the looks category, and he's a cop to boot. Fucking hot!"

"Girl, I didn't even notice," I said.

"Liar. Bet we haven't seen the last of him."

I started to ask Erick his thoughts on me staying longer and sending them home alone the following day when he looked at my watch on the table next to my bed.

"It's after midnight, Sara. Our first Christmas together. Merry Christmas."

"You, too."

"Don't forget to call your mom in the morning, and tell Matty to do the same," I said as I hugged him.

"Are you practicing being mom for Britney?" he said with a grin.

He left my room to return to his own where I knew Matty was waiting for him.

Oddly enough, I had felt like the mom on this trip. Guess I had some parental instincts inside of me somewhere ... they hadn't all died ten years ago.

My phone buzzed with a text message.

Sara, you deleted that creep ... don't even look at it.

But I did. And it wasn't Steve.

It was Brent.

He wanted to be the first to wish me Merry Christmas. And he didn't know that my guy who had been there for me through so much had only beaten him by seconds. I sent a text back and wished him pleasant dreams. I turned off the light and listened to the wind howling above the attic ceiling. I began to think about the dreams that had filled my brain for the past year. So many parts had been answered, but one remained. It wasn't a big deal anymore, but I still wondered why I was a man in the dreams. I had no desire for women ever in my life. That was obvious with my string of loser men. And then there was Brent – Brent who came into my life in one huge swoop. Who was such a wonderful provider for his little girl. Who was so strong after his wife had died. So strong in choices he made in his life.

Strength.

It's something we always attribute to a man. Maybe I had been looking for that kind of strength to visit my past. Lord knows I needed it. And just perhaps I thought I had to be a man in order to do what I had done– at least in my dreams. I didn't know. But I had to discuss that with Dr. Pingleton at some point. Whatever the case, I knew then that a woman could be just as strong. I had plenty of examples where I had witnessed it: Ida and her family, Hahn and her past, and Sara Butler who took up a new life at the age of three to make something of herself.

I looked out the window at the star-filled sky and thought of the star points on Pingleton's ceiling that had helped lead me to Maine – a very, very wise man, that doctor. And I was happy to think that another man I hoped I would be dreaming of that night was looking at those very same stars in the Maine sky.

CHAPTER THIRTY-SEVEN

No dreams ... that I could recall.

Christmas morning in Maine was a magical thing. The four Arizona folks got their white Christmas. We witnessed children opening up their gifts and tearing through the paper like banshees around the fresh smelling pine tree in the parlor. And Ida was thrilled with the glass angel that I gave her. But never one to be outdone, she returned with a wrapped gift for me. I opened the box to find the beautiful handmade doll from my room made of all those quilt patches. I hadn't even noticed it was missing the night before when I had retired to my room. But being the unbelievably kind person she was, Ida had taken the time to surprise me.

"Something to remember me by," she said, hugging me.

"How do you ever think I could forget you?" I asked. "You're like the family that I have never had."

"I'm honored for you to think of me like that," she said.

I walked away, looking at the handmade doll and thought how much the doll was like me – all patched together with different quilted pieces to create one thing. The time and love that Ida had put into making it was the same that so many people had done in my life without me even knowing it, slowly sewing me together to create a fuller person. I thought it was a wonderful present.

There were Christmas traditions in that house that I, for one, had never participated in. After presents were opened, the final gift under the tree was hidden in the house, and people scrambled to look for it. Then, the guys helped chop more fire wood for the stove while Hahn and I spent the time in the kitchen with the women. Of course, Hahn thought it seemed sexist, but I didn't care. I was thrilled to have the opportunity to bond with other women, even over something like cooking. We cooked, played the radio, and shared stories about what else … men.

The Christmas lunch was a feast fit for a king, and I knew I'd be in a coma for sure. I had never eaten so many carbs in my life. Oyster stuffing, a huge turkey, fresh cranberry sauce, regular mashed potatoes, candied yams, and the list went on and on. Erick, Hahn, and I would have to do some major working out to rid ourselves of it once we were back in Phoenix. But Matty was like a 33-year-old kid in a candy store.

"Back to Veggie Delight as soon as we get home," Erick whispered to me.

"I heard that," Matty said, smacking him on the arm.

Ida's kids were very nice to us as strangers, and the children didn't mind that they were moved to a kids' table to make room for us at the main table. The desserts came and went, and people seemed to disappear around the house to go take naps. We packed up our bags, loaded the car, and said our goodbyes to the family that had made us feel not just incredibly wanted, but part of them. I was completely overwhelmed by the feeling of belonging I had in that house and desperately hated the thought of leaving. I was surrounded by loving, caring people who didn't seem to mind that we were not their blood relatives. I didn't want to lose the incredible feeling I had.

"Are you sure you all don't want to stay one more day?" Samuel asked.

It was my chance. The moment to turn to my three friends and tell them to go on without me and that I would join them in Phoenix. But just as the words were about to come out of my mouth, I realized I already had a family that was not blood related. Those three members of our mafia were my true family. Not Charles or Lois or any of the people in Boothbay that I didn't know. Sure, they had welcomed me with open arms, but my friends knew me and still loved me. Each of us was a strange outcast in our own way, but luckily had found each other. And I was ready to start a new adventure on the ride home with all three of them.

"We need to get back on the road so that we can make it to work next week," I said.

"You come back anytime you want, dear," Ida said. "But try the summer next time."

"We will," I said, hugging her strongly. "Now, I have an honest to God good reason to come back. Thank you, Ida. For everything."

"I hope you can let go of the past," she whispered in my ear. "You have a wonderful future ahead."

I felt as if I could cry as I was saying goodbye to Ida, so I quickly walked away to get into the car while the others said their own goodbyes. The guys made sure all our bags fit in the trunk, and we situated ourselves in the car with the men in the front and women in the back.

"I'm not sure I agree with this whole 'women sitting in the backseat' thing," Hahn said.

"You'll get a chance to drive," Erick said.

"So, Hahn, let me tell you road rules for the trip," Matty said as we pulled down that long drive from the Q&D.

There on the street waiting was Brent's truck.

My heart began to pound, and I no longer heard the conversation in the car. Britney was sitting inside, and Brent was leaning against his cab door with his arms folded, trying to stay warm. I rolled down the window and shouted at him.

"Are you nuts? It's freezing!"

"Just wanted to say goodbye."

"So I didn't scare you away last night, huh?"

"What? I'm a cop. I don't scare."

And there was that twinkle.

"Did you like your present?" he asked.

I had decided to save the gift for the drive home, but reached into my purse and pulled it out, looking at the guys in the front seat and Hahn by my side.

"Get out there with him," Matty said.

I opened the door, and Brent pulled me out of the back of the car and gave me a bear hug.

"You're so cold," I said.

"Well, I called Ida, and she said you were leaving 20 minutes ago. So I've been standing here a while."

"We took some time trying to get away. No one wanted to leave."

"I don't want you to leave either," he said.

I couldn't believe this man was saying this to me. I blew Britney a kiss in the car as she held up an iPod to show me through the window.

"She must love that," I said.

"We'll just wait to see what all music she puts on it. She's six going on 13."

"Girls mature faster than boys, remember," I said.

I started to open the present, and he stopped me.

"You know, it's my job to take care of people," he said. "I want to make sure people are safe, can find their way. I know it sounds silly."

I touched my hand on the side of his face to calm him.

"Nothing is silly where you're concerned."

You don't even sound like the old chick I used to know.

I opened it and pulled out a compass. It wasn't fancy. It wasn't an engraved trinket. It was thoughtful and such a nice gift, and it made me smile.

"Just so you can find your way back up to me," he said.

"I have GPS," I laughed.

"That would work, too."

He kissed me long and hard – leaving the taste of him in my mouth, while his memory would be etched in my brain. That kiss said so much. About what we had meant to each other, about coming back, about trying to see if it would be enough to get us to know each other better and continue the connection we already felt. While he held me tightly in his arms, I could already feel the void that I knew I'd experience once I left his side.

The truck horn blew, and we looked up to see Britney making faces at us, causing us both to laugh.

"Next time, I fly here," I said.

"Or ... I fly to you."

"That works, too," I repeated.

"Be careful on the road, and call me when you get home ... just so I know you got there safely."

"Thank you for a wonderful Christmas," I said, not wanting to budge.

"No, Sara. Thank you. No one here has been able to get me to enjoy ... to even try ... well ... just thank you."

One last kiss, and then, I ran over to Britney's side of the truck to hug her a final time. I looked up at the seagulls circling overhead that had taunted me so much in my dreams. Suddenly, they seemed to be singing to me instead. I was so happy that through my own quest, I was able to help Brent without even knowing it. I got in the car and watched he and Britney pull away, and we were back on the road.

"You okay, girl?" Erick asked from the driver's seat.

"I am more than okay," I said as Hahn grabbed my hand.

"You were different with him," she said. "You let go of some of that edge. This edgy bitch can tell."

Again, the old sage was right. I was a calmer person Brent had allowed to be unleashed. I got the answers that I was seeking. I confronted my past and came out a much better person for it. I still had work to do, but I had my guys and Hahn. Ida back here in Maine. A hot cop to call, visit – see where that would go. And a future to look forward to.

"So where are we stopping for dinner?" Matty asked.

"Bi-otch ... don't even start," Hahn said. "Big bad Hahn is here now to take control of these road antics I heard you pulled on the way here."

"I'm scared," Matty joked.

"I am not eating again for a year," Erick said.

"What if I can build your appetite up again like last night?" Matty said.

"What happens in Maine stays in Maine," Erick said.

That's what Ida had told me, too. Leave it behind in Maine. And I planned on it ... at least some of it. Hopefully, not the

Q&D folks or Brent. It didn't matter if the paperwork was waiting for me at home from the child protection office in New Mexico because I already had my answers. I knew who I had been, and I knew who I had become. Whoever came up with Sara Butler did right by me, and I'd love to thank them for it.

You've had a great life ... be happy.

My phone buzzed with a text.

"So soon?" Matty asked. "He just left you."

"It's Steve," I said, looking at the phone. "Giving you one more chance: as X-mas present."

"Ewwww ... he wants some Christmas booty," Erick said.

I didn't want the man near my booty ever again, but Hahn grabbed my phone and was texting him back before I had a chance to respond.

"New Year's Resolution. Your skanky prick stays far away from Red's bed. Lose my number," she said.

Hahn plopped the phone back in my lap.

"What?" she said. "We don't need him pestering our girl."

"I couldn't have said it any better myself," I said.

The guys cracked up, and Matty gave Hahn a high five. I realized Brent helped me believe I was worth so much more, but I knew my closest friends could still bring out the crazy chick now and again.

"I think we should drive home a different way since more snow is forecast in the Midwest," Erick said.

"It's been a strange month with blizzards and snow all across the country," Matty added.

"Just in time for our road trip," Erick said.

"Oh goody," Hahn quipped. "Snowy road trip."

"But at least we can see other parts of the country if we head south and then westward home," Erick said.

"I can input a new route into this PS of G," Matty said.

"Now, that one doesn't even work," Erick said. "I take your strange talk, but that one doesn't make sense."

"Oh, and everything you say always makes sense?" Matty said.

"He has you there," I said.

I knew I'd be re-programming my own GPS as well. A new route for Sara was coming at the start of the approaching new decade. Starting on the road trip home, I would be rising from the ashes of my past as I headed back to Phoenix a new woman, a woman who didn't have a need to look backwards in life – only forward.

And hopefully, that negative voice inside would stay quiet and let me make my own decisions for myself.

"Let's sing Christmas Carols," Matty said.

"Whatever you guys want," I said. "I ain't calling the shots on the way home. I'm just enjoying the ride."

ACKNOWLEDGEMENTS

Like Sara's journey in the book, with each story I write, I take a new journey myself. And my car is just as "full" with an assortment of friends and people who have aided me on my trip. To my good friend, Donna, who gave me my first great memories of Maine! Thank you. To Bruce, who helped with all those "show-tunes" on the road trip – glad you have that crazy catalog in your brain. EMR, your edit of this novel makes me a better writer. To Melanie, who did the copy edit prior to publication – eyes like yours are so greatly needed! For my wonderful other half whose support and encouragement went beyond other writings as you were right there discussing and defining the background elements of Sara's life with me on this one. I'm lucky to have you in my life every single day. To NaNoWriMo for the yearly November writing challenge they make which started this entire book a few years ago. To all those friends and colleagues who read early versions and gave such valuable feedback – I can't thank you enough. And to my wonderful family, who not only encourages me in what I do, but gave me such a varied background in my life that things we may have encountered at some point usually find a way into my writing. Love you all! Lastly, in getting in touch with my "inner female voice" – there have been many women who have inspired me. I can't list them all, but here are a few: Allison, Angie, Bee, Cheryl, Ellen, Gwen, Jamie, Jodi, Kate, Kathi, Linda, Lisa, Liz, Lori, Lynn, Martha, Melissa, Nancy, Pamela, Patti, Penny, Sandra, Shirley, Suzanne, Tami, Terri, Tiffany, Traci.

About the Author

Gregory G. Allen is the author of *Well with My Soul* (multi-award-winning finalist), *Proud Pants: An Unconventional Memoir* and the children's picture book *Chicken Boy: The Amazing Adventures of a Super Hero with Autism*. Allen loves to write of adversity and diversity and has had numerous short stories and poetry published in anthologies and websites and is a contributor to several online publications. He has been in the entertainment business for 20+ years as an actor, director, writer, and producer; is an award-winning writer of musical theater with over ten shows that he has served as book writer and/or composer/lyricist produced on stage; and has been the recipient of musical grants from BMI, ASCAP, and the Watershed Foundation. He lives in northern New Jersey with his partner, Anthony.

DISCARD

CPSIA information can be obtained at www.ICGtesting.com
Printed in the USA
BVOW041921160512

290417BV00003B/2/P

9 780983 604945